THE SILENT DAUGHTER

EMMA CHRISTIE

WELBECK

Published in 2020 by Welbeck Fiction Limited,
part of Welbeck Publishing Group
20 Mortimer Street London W1T 3JW

Copyright © Emma Christie, 2020

Cover design by: Micaela Alcaino
Cover images © Kirill Sakryukin/Trevillion Images (front)
© Shutterstock.com (back)

The moral right of the author has been asserted.

A CIP catalogue record for this book is available from the
British Library

Paperback ISBN: 978-1-78739-493-3
E-book ISBN: 978-1-787-39-501-5

Printed and bound by CPI Group (UK) Ltd., Croydon, CR0 4YY

10 9 8 7 6 5 4 3 2 1

For Mum and Dad

This book isn't about you, or me.
But it's for you, from me.

With all my love, always.

I killed Ruth Morrison.
Do I feel guilty? Yes.
Do I regret it? No.
Would I do the same again? Yes. But sooner.

CHAPTER 1

Chris Morrison held his wife as close as tubes and wires allowed.

The worst reaction was no reaction at all. Not a flinch, not a sound. The metal bars at the side of the bed dug into his legs when he tried to lean in closer.

He wished for home and for no space between them.

Her mouth was hanging open under the plastic mask, dried saliva like mould on her tongue. He flushed, felt an intense embarrassment for the woman in his arms. Beauty had left every part of her. Even that mouth that perfectly fitted his, silenced now by bad luck or bad timing; some force stronger than she was.

The word *accident* hadn't registered at first.

He'd been up north for a weekend's winter hiking when he'd answered the call, heard a stranger with an Eastern European accent saying his wife's name in a way he'd never heard it pronounced before. Then he'd heard the words *fall*, *head* and *coma*; had been advised to go to Edinburgh Royal Infirmary as soon as possible. An officer would meet him there. Ten hours later he was still there, holding a lump under starched white sheets that police and doctors referred to as Your Wife.

It was so bloody impersonal. *Her name is Maria.*

If it had been him in the hospital bed, Maria would tell him to focus on all the parts of his body that were healthy. *You should be grateful that's the only thing that's wrong with you*, she'd say.

I know, love, I know.

But what if there were no healthy parts left? What did you focus on then? He looked at Maria, a bruised, bloated version of herself, her breath and blood trapped in plastic tubes. Maria, moving only on the inside, the fight of bloody, pulsating organs neatly packaged into polite beeps and jagged little lines on a screen. And all of this because she went for a run.

It was incomprehensible to think he could lose his wife because she'd missed a step or tripped on her laces or slipped on a chip wrapper dumped by a student. Was that really all that had happened here? Maria had just fallen?

He struggled to believe it.

When he'd pushed the police for more information he'd been fobbed off, told to be patient. And all the doctors offered were the same phrases he'd written a thousand times as a news reporter – 'critical condition', 'potentially life-changing injuries', 'some chance of a full recovery'. All of them utterly meaningless, impossible to measure. But it was the night nurse's words that had stung the most. She'd tucked in the corners of Maria's sheets then squeezed

Chris's hand so tightly that his wedding ring had left a mark on his middle finger.

If I were you, she'd said, *I'd start phoning the family*.

He didn't need to ask why.

The call to Mikey had been quick, though not painless. He was on his way. But it was never as straightforward with Ruth, was it? He'd tried her mobile dozens of times already. It went straight to voicemail without ringing, suggesting it was either switched off or that she didn't have any signal. He'd left messages that he hoped gave no suggestion of what was really wrong. Once she called back he'd explain, assure her she shouldn't feel guilty for being so far away. Anyway, miles meant nothing, would disappear with a flight.

The distance between them would not.

Chris heard the buzz of a fly, felt sick when it landed on his fingers. Could it sense Maria there? He'd used water and a paper hankie to clean blood off Maria's cheeks when he arrived, tiny spots missed by nurses but not by the man who'd woken up to that face every day for more than three decades. He'd washed his hands a dozen times afterwards then scrutinised every line and crevice under the harsh bathroom light. He did not want pieces of his wife stuck under his fingernails. But Christ, she'd always be there. On him, in him.

He closed his eyes and pressed his nose and lips to her cheek, thinking of the tiny soft hairs in the nape of her neck that he loved and she'd never seen. That part of her was for him only, hidden from the world under thick black curls that

3

grew from Spanish roots. Tears came when he took a deep breath, sucked in the scent of her. There it was, the only part of Maria that remained unchanged. He took another long, deep breath, then leaned over the side of the bed to vomit.

CHAPTER 2

Chris was slumped in a plastic chair, fighting sleep, when he heard a polite knock on the door. Knock-knock. Pause. And then the same again. It had to be Mikey. Chris had told him to stay home until the morning but he'd refused. He knocked again then gently pushed open the door. He was half-Spanish but so bloody British. *My mum is dying – but don't worry, I didn't forget my manners.*

Chris kept his eyes closed, feigned sleep.

Shoes squeaked on polished lino, then Mikey groaned. 'Mum?'

It was the first familiar voice Chris had heard since all of this started. Well, apart from his own. He was surprised how natural it felt to talk to Maria when she was unconscious. Still, he'd curse himself when he automatically capped one of his stories with a question, an accidental request for affirmation. *Right? Wasn't it? Remember?* There was never a silence longer.

He'd been embarrassed when a doctor had walked in, caught him talking about the weather up north, how close he'd come to crashing the car when he'd hit black ice. But the doctor clearly didn't give a shit about the content of his stories. He'd glanced at a clipboard hooked over the end of Maria's bed and, as he wrote a note in red pen, he'd assured Chris conversation was good for People In Your Wife's Condition and was Perfectly Normal Under The Circumstances.

Chris pictured others exactly like himself in the rooms either side of Maria's, every one of them grasping the hands of the dying and the dead, saying things they'd never have dared say if they thought there was a remote chance their beloved could actually hear. It was pathetic. Chris wondered if they imagined the responses too, same way he did. Maria's voice flooded him.

You know your problem, Chris?

Tell me.

You filter your feelings.

Meaning?

Meaning you feel something but, instead of expressing it, you judge it; wonder if it's the right thing to be feeling. And you worry other people might judge you for it too. But it's nonsense. I won't love you less for being honest.

You don't know that, Maria.

Try me.

And so he'd spent the past few hours trying to unclog a filter so choked with the residue of The Unspoken that almost nothing got through, especially the fear that weighed him down the most: he'd failed to protect his family. *Again*. That was why he was sitting at the side of another hospital bed, and on the edge of another loss.

And, just like that, he was thinking again about That Day, fifteen years ago but fresh as ever. He remembered how quickly the blood had cooled and dried on his fingers; the bath he'd had later, rubbing matted hair between his fingers to remove every trace of it, of her. By that time the blood had been hard and black but the hot water had resurrected it, turned the crust of blood to shiny droplets of rust on his skin that dripped off and blended with the water. He remembered squeezing a sponge that dripped red, watching stained water swirl and gurgle around the plug hole. It left a dirty ring on the white ceramic long after he'd pulled the plug.

Those were images that would never shift.

'Dad? Are you awake?'

Mikey gently tapped Chris's arm until he opened his eyes, blinking for effect. 'Thanks for coming,' he said.

'Couldn't sleep anyway,' said Mikey. 'Are you doing okay?'

'Not really,' said Chris, thinking about all the times he'd asked that same question, interviewing someone who was clearly falling to pieces. It was polite to ask. But there was no place for manners here, now, in this room. People often asked him if human suffering got easier to deal with the more he wrote about it – then quickly answered their own question before he had the chance to. *I suppose it's something you just get used to*, they'd say, and he'd agree, because nobody wanted to know that he never had.

The bed wobbled when Mikey leaned down and kissed his mum's cheek, then held her hand. He looked awkward and the gesture seemed forced, somehow inappropriate. Chris pulled himself out of the chair, stood facing his son on the opposite side of the bed. Mikey hadn't shaved, looked hungover.

'What happened to her?'

'Police claim she fell,' said Chris. 'Smashed her head on stone steps.'

'Where?'

'Fleshmarket Close.'

'Jesus.' Mikey's face crumpled. 'They're steep, those ones.'

'Aye, but you know as well as I do that steps don't faze your mum. The more the better, she'd say. That's precisely why she makes the effort to go running in the Old Town. She could easy go for a run near the house, but it's too flat for her liking.' Chris pictured her, at home and on holiday, seeking out routes with steps and stairways, letting out an occasional whoop as she was forced to dart to one side to avoid dog shit or a puddle or a discarded kebab box. She was a proper bloody expert.

'Was she racing?'

'Another 10km,' said Chris.

'Who found her?'

'Not sure.'

'And they think she tripped?'

'Aye,' said Chris. 'They're checking CCTV to confirm, but the officer told me that's a formality. They think it looks like an accident, plain and simple. They're certainly not treating it as a criminal investigation.'

'And what – you think they should?

'I'm not sure, Mikey,' said Chris. 'But I know your mum. And I know she wouldn't *just fall*.'

'Och, here we go.' Mikey sat down, stared at the floor. Chris watched his son's back rise and fall. His breaths were short and fast and shuddering, nothing like the perfectly symmetrical inhale and exhale created by Maria's ventilator. You could play music to the rhythm of that mechanical breath and never lose the beat. He couldn't bear it, scoured his brain for a question to ask, anything that would smother the sound of that machine, and what it meant.

'Have you told Rachel?'

Mikey nodded, started chewing the nail on his ring finger.

'Will she come to the hospital?' Chris hoped not, and hoped it didn't show. Mikey's wife was a challenge at the best of times, let alone the worst.

'She said she'll stay home for now,' said Mikey. 'Thought it was better if we had time on our own with Mum. You get hold of Ruth yet?'

Chris shook his head. 'Still no word,' he said. 'I've left voicemails, but—'

'She's in a different time zone.'

'Aye.'

'And anyway, it's Ruth. You know what she's like.'

Chris wanted to say, *Do I?* but opted for a silence he then couldn't break. Mikey opened his mouth a few times to speak, then snapped it shut. When he managed to speak he whispered, as if he didn't want his mum to hear.

'Dad . . .?' Mikey averted his eyes. 'Have you contacted Uncle Mateo?'

'Not yet,' said Chris, flushing at the mention of that name.

'Shouldn't take him long to get here from Barcelona.'

'If he can be bothered,' said Chris.

Mateo was Maria's only brother but he was fifteen years younger than she was – and just ten years older than Mikey. Their parents had referred to Mateo as *a late surprise* but he'd interpreted it as *unwanted* and spent his life struggling to escape that self-imposed curse. These days Maria referred to him as *troubled*, and Chris called him all manner of different things, none of which were complimentary. But, whatever label he gave him, Chris was sure of one thing.

He did not want that man here, now.

'You should probably call him,' said Mikey.

Chris felt his jaw tighten. The ventilator whooshed. Maria's chest rose and fell. Mikey looked as if he was going to speak again but instead he bit down on his bottom lip, stared in silence at the bed where his mum lay, stilled. Maria, as she was. She'd never lost that touch of the exotic, would have sold a million packets of cigarettes if they'd stuck her face on the poster. Her skin was the precise colour of cinnamon sticks, Nature's gift for life despite the fact that she'd spent most of her days in Scotland, under white skies. Maria had passed those traits to Mikey and Ruth, along with bodies made for swimming and a love of all legumes.

But they had Chris's eyes, the pair of them. Restless; searching for whatever was going on behind them; eternally irritated by pollen and serious conversations.

He looked at Maria now, her eyes sealed again with that hard yellow crust. When he'd first arrived he'd tried to scrape it off with his nail, but the nurse had told him to be gentle, brought cotton pads and a little bottle of antiseptic gel, showed him the best way to clean her. He'd done exactly as the nurse said, then felt sick, like an embalmer. But it was still easier than talking to Mateo.

He reached for the pads and gel to keep his hands busy. He flipped the lid open and took a sniff then closed it again and turned the bottle in his hands, feigned interest in the ingredients listed in tiny writing on the label. But they were cheap avoidance tactics, and they failed. He had to call Mateo.

Maria would have his number in her mobile.

He got up and went to the wardrobe, pulled out Maria's running jacket. She'd chosen it specifically for its useful pockets, including a long one in the left arm that perfectly fitted her phone. But it wasn't where it should be – and that wasn't like Maria. *A place for everything*, she always said, *and everything in its place*. He pulled the jacket off the hanger then started opening other pockets, felt uncomfortable pushing aside paper hankies and receipts for things she'd bought when he wasn't there. But it paid off. Her phone was tucked into the inside pocket.

The screen was black, and when light hit the shiny surface he could see traces of Maria's fingerprints; the last places she'd touched. He couldn't bear it; pushed the home button to get rid of them. Instead he was asked for a six-digit password. He entered the date of their wedding anniversary but for once Maria had chosen a different combination. He tried again and got the same result.

'Any ideas what your mum would use for a password?'

Mikey looked up, shrugged. 'Ruth's birthday?'

'Worth a try.' Chris typed in the date but the screen stayed locked. 'Any other ideas?'

Mikey sighed. 'Give it here, Dad.'

He leaned over the bed to take the phone then gently lifted his mum's hand and pressed her thumb on to the home button. The screen lit up.

Chris felt a lump in his throat, swallowed hard to flatten it.

The background image on Maria's phone was an old photo of the four of them – a close-up, but bits of their faces were obscured by icons and by cracks that made jagged webs on the screen. Chris, Maria, Mikey and Ruth, together, but split into pieces.

He would not allow it.

Chris pushed the contacts icon, started searching for Mateo's number. He hadn't seen or spoken to Maria's brother for years – in fact, he'd avoided Barcelona altogether since That Day. But he could still picture him. He and Maria looked alike, but Mateo's skin was dull and waxy and his smile was joyless.

The first number Chris found was AaaaaaaaRuth, at the top of Maria's contact list. Ruth, always number one. He felt the familiar flutter of resentment in his chest, a big red warning flag threatening to unroll.

Notice me, it said. *Acknowledge me.*

But Chris was a master of looking the other way. He kept scrolling, all the way to Z, was surprised Maria had so many contacts he didn't recognise. They'd be friends from yoga, maybe, or folk from that meditation group she'd started attending on Thursday nights. Whoever they were, they were not Mateo. Talking to his brother-in-law would have to wait.

He went into the settings and changed the PIN number to their wedding anniversary, then put the phone to sleep, and wished again that he could do the same with the memories of That Day fifteen years ago. He and Maria, getting back to Mateo's flat later than intended, finding empty rooms and an open brandy bottle. Chris remembered the fear that had shredded Maria's voice when they'd first realised something was wrong: that Ruth was not where she should be.

Ruth, she'd said. *Where's Ruth?*

He imagined her saying the same now if she woke up from her coma and realised Ruth wasn't there. He could avoid calling Mateo, but Ruth needed to know. She'd need to cross the Atlantic to get here and, knowing Ruth, she'd be miles from an airport. But she'd have to start making her way home, right now.

He picked up his phone and dialled her number again, trying to ignore the words that clung to the end of every thought in his head. *Before it's too late.*

Me and Ruth started back in the days when she'd share snot and saliva and clothes and a bath with anyone who asked. She would run around naked at the beach and the park and at home without any concept of why anybody might stare or pass comment. We were inseparable and, back then, nobody minded.

When I was there, Ruth would push aside those nervous, shivering boys who stood at the edge of the harbour with their toes curled over the edge and their necks stretched forward, eyes wide as they surveyed the frigid grey water six feet beneath them. I'd give her the nod and she'd throw herself into the sea before any of them. When she pulled her sleek body out of the water her dad would cheer and her eyes would find his right away, as if their heads were joined by an invisible string that neither wanted to break, even for a minute. She'd be happy she'd listened to me, and I'd be happy she'd done what I said.

When I was there, Ruth would chase me until her breath was hard to catch, then she'd lie on her back on the grass and stare at the clouds changing shape. I'd lie with her, me and Ruth and our heartbeat and a white sky with blue always hidden underneath. I'd tell her that the sky would always be the same, no matter where we decided to lie or how scarred and wrinkled our bodies became, and she'd agree and I'd be happy she saw the world through my eyes.

Then, she did not question what we had.

Then, there was no blood on her hands, or mine.

CHAPTER 3

Mikey handed Chris a coffee and a croissant, then moved to the other side of Maria's bed and sat on a plastic chair he'd swiped from the visitors' room. He'd slept in there, sprawled on the floor. Chris had stayed with Maria, anxiety gnawing every part of him. His body craved sleep but his mind angrily protested.

'Still no word from Ruth?'

'Nothing,' said Chris, glancing at his watch. 'And that's twenty-four hours since your mum's accident.'

Mikey nodded, then both of them stared at Maria's chest, rising and falling, rising and falling. The sound of the ventilator reminded Chris of snorkelling and he let his mind carry him to the sea, a world without walls. When the kids were younger they'd all go out together in the boat, Maria at the controls while Chris checked their equipment then helped Mikey and Ruth squeeze into their little wetsuits. They had no fear back then. They'd just leap over the side of the boat and let the sea hold them, transform them from standing humans into floating ones. He closed his eyes and pictured Maria in the sea – but suddenly she was sinking, hair billowing like seagrass, lifeless limbs lifted this way and that by invisible currents. He imagined her body breaking down little by little, giving life to the underwater world where she felt so at home. It was graceful, almost. But Chris knew what really happened, had stood on the harbour taking notes for the front page exclusive as officers stood knee-deep in frigid waters dragging bloated bodies from the water. Big fat rotting balloons, faces ten times their original size, eyes pecked out by the gulls.

Stop, Chris. Stop.

He was relieved when he heard the rattle of the nurse's trolley in the corridor, followed by a single knock on the door and a *Good morning, gentlemen!* that was far too cheery for the circumstances. She asked for five minutes with the patient. Heads nodded, chairs scraped, and they were out.

They left and walked in awkward silence down the only corridor in the whole hospital with a carpet. Colour choice: the blue of a dead man's lips. It connected the head injuries ward to the intensive care unit. How could Maria be here? So far there was no real update on her condition – and nothing at all from the police. She ran, she fell, she smashed her head on stone. That was it?

The police said there was no evidence of foul play – so far – but the reporter in him didn't believe it. So what was the alternative? It was the classic question, a cliché he cursed himself for thinking, never mind asking.

Did she fall or was she pushed?

He walked away from that thought and opened a glass door on the other side of the corridor. It led to a sad little garden that would once have been the haunt of smokers but was now a Designated Fresh Air Zone, according to a sign paid for using taxpayers' money – with the sole purpose of telling people they were now, officially, outside. Back in the day Chris would have made a decent article out of it, found out how much the sign cost and let the public know the ridiculous ways their cash was being spent. Give readers something new to whinge about and they'll lap it up, thank you for dragging their attention away from the things that really matter; the stories that really hurt. It was easier to read about corruption and political inadequacy than it was to digest a single paragraph about a human just like you, no longer being.

Was that what would happen here? Maybe. The first report he'd read about Maria's accident was tucked into a 'News in Brief' column on the online version of the paper, a three-liner neatly summing up his family's misfortune.

A woman was found with serious head injuries yesterday in Edinburgh city centre. The 58-year-old, named locally as secondary school teacher Maria Morrison, was transferred by ambulance to Edinburgh Royal Infirmary.

He'd written hundreds of them during his career, probably read thousands. But this time he was part of it. This time he wasn't just watching someone else's life go wrong, from a distance. This time the blood and the skin-marks on the road belonged to Maria. And if he didn't get hold of Ruth soon he'd be the clichéd *worried relative* appealing for her to get in touch. He desperately wanted to reach Ruth before the news found its way to her from someone else. He paced circuits around the tiny garden while he called Ruth's mobile, got nowhere.

'Still switched off,' he said. 'I'll try from your mum's phone.'

'Och, there's no point,' said Mikey. 'It's not exactly unusual for Ruth to be out of touch, is it? Especially when she's off on one of her big trips. The only difference here is that you actually *need* to speak to her. If she chose to switch off her phone on any other Monday morning you'd think nothing of it.'

'Maybe.'

'Maybe my arse. This is standard Ruth behaviour.' Mikey let his head fall back, stared at the square of cloudy sky above them. 'When did you last speak to her, anyway? And I mean an actual phone call, not texts or emails.'

Chris screwed up his face. 'Not for months, I suppose. You?'

'She's not phoned me once since your birthday weekend,' said Mikey. 'I follow her photos online but these days that's about as close as we get.'

'Have you two have been arguing again?

'No worse than usual,' said Mikey.

'To be honest, I don't think she's ever forgiven you for chopping her bloody hair off before the school play. Christ, your mum was furious.'

'The famous Cinderellagate scandal,' said Mikey, and for a moment both men smiled at the memory. '*Lead actress scalped by raging brother*.'

'Poor wee mite,' said Chris. He remembered Ruth's teary face when she came downstairs, one pigtail detached from her head and clutched in her little hands, bobble still attached. She'd been playing with Mikey's computer games without asking, accidentally broken the console when she kicked over her drink. When Mikey realised, he'd taken Maria's scissors from the office drawer, chopped off her hair on one side as punishment. Chris and Maria were livid, Mikey was grounded, and Ruth was forced to wear a wig when she played the lead role in Cinderella the week after. 'She did well in the end, didn't she? Good actress, Ruth. But she got lots of stick thanks to your handiwork.'

'Och, Ruth could handle it,' said Mikey, then he crossed his arms around himself as if he'd suddenly got cold. 'Anyway, I'm going to check on Mum.'

Chris watched him go, then called Ruth's number again. It went straight to an automated message informing him the phone was turned off, then switched to voicemail – same as every other time he'd tried. He pulled out Maria's mobile, repeated the process, and got the same result. He sighed, knew he had to be patient. Ruth would switch on her phone eventually. Wouldn't she?

Some questions were better left unanswered.

He distracted himself by checking for messages. Emails nothing, texts nothing, social media, nothing. He opened his notepad, wrote down the time he'd tried contacting Ruth then the words *No Progress*. He'd persevere, repeat the process every hour until he got hold of her. He was tempted to call her mobile yet again but instead he stuffed both phones in his pocket and went back inside.

The door to Maria's room was closed when Chris got there. Fear burst to life like a struck match in his chest when he heard shrill electronic beeps coming from inside. The machines that were keeping Maria alive had softer sounds, at least when her heart was beating. *Christ*. His pulse raced in his fingertips as he pushed open the door. Mikey was being consoled by a woman Chris knew – but only from crime scenes. Her police radio beeped again and when she looked up she nodded to him in recognition, but her expression was grim.

'Please follow me,' she said. 'We've got some news.'

CHAPTER 4

Farida McPherson turned her chair round so she was facing Chris. She'd flashed her police ID to a man who was charging his mobile phone in the visitors' room and when he left she'd closed the door, suggested Chris take a seat.

She had a face that did not match her manner. The skin around her eyes and mouth was inexplicably smooth, looked airbrushed even under the harsh glare of tube-lighting. If Maria had been awake she'd have admired it when she thought Farida wasn't looking, then commented on it later when she and Chris were alone. *It's her heritage*, she'd say, and hope such generalisations didn't make her racist.

The vast majority of police officers Chris had encountered in his career were lumbering males who effortlessly slipped into the clichés of their profession. Smokers, drinkers, swearers. If their outline was drawn in a thick-tipped marker pen, Farida's was created with a recently sharpened pencil, something with a sleek, smooth tip and no smudges around the edge.

And yet, she effortlessly filled any room she walked into, held herself in such a way that she transmitted a clear, unmissable message. *Don't fucking mess with me.*

She handed Chris a coffee he'd said he didn't want. Chris had met Farida dozens of times as a news reporter, but they'd rarely spoken without a flapping line of tape between them. *Police side. Press side. Don't you forget.*

Now there was a little white table between them. It heaved under an untidy pile of magazines, pages curled and soiled by greasy fingers. On the wall beside them a string of coloured Christmas lights had been draped over an information board.

'So . . .' Farida leaned forward, focused on Chris. 'How is Maria?'

'Stable,' said Chris, and Farida nodded as if that meant something. If Chris had written that word in an article his editor would have torn out the page and brought it to his desk, asked him to underline the problem word, the one that could not be measured, that created questions instead of answering them. *Stable?* he'd have said. *Compared to what?*

'Stable's good enough,' said Chris trying to gag the voices in his head. 'The nurse says her body is responding well to treatment, whatever that means.'

'That's something,' said Farida. 'Now let's talk about the incident.'

She took a sip of coffee, flinched as if she'd burnt her lips then set the cup down on the table, eyeing it as if it were hot on purpose. 'Your wife has sustained very serious injuries,' she said. 'We hope and expect to quickly eliminate any suggestion of foul play. We've already obtained images of your wife from council CCTV cameras located close to the place she was found. We've also asked businesses to allow access to their security recordings.

'From what we have so far – I can confirm she was running on South Bridge moments before the incident. She turned left onto the Royal Mile and immediately right on to Cockburn Street. She then turned right again, into Fleshmarket Close. The steps lead down to Market Street. You know it?'

Chris nodded.

As a news reporter he'd walked every inch of the Old Town and he and Maria used to spend weekends in city centre museums and parks when the kids were wee. These days, they lived in the suburbs and rarely went in – unless Chris was writing a review for the paper or when friends came to visit the city.

But Maria still loved to run there sometimes, couldn't resist the endless beauty and mystery of the Old Town and its intriguing closes – narrow alleyways that connected the Royal Mile to the lower parts of the city.

They were mostly dark and damp and dripping with stories of the ghosts who walked there. Fleshmarket Close was no different. The top end was a slope – but the close was best known for several flights of stone steps that sliced steeply between tenements, stretching from Cockburn Street to the train station.

Chris pictured Maria running, stumbling, falling, then coming to rest face down and bleeding halfway down those steps. 'Who found her?'

'Staff from a nearby business,' said Farida. 'They alerted the emergency services and were happy to give a statement to officers. But, from what we've seen on CCTV so far, there was nobody else around and there was no traffic. Most of that area was temporarily closed off for the race.'

'Hang on,' said Chris. 'Does the race divert down Flesh-market Close?'

'No, it does not.'

'Then why did she turn off? I don't understand why she'd leave the route,' said Chris. 'I also don't understand how the street could be empty when there were a few hundred runners signed up to race. It doesn't make any sense.'

'That's just it, Chris. Maria wasn't running the race.'

'What do you mean?'

Farida leaned so close he got a whiff of her perfume.

'The area where Maria was found is on the very final stretch of the race route. But at ten a.m. all the other runners were miles away, at the starting line.'

'So was Maria running late? Heading back in that direction?'

Farida shook her head. 'Maria was running in the opposite direction, *away* from the starting line. Contrary to initial reports, I can confirm that your wife was *not* competing in the race at the time of her accident.'

Chris screwed up his face. 'That makes no sense. She was dressed in her running gear when she was found. Her trainers are here, and her running jacket. That means she definitely intended to run when she left the house that morning.'

'It's definitely her in the footage.'

'But why was she there?'

'I'm afraid I can't help you with that,' said Farida. 'And I must stress that her reasons for being there are not relevant to our investigation. As far as we can tell so far, it's looking like a very unfortunate accident. The streets in the Old Town are treacherous, especially after rain. As I said yesterday, my suspicion is that Maria slipped. It certainly doesn't look as if anybody else was involved.'

Chris took a sip of coffee, tried to ignore the bitterness on his tongue and in his chest when he realised Farida was packing away her notepad and preparing to leave. He reached out, touched her arm.

'And that's it? Investigation closed? You must be bloody kidding.'

'Come on, Chris. You know how these things work.'

These things. Chris wanted to punch someone. Everything was so bloody impersonal. To them it was just another sad case that would be closed and forgotten as easily as any other; just another incident with a number and a barcode on the file. If it was *just an accident*, the police and papers and public did not care.

But what if it wasn't?

He stood up and started pacing the visitors' room while Farida finished gathering her things. She paused in the doorway before she left and wished Chris and his family all the best. *All the best*. It was such a simple thing to say, written automatically on emails and letters and pegged on to the end of forgettable phone conversations. It was meaningless to most, an empty cliché uttered without any real desire for goodness; just something to say. Chris felt suddenly dizzy and alone and the opposite of who he wished he was. He steadied himself against the wall and longed to be solid. *All the best* was beyond his grasp; was not what he'd allowed his family to become. Time and time again, he'd failed to protect the ones he loved the most. *You can't let it happen again, Chris.*

He waited for the dizziness to pass then walked, unseeing, through other's people's muddled lives. Hospital life flowed around him, floor after floor of grief and miracles that would never affect him. Everyone there was consumed by their own personal tragedies, spared only momentary thoughts for the suffering of all the people outside their direct scope of vision.

But every room held a story. He pushed open the door to Maria's room, more confused than ever about how and why his wife's story had ended up here.

There was no sign of Mikey. Chris checked his phone, found a text to say he'd gone home to rest, see Rachel and take a shower. *Christ.* What happened to staying with his mum? It was hardly a big ask. Surely he could have waited with her until he knew Chris was back in the room. He called him, pissed off – but it went to voicemail. He hung up without leaving a message.

Chris leaned over Maria's bed, gave her a hug that was awkward and one-sided, bones all in the wrong place.

'Why were you there, love? Why didn't you race?'

Beep, whoosh, nothing.

When Chris straightened up, a few matted strands of Maria's hair came with him, stuck to the buttons on his cuff. They snapped when he tried to pull them free, one part clinging to his sleeve, the other in his hand. He paused for a second then let them go, watched them drift down to the floor; the only part of Maria that was already dead. He was still staring at those tiny pieces of her when he heard muffled music nearby – some cheesy crap by Abba. He tried but failed to ignore it, and it was halfway through its cheerful chorus when he realised where the sound was coming from.

It was Maria's phone, ringing in his pocket.

Ruth was popular at primary school, even with the bad kids who had food stains on their jumpers and jotters without covers and cans of Coke at playtime. People liked her and, when I was there, they liked me too.

Ruth didn't look at me and see all the parts she'd want to change.

In fact, changing hadn't even occurred to her until the day a big boy asked her about me and Ruth hadn't yet learned to lie so she said yes and he told her I was a total freak and everyone laughed and she wanted to defend me but didn't.

And so shoulds started to shape her.

When Ruth was with her friends I'd keep my distance, keep our secret just that. But she'd always let me in when everyone else was out. I'd put a chair against her bedroom door, smile when her school skirt dropped to the floor.

Afterwards we'd lie in Ruth's single bed and imagine the lives lived beneath and above us, creating images from the blend of sounds that seeped through open windows and thin walls. The whirr of washing machines, the rattle of plates and cutlery in a sink, a blend of voices from films and the fake applause from game shows. A foreign woman shouting abuse down the phone. Laughter. Arguments. Doors closing, defining moods.

It took Ruth years to recognise the sound of the neighbours having sex or to understand what that actually meant or realise it was something that she should be ashamed to listen to. Her mum set her straight on that one.

Sometimes if we kept the window closed all afternoon my sweat would rise up and cling to the window and the glass would squeak when I reached up and wrote my name in the fug. Ruth would smile when she saw it, then panic and wipe the window clean, leave no trace.

Gone! she'd say. But not forgotten.

CHAPTER 5

Chris was confused when Mikey woke him up with a gentle nudge and a cheerless *good morning*. Just for a moment Chris forgot what had happened and why he'd slept fully dressed, in that plastic chair. Then Mikey sighed and the ventilator puffed and his heart felt as though it was being wrung dry.

'Any updates, Dad?'

'Nothing good.' Chris had sat alone by Maria's bedside since the previous afternoon, leaving only for the loo and a few trips to the canteen for sandwiches that all tasted the same.

Chris stood up and opened the blinds, gazed out at fold after fold of dark grey clouds that looked ready to burst any second. When he picked up the yellow hospital blanket he'd slept under his notepad fell onto the floor, still open at a *To Do* list he'd started writing before he dozed off.

Mikey picked it up, frowned as he read it. 'Trace silent voicemail?'

Chris nodded. 'Someone called your mum's phone yesterday afternoon, after you'd left. Unfortunately I didn't answer on time. It switched to voicemail but they didn't

33

leave a proper message – just a few seconds of static, then they hung up.'

'Did you call back?'

'The number was withheld,' said Chris.

'Do you think it was Ruth?'

'I hope so,' said Chris.

'Who else could it be?'

'That's the big question, Mikey.' Chris reached for Maria and held her hand, remembering the simple but now unreachable comfort of her fingers entwined in his. 'We've had some calls to the house recently. Silent ones.'

'How many calls are we talking about?'

Chris puffed up his cheeks, let the air out slowly. 'Four or five maybe, in the past month. We didn't think anything of it, really. We tried calling back but – surprise, surprise – it was a withheld number. Your mum laughed it off, said it would be someone wanting to sell me a timeshare now I'm in my sixties.'

'So you didn't tell the police about it?'

Chris shook his head. 'We thought about it, but in the end we didn't bother. I know it happened again this week-end though, when I was up north. Your mum texted me on Friday night, said she'd had another one. She didn't seem too worried and to be honest I hadn't thought about it again until I got that silent call to her mobile yesterday. But *that*, combined with . . . *this* . . .' He glanced at Maria, squeezed her hand even tighter. 'It doesn't sit right, does it?'

'Please don't make this more of a drama than it already is.'

'I'm not *making a drama*, Mikey.'

'You could have fooled me. How about you focus on logical explanations for once? Mum was running too fast and she fell. End of story.'

'I hope you're right.'

'And the calls to the house could be anything. Sales, surveys, wrong numbers. It doesn't mean it's the same person who called mum's mobile yesterday afternoon. Has she had silent messages on her mobile before?'

'Not as far as I know,' said Chris.

'Then I'm sure it's a coincidence. Either way, you should contact Mum's mobile phone provider and see if they can trace it, so we know for sure.'

'I called them yesterday afternoon – they were predictably useless. I left a message with Farida McPherson as well but she's not responded yet. Probably thinks I'm mad. And I decided to phone Sandy too. If anyone can help with this kind of thing, it's him and his famous contacts book.'

Mikey tutted. 'So I'll just go home again, will I?'

'Don't be daft.'

'I don't see why Sandy needs to be involved, Dad. This is a family thing – and Sandy's an even bigger headline hunter than you are. He loves a drama.'

'Enough, Mikey. He's coming. And he'll help.'

Sandy Hamilton was Chris's most reliable friend, mentor and bullshit detector. He'd trained Chris when he'd started out as a cocky news reporter almost forty years ago. It was Sandy who'd taught him how to sniff out the most important line in a story, to identify the one key quote from an hour-long interview. It was Sandy who'd ranted at him when he made mistakes and who'd forgiven him if he learned from them. It was Sandy who'd nominated him for the chief reporter role and all those awards he'd won. And it was Sandy who'd noticed how grief had changed him after That Day; how he was immersing himself in other people's tragedies to avoid confronting his own.

The editor had noticed too, eventually.

In one year Chris had fallen from deserving star of the regional press awards to someone who was branded as *clearly unfocused* – a condition that, *while understandable*, had led to a series of errors in his articles that had undermined both him and the paper. Translation: *you're a liability*.

The solution was paid rest, to help him recover – but when he returned to the office six months later he was forcibly removed him from the front line of news and shunted into a *stress-free* job with the features department.

There would be no more knocking on doors or chasing ambulances or murder trials. Instead he'd write property supplements and light-hearted culture reviews. *The boredom will kill me*, Chris had said.

Sandy's reply? *Aye, but it'll save your life.*

Just like that, their days of working side by side on breaking news were over, but the connection was never lost. He was family in all but blood.

'When's he arriving?'

'As soon as he can escape the office.'

Mikey scowled. 'Well, I'll be in the visitors' room if you need me,' he said. 'I've brought my laptop, thought I'd post a public message on Ruth's social media and maybe send some private messages to her followers. I'll go through all her recent posts as well, see if we can pinpoint exactly where she is.'

'That'll help too,' said Chris, then shook his head once Mikey's back was turned. The boy expected an award every time he did something nice.

He picked up his notepad from the bed, relieved Mikey hadn't turned to the page after his *To Do* list. Chris had written and underlined the title – *Why Ruth Hasn't Responded* – but the rest of the page was blank. The empty space taunted him, dared him to write what he'd have thought if the story had come in over the wires. It was the kind of case that would have sent a thrill through him as a reporter; something to bring a bit of excitement to the dullest of news days.

Young woman, missing.

She'll be a deader, Sandy would say. *Best leave space for a photo*. Chris would then sum up the torture of ordinary families in eight column-inches, proud of his ability to portray their suffering without exceeding the word limit. But Ruth was different, wasn't she? Nothing about her life was ordinary.

Between March and September she was a freelance tour guide, leading groups of Americans on educational tours across Europe. She often worked back-to-back trips, meaning there was very little scope for visits home or spending money during that time. By the end of September her energy supplies would be empty but her bank account full, so she'd exchange her suitcase for a backpack and head off travelling on her own, usually to remote places where worried parents wouldn't dare to tread. This year she'd chosen to travel in Mexico and Central America. It was now mid-December, so she'd been travelling for weeks on end already.

Whenever she was on the road – for work or for adventure – direct contact was reduced to a minimum. *No news is good news*, and all that. So long as she kept posting photos on social media, they were to assume she was fine. And if she went silent for a few days or weeks, chances were she'd opted for some off-grid adventure and would get in touch when she could. Just because she had a mobile phone, it didn't mean she had signal or credit or a place to charge it. Just because she had an email address, it didn't mean she had access to a computer or WiFi. Just because there were phone boxes in towns, it didn't mean they were in working order – or that it was safe to go outside and use them. And just because she was their daughter, it didn't mean she would behave as they wished.

They'd developed a system over the years whereby Ruth would be the one to instigate contact if and when she was able to do so. Maria was banned from sending texts and emails full of questions for the simple reason that she worried herself to death when she didn't get a reply – the same way Chris was now.

All of that brought him back to the same conclusion – if Ruth were aware he was trying to contact her, she'd have been in touch. Once she received their messages, she'd respond. Simple. Nothing to worry about. Perfectly logical. In the meantime, all he could do was be patient and stubbornly ignore all explanations offered by the part of his brain that was trained to sniff out headlines. The same rules applied to Maria's situation. Stay calm, stick to facts.

Chris spent the next hour staring at Maria, her hand held in his; her life held in place by machines and drugs he'd never understand. Could she really hear him when he talked to her? What would she tell him if she could speak? His mind was a whirl of questions but he was sure of one thing – if there was a connection between Maria's fall and those silent phone calls, he'd find it. He wouldn't let her down again – and he'd start by getting Ruth home, now.

He grabbed his pad and headed to the visitors' room, found Mikey hunched over his laptop. The screen was filled with the image of a smoking black peak against a blue sky, solid but still moving, soaring but still growing taller. Chris recognised the image only because Ruth had posted the picture a few days ago – with a hashtag telling them it was the youngest volcano in the world. It was hard to imagine these things still happened: the force and fury of nature, hidden under the crust of the earth for millennia then pushing up through the earth and bursting through solid rock, scarring a rocky mountain landscape that had looked the same way for centuries. Now a desert of sharp black sand seeped over grass and fields and ant hills and the twisting trunks of ancient trees. The sand pushed its way into houses, swallowed churches right up to their steeple.

Mikey had his back to the door, eyes on the screen.

'Knock, knock,' said Chris.

Mikey glanced over his shoulder. 'Come on in.'

Chris sat down beside him, made sure no part of them was touching. 'You made any progress?'

'Kind of.'

'Meaning?'

Mikey sighed. 'I've been taking a closer look at the photos Ruth's been posting, trying to piece together her route over the past few weeks. I figured that if she doesn't get in touch soon we could try to contact people in the places she's been, see if they know where she was heading. I've made a list of hostel names she mentions, local companies she's taken excursions with – that kind of thing.' Ruth always preferred to travel alone but occasionally signed up for day trips with small tour operators offering experiences that were impossible to organise independently. Mikey turned his screen towards Chris. 'This is the last photo she posted. Some volcano in Nicaragua. Ruth hiked up then surfed back down. Loads of companies offer the same trip but hopefully the one Ruth used will remember her and might even know where she planned to go next.'

'When was that?'

'About four days ago.'

'She could be miles away by now.'

'Or she could be planning another excursion with them today. We won't know until we ask, will we?' Mikey checked his watch. 'They won't be open yet but let's search for all the companies that offer that volcano trip. And the moment it hits nine a.m. in Nicaragua I'll call every single one of them.'

The two men worked together at Mikey's laptop, noting the name and number of all companies that offered the same excursion Ruth had just done.

They clicked from one website to the next, had almost filled a full page with contact details when Chris stopped, leaned closer to the screen. He'd just opened the main page of a tour company called Sand Safari. Just like all the others, they'd used an image of the volcano as their central image. But Chris had seen this one before. He grabbed the mouse, flicked back to Ruth's Facebook page. 'They've used Ruth's photo,' he said. 'Look, Mikey. This is the one.'

Mikey pulled the laptop closer to him, adjusted the size of both boxes so the Sand Safari web page and Ruth's Facebook feed were open side by side.

'You're right. They're identical.' Mikey sighed. 'How did I miss that?'

'Fresh eyes, that's all.'

'I should have noticed.' Mikey cleared his throat to smother a wobble in his voice. 'So if they're using Ruth's photos on their site it means she *must* have done the trip with them – then maybe she emailed her best images to them afterwards?' He quickly checked the time difference on his laptop. 'It's still too early to call – let's go and grab some lunch, then I'll phone them. This might lead us right to her.'

They brought rolls and tea back to the visitors' room then ate in silence, watching the clock, willing time to move faster. Chris's stomach churned when Mikey finally pulled out his phone and dialled the number for Sand Safari, hoping the office would have an early start.

The call was answered quickly and Mikey launched into rapid Spanish, losing Chris after the initial *hola*. Maria had always spoken to both kids in her native tongue and the three of them would disappear to Barcelona every summer to immerse themselves in it completely. Maria's teaching job meant she had the same time off as the kids, so they'd pack up and fly off as soon as school was done, stay with Mateo in the same rambling apartment that Maria and her brother had grown up in.

Mikey and Ruth had been fascinated by their young uncle. He was the only grown-up they knew who'd buy sugary cereals and let them watch 18-rated movies and splash out on tickets for theme parks. They were intrigued by Mateo's computer programming job, too, would drag chairs from the kitchen through to his home office, watch in amazement as he created colourful animations on the screen. Chris was less impressed by his career choice, mainly because he didn't take on enough work to sustain his lifestyle and he expected his sister to fill in the gaps with *temporary loans* between projects.

The financial deal between Mateo and Maria would usually have been struck by the time Chris arrived in Barcelona towards the end of the holidays. And by that time the kids would be so used to speaking Spanish to all adults that they'd do the same with him. They'd look disappointed when he answered in rough-edged English. Chris had studied Spanish for years yet failed to retain anything more than the most basic phrases. When the kids were wee they'd drive him mad with secret conversations in Spanish whenever he looked after them on his own. He felt just as lost now, listening to Mikey on the phone, as he had back then. The only words he recognised now were *Ruth* and *Morrison*, repeated over and over by Mikey then spelled out, slowly.

Silence followed.

Chris tried to attract Mikey's attention but he waved him away.

After a few more repetitions of Ruth's name, Mikey started shaking his head, sucked his lips inside his mouth. There it was, the Morrison family mechanism for tear-prevention. Tried and tested, never failed. *Bite down hard enough and the tears won't come, son.* He did it when they were burying the dog in the garden and when they went to visit his gran in the hospital the week before she died. He did when he missed that penalty that meant his football team lost the city cup. And he was doing it now, staring at that photo on his laptop with a phone gripped in his hand and his mum half-dead across the corridor and his sister gone AWOL and his dad staring at him and his jaw clenched tightly shut. The technique worked, stopped the tears.

But bad news came all the same.

Chris sat down, closed his eyes, and waited.

CHAPTER 6

Mikey sat with his head bowed, phone pressed against his ear. Beside him on the table was the list he'd made of all the places mentioned on Ruth's Facebook and Instagram in recent months. Sand Safari was already scored out. The staff had checked their files when Mikey called but insisted they had no record of any client called Ruth Morrison. They couldn't explain why Ruth's Facebook photo was identical to the photo on their website but told Mikey it was the typical panoramic view from a popular lookout spot that all tourists visited.

Conclusion? It was probably a coincidence.

'Coincidence my arse,' said Chris.

Mikey volunteered to call all the other hostels, restaurants and tour companies Ruth had photographed or hashtagged in the past few months. Someone, somewhere had information about where Ruth was or had been or was planning to visit. They just had to persevere and stay positive. But hope faded every time Mikey scored off another name and every time Chris checked his mobile phone for updates.

Why hadn't Ruth looked at her phone yet? It was so bloody frustrating. She seemed obsessed with plastering details of her life on social media but when it came to actual contact she was utterly useless, and getting worse. Chris reread the few emails and texts she had sent them in recent months, hoping to find a way forward: mention of places or people they could contact. But the only conclusion he came to was this – the words written by Ruth said nothing at all.

Life was amazing. Places were beautiful. Food was fantastic. People were so nice. Weather was great. She was having The. Absolute. Best. Time. Ever.

All of them were things that could not be measured.

It was a while now since she'd written them an actual letter, but he remembered feeling the same when he read her accounts of life at university. He had loved picking up the post from the front door and seeing Ruth's distinctive handwriting on an envelope. He and Maria used to open her letters together, watching each other as they read; knowing which parts would make the other one laugh. Afterwards they'd make comments like *she seems to be getting on fine* and at the time that was good enough. They were happy just to hear from her, to know she'd made the time and effort in her day to think of them and spend money on a stamp. But Chris had often reread her letters later in the day with a coffee and the eye of a journalist and he'd see what wasn't there. She'd describe the old-fashioned lecture theatres where she took classes, detail her strict study routine, maybe tell them about some new dish she'd just learned to cook. Again, she'd use words like *lovely* and *interesting* and *nice*, but it was all so bloody polite.

To be fair, she'd probably learned the technique from him. It was life, filtered; like a news story carefully moulded to fit the views of its readers, to cause no upset and present a picture that matched what they wanted to believe. Ruth's letters were too rosy, too positive, too bloody happy.

When he'd mention it to Maria she'd roll her eyes, tell him to remove his news reporter hat – and his miserable Scottish pessimist hat while he was at it. *You should be happy she's happy, amor, not picking her words apart.*

I know, but—

No buts. She's moved on, got past it. You should try doing the same.

And, just like that, Chris would be stung into silence.

The letter-writing had continued during Ruth's big backpacking adventures through Europe after she'd graduated. She'd write them page after page of A4, describing the worlds she was travelling through and temporarily building her life within. She'd punctuate her letters with phone calls home, but they'd always been a rarity owing to different time zones and crap phone lines. Her letters stopped for good when she started travelling further afield, and staying away for longer stretches of time. Paper and pen, treasured for so long, died a technology-induced death. She shifted her focus to email, then long comments on social media, then pictures with short comments. Now, mainly just photos.

Her life had become a stilled image, her voice a hashtag.

Chris would barely pass comment when Maria slid her phone across the table at breakfast, gently demanding he show interest in the latest picture Ruth had posted, hashtags beneath. He'd look, nod, smile, try his best to be interested.

Not just *look* interested, *be* interested.

Chris loved photography, but Ruth's photos bored him for the same reason her letters did. They rarely told a story. There were church steeples reaching up into blue skies, ancient doors with peeling paint, exotic meals not yet eaten, a beer in a branded glass, two bare feet with the sea and sunset and the horizon behind. He could look at thousands of them and be none the wiser about how Ruth actually felt or what had moved her to capture that particular image.

It had been so different when she was little. Sharing came naturally then, with ease. When they were down the beach or out on the boat she'd tug his hand and tell him to *look, Dad, look*. They'd stare at the sea and she'd tell him she wanted to spend her whole life right there with white horses and the slimy seaweed that tangled in her toes and salt that dried on her skin, made her arms sparkle when she held them up to the sunlight. *A world without walls*, she called it. When she came home from school or from a friend's house she'd chatter non-stop, wouldn't shut up until Mikey poked her in the ribs or Maria shushed her. Chris would do what he did best and listen. He loved the endless energy of her and she loved it when he laughed and told her she'd have been a nightmare to interview: her rush of stories and observations and laughs and memories and ideas tumbling out faster than any shorthand master could ever catch.

He thought of all the old family albums at home, how they'd cringe and howl with laughter when Maria brought them out. Every photo triggered a memory, part of their shared history. Often their stories wouldn't match and that would make them laugh even more, each of them remembering different details of the same moment. But there was none of that in Ruth's collection.

Ruth shared images, but not the life behind the camera.

'Another dead end,' said Mikey. He tossed his phone on to the table and scored out another name on the list. 'That's more than half of them ruled out. The restaurants from her photos don't have a clue who she is and the hostels all tell me they're not allowed to give out client details to strangers. Which means all we've got so far is the big fat *no* from Sand Safari – and that was the one call I thought would lead us right to her. But you know what? I think we need to ask them to check it again – and I think you should phone this time.'

'Me? I don't speak Spanish.'

'I'm sure they'll speak English and actually, they might respond better to you. Phone again and innocently enquire where they got the main photo on their site. No mention of Ruth. If they say it came from a client, ask for the name.'

'Is that not exactly what you just did?'

He sighed, shook his head. 'I think I messed up, sounded a bit accusing. To be honest they probably didn't hear much beyond the word *desaparecido*.'

'Desa-what?'

'*Desaparecido*. It means "disappeared" in Spanish. *Los Desaparecidos* refers to The Disappeared – all the people who go missing during civil wars. But more recently it's been used to describe all those thousands of women who've gone missing in Central America, mainly in Mexico. I'm sure you've read about it – or written about it. And before you get paranoid – I'm not suggesting Ruth's involved in any of that shit, I just realise now that it was a mistake for me to use that word when I phoned. Total conversation-stopper. My own stupid fault.'

'You're not stupid, Mikey.'

'You think?' He cut eye contact, stood up, handed Chris the phone. 'I'll go and sit with Mum while you phone. It's worth a try, Dad. If there's one thing that would help Mum wake up it'd be hearing Ruth's voice out of the blue, telling one of her travel stories.'

'She'd like to hear your stories too, you know.'

'I know, I just . . .' Mikey shrugged.

'It's hard for all of us.'

Mikey pressed his lips so tightly together they almost disappeared. Then he turned and left, head down, swallowing so hard Chris could hear it.

Chris watched him go then dialled the number, staring at the volcano photo on Ruth's page while the phone rang, zooming in so he could better see the details. The black dust that hung in the air behind one of the surfers, trailing him on his descent like a thick swarm of flies. The pained exhaustion on the face of someone hiking back up, surfboard hauled up on to their shoulders. The way sunlight bounced off the windscreen of a pick-up truck waiting at the bottom of the slope. And then he saw something else. Tucked into the bottom right-hand corner, almost invisible against the black sand, was a tiny grey rose.

When Chris went out hiking he loved to see flowers and plants growing in inhospitable places: a burst of colour on the rock, soft leaves pushing through a solid. But that wasn't this. The rose in Ruth's photo was made of pixels, not petals. The rose in Ruth's photo was not real. It was a copyright symbol.

'Christ,' he said, hanging up the phone.

He closed the image of the volcano and flicked through the other photos on Ruth's Facebook page, zooming in to search for the one detail he'd never noticed when he looked at them on the tiny screen of his mobile phone. Now, he saw copyright symbols on almost every photo. It was so obvious, so blatant a deception. Aye, the icons were all different, but they all said the same thing.

The photos Ruth posted were not her own.

And why did that matter?

In the absence of words and phone calls, photos were the only thing they had that tied Ruth to a specific place and time. Without them, she could be anywhere.

CHAPTER 7

Mikey was sitting stony-faced at the side of Maria's bed when Chris got back to the room, and the only sound apart from the beep of machines was the muted scrape of tooth on tooth in his mouth. 'What took you so long?'

Mikey had clearly been crying but Chris pretended he hadn't noticed, kept his eyes elsewhere. 'Something's going on,' he said. 'Ruth's been posting photos she didn't actually take. She's stealing them from other sites.'

'Says who? Sand Safari?'

'I haven't called them, Mikey. I didn't need to. Look.' He sat the laptop on the bedside table, pointed to the grey rose icon in Ruth's volcano photo. 'It's a copyright symbol – and this isn't the only one. Remember the photo of the big blue flowers? The one of that church decorated with balloons? The one of the old man selling corn? They've all got different copyright symbols. Easy to miss, but they're there. This comes up all the time at the paper when the photo desk tries to use online images to accompany a story. They can't use them, but Ruth can, and has.'

Chris had studied every image posted by Ruth, only giving up the search when he reached the family photo taken on his sixtieth birthday weekend, back in March. That was the last time they'd seen her. Maria had forced Ruth to be part of the photo, despite her usual protests – then posted it publicly on Ruth's Facebook page. And there they were, the four of them, smiling together. Maria, Mikey and Ruth with their wild, dark hair and skin that made every Scottish person jealous. They were so bloody Spanish, the three of them – a trait that was even more obvious with Chris standing beside them in his kilt. Maria, effortlessly elegant in jeans and a hand-knitted jumper. Mikey with that beard he proudly claimed he'd grown in a week. And Ruth? She'd made the effort to be there – and that was enough.

But that was it – the only moment in any of those photos that Ruth had actually witnessed in person. The other photos were not hers.

'The ones that aren't copyrighted have been copied from other sites – blogs and things. I did a few searches of the place names and got hundreds of images for each. Ruth must have done the same: picked out the photos she thought we'd never see. The majority of her images were buried in web pages most people would never look at. She's copied forgettable images from sites with very few hits. She's made an effort, I'll give her that much.'

Mikey pulled the laptop on to his knees and for a few minutes he flicked through Ruth's posts, zooming in on every photo until he found the part that should not be there, the evidence that all was not as it should be.

'But what's the point of her doing this? What's she trying to prove?'

Chris saw the wee boy hiding behind a man's beard and his eyes stung. 'Your guess is as good as mine.'

'And if she's using all these sites that nobody ever looks at, then why did she decide to post one from the Sand Safari site? That must get loads of viewers.'

'Maybe she just got lazy,' said Chris. 'Nobody has questioned her in nine months so she probably thought she'd get away with it. At least it explains why Sand Safari have never heard of her. She's never been on one of their day trips.'

'You don't know that for sure,' said Mikey. 'And as for the reason she's stealing photos . . . maybe the camera on her phone broke. Or maybe her mobile got nicked. And that would explain why she's not answering your calls, too. Makes more sense than your theory.'

'You think? Sounds like blind optimism to me.'

Mikey sighed. 'It was just a suggestion.'

'If she didn't have her phone she'd have let us know, by email.'

'I suppose you've got a better explanation?'

Chris clenched his jaw, hoping that was enough to stop the words from escaping. Tears stung his eyes, threatened to fall. What would Maria say? He knew the answer to that one, could almost hear her voice, soft and stern at the same time. *Pull yourself the fuck together, Chris.* She could be vicious when she wanted to. She swore sparingly, but to marvellous effect. Her *fucks* were never gratuitous, never down to habit.

'Dad? Just say it. What do you think's going on?'

Chris looked at Mikey and at Maria, both of them entirely out of place in that room. His son and his wife did not belong here, like this. They deserved to be kept safe and at ease. That was what he'd promised all of them, wasn't it? His mind took him back more than three decades and once again he saw Maria's face when she came out of the bathroom at the flat holding the little white stick that told them life was changing, and for the better. He'd vowed then that he'd protect her, and the new lives they created. Mikey was born and adored, delighted when they told him he'd soon have a wee sister to look after. Heather. Born one week, died the next. The day it happened, Mikey had kept asking why the door to the nursery was still shut; why he and Maria were so quiet . . .

'Dad? I asked you a question.'

'I heard.'

Chris looked at Maria, remembered her muted struggle with the grief of losing Heather. Ruth, another daughter, had helped bring not just joy, but peace. He couldn't stand the thought of her enduring another loss; could barely bring himself to say the words in front of her.

'I'm worried something's happened to Ruth.'

Mikey looked away, shaking his head. 'Please, don't start. There must be a logical explanation. Maybe she's stealing other people's pictures because they're better than hers. Mum used to buy postcards on holiday then stick them in the album beside the photos of us, remember? We used to take the piss but she always said the same thing – *other people take better pictures*. This might be Ruth's version of the same habit. Like mother, like daughter.'

'I doubt it,' said Chris. 'And anyway, your mum didn't pretend she'd *taken* the pictures in the postcards, did she? That's the bit that worries me the most. Why would Ruth present these photos as her own? She wants us to think she's there – but in fact she could be somewhere else entirely. If she's trying to hide where she really is, then she's done a fine job. Mission accomplished.'

But still, Chris was stuck on the why.

Again and again his thoughts were dragged towards the explanations that hurt the most, his mind like a small boat fighting invisible currents. He tried to pull it back to safe, shallow waters. But nature was stronger than he was.

Maybe it wasn't Ruth who had posted the pictures at all.

Maybe someone else had – someone who wanted the world to believe Ruth was perfectly well and happy and exactly where she should be.

But who?

Puberty brought Ruth oily skin and acne and my eyes lingering on the parts of her that now swelled. Ruth's mum bought her first bra and left it, unannounced, on the end of her bed along with sanitary towels and a little book called Girl To Woman *which helped reinforce the most important fact of life.*

Sex is embarrassing and should not be discussed.

The book had colourful diagrams of insides and outsides and a sketch of a mum and a dad and the little person they'd created by following the simple instructions. And so Ruth learned about desire, and why she should fear it.

But it wasn't me she was afraid of. Not really. She was afraid of everyone else and what they'd say if they knew about me and her, the secret we shared.

This Is Not Right, she'd say. Me and you are no longer right.

But she didn't mean it. I know because somewhere between the struggle and the shame and the pushing me away and the keeping quiet, her words disappeared and her body spoke, said that when I was in her she felt complete.

But, of course, that did not mean we could not be broken.

CHAPTER 8

Chris was in the canteen when Sandy arrived, dressed as ever in his green tweed suit. His build was what Chris's mother would have described as *solid*. Not skinny, not fat, not somebody you'd challenge to an arm-wrestle. The colour had drained from his trademark ginger hair before he reached forty and he'd been called *the white fox* ever since, by friends and rivals alike. Aye, he could be sly when required, but more than anything Sandy brought with him a palpable sense of calm.

He nodded to Chris. 'I won't ask how you're feeling.'

'Wise man.'

Sandy sat opposite him. 'Anything new?'

'Not since my last message. Sorry for bombarding you but Mikey shuts me down every time I suggest there's something wrong.' Chris stared into his mug of tea, let his eyes drift out of focus. 'I know you'll tell me not to speculate. I know I need to focus on facts. But I can't shift the feeling that it's all connected somehow. Maria, Ruth, the silent calls, those bloody photos.'

Sandy nodded slowly, eyes following a departing ambulance through the window, sirens screaming. A potential life-changer for a stranger, a potential headline for him.

He pulled out his notepad and pen, fingertips automatically feeling for a folded corner – marking the next clean page. 'I'll do my best to trace your mystery caller, and then – if you want me to – I'll do some digging on Maria's accident and on Ruth, see if I can help you make sense of it all. You must be desperate to get to the bottom of this, Chris, but make sure you look after yourself as well.'

'I'll be fine.'

'I've heard that one before.'

'And what's that supposed to mean? Christ, the last thing I need is you dragging up old ghosts.'

'They're not old if you're still haunted by them.'

'Enough of the puns.'

For a few moments the men stared at each other, then Sandy spoke, his voice softer now. 'How are things between you and Ruth these days anyway?'

Chris's jaw tightened. 'You want the honest answer?'

'Always.'

'It's a struggle.' Chris stared straight ahead, as if holding his eyes still would stop tears spilling over. 'You know when you meet an old pal in the street and you quite fancy a chat but it's obvious they're desperate to get away? That's the kind of conversation me and Ruth have all the bloody time. Totally stilted.'

'Is she more relaxed with Maria?'

'She used to be, but she doesn't really open up to either of us anymore. I just hope there's someone she can turn to, you know? I worry about her.'

'Chris . . .' Sandy sighed. 'Do you think she might have tried it again?'

Chris closed his eyes as gently as he could but the memory of it was there, waiting. The terrace, the blood, the knife, and Ruth in the middle of it. He focused on keeping his forehead smooth and his jaw loose and his breathing steady. *Panic isn't every part of you, Chris.* That was what Maria always told him. But when it took hold Chris felt as though his body was burning on the inside. It was a thundering chaos of vicious thoughts, it was blood and lungs and eyes moving far too fast. It was loneliness and terror like no other, every time.

'I honestly don't know,' said Chris. 'But I can't stand all this sitting around, all this endless waiting. I've been staring at Maria for two days and I'm no closer to understanding why she's here, or why Ruth's not. None of it makes sense. But it seems like nobody's doing anything to try and join the dots.'

'I'm here to help with that.'

'You're a pal. One of the good ones.'

'Enough of that. If you get sentimental on me I'll be out of here before you've finished that tea.' He clicked the end of his pen, wrote the date on a fresh page. 'Let's get started. Does Ruth still own your old flat in Portobello?'

Chris nodded. 'Lets it out short-term and stays there when she's home.'

The mention of their old home in Portobello conjured up memories of Ruth when she was little – the way she'd plonk herself on to the kitchen floor and demand he clean the sand out from between her toes after a trip to the beach. Later he'd catch her standing barefoot on the draining board, smiling to herself as she stared out of the window towards the sea, hands smudging the glass.

'Earth to Chris?' Sandy waved a hand in front of his face, dragged him back to the present – and the fear of another daughter confined to the past tense. 'I said – have you been down there to knock on the door?'

'We'd know if she was in Scotland, Sandy.'

'That's not what I asked.'

'Then no, I've not been down there, but—'

'So you don't know for sure, do you? Never assume anything, especially the highly unlikely and the highly illogical. You've been out of the game for a while but I thought that message would have stuck.'

Chris tutted. 'You're right. I'll go.'

'It'll do you good to get away from the hospital for a wee while,' said Sandy. 'But before you go – does Ruth have any boyfriends, past or present?'

'I don't have a clue. Mikey might know.'

'I'll ask him while you're out. She's a freelance tour guide, right? Have you spoken to the companies she usually works for?'

'Not yet,' said Chris. 'But she only ever works for one. Trobador Tours.'

'Then call them on the way to Ruth's flat,' said Sandy, then he closed his notepad and stood up. 'What are you waiting for? Go. Now. I'll go find Mikey.'

Chris headed for his car, feeling a surge of determination.

With Sandy's guidance, Chris had tracked down hundreds of people during his years as a news reporter – and that was long before the internet was invented. He'd start the day with a name and nothing else. He'd get out of the office and start asking questions and always – always – he'd find something to move the story on. Someone at a garage or a church or a shop or a bar would recognise the name and have a vague idea where the person lived or where their brother worked or where their mum drank on a Thursday. Each life was a vast jigsaw, a seemingly endless series of connections. His success as a news reporter had been testament to that. So, if he could track down total strangers in a single afternoon without the help of technology, finding a member of his own family in the internet age should be a piece of piss.

Right, Chris? Right.

CHAPTER 9

The car smelled of boot polish. Chris's hiking gear was stashed on the back seat exactly where he'd left it two days ago. His jacket and headtorch and hiking pole, relics from a past life that already seemed achingly distant. He distracted himself with his phone, found a number for Ruth's employer and set it to hands-free as he drove towards that flat he and Maria had made their first home.

The woman who answered clicked some keys and tutted louder than necessary then said she was very sorry but she had no record of a tour guide called Ruth Morrison. When Chris suggested she double-check, the woman sighed and told him it wasn't really her job, then asked him to hold the line while she transferred him to the tour guide manager in Boston. Cue a pop song Chris had never heard, on loop, punctuated by an unnaturally cheerful American voice trying to sell him holidays with Trobador Tours. He'd heard it three times when the line clicked and from the void came a voice.

'Mr Morrison? Good morning to you! Well, good afternoon for you, I suppose. You're one meal ahead of me.' His accent was half-Irish, half-American; his tone, unbearably enthusiastic. 'My name's Montgomery but please, call me Monty. Suits me better. Now how can I help? Lesley in London says you were asking about one of our guides?'

'Aye. Ruth Morrison. My daughter. She's been freelancing with you for about six years, ever since she graduated. But there seems to be some confusion. Your colleague in the London office says there's no record of Ruth but—'

'Can I interrupt?'

You already have, pal. 'On you go.'

'Before you go on – of course I know Ruth Morrison.'

'You do?' Relief flooded Chris's body. 'Thank Christ.'

Monty seemed vaguely amused. 'It was me who employed her, you see, back in the days when I worked in the UK office. I did recruitment and training back then, all the fun stuff. But I'm based in the States now, operations side. I was sad to see her go but it's the nature of the business.'

'Go? Go where?'

Monty laughed. 'I mean I was sad she had to leave us.'

'She left? When?'

'Just before the season started this year. Middle of March.'

'Christ.'

He pulled over, too quickly. The bus behind him honked its horn and he got a death stare from a granny dragging a tartan trolley along the pavement. He ignored both. He cut the engine, took a few deep breaths before he managed to push out the words.

'So you're telling me Ruth hasn't worked for you all year?'

'You didn't know?'

'No. I didn't bloody know. Why did she stop working for you?'

'Well – it wasn't exactly her choice.' Monty started to say something else, then hesitated. 'Sorry to ask, but did you say you're Ruth's father?'

'I am, aye.'

'And she didn't mention this?'

'Nope. What happened? She's been freelancing with you for years.'

'In a nutshell? Ruth let us down, badly. She got in touch the day before her first spring tour and said she couldn't do it – then proceeded to cancel every single one of her assigned programmes. We were stunned. She must have known we'd struggle to cover so many days without any notice. A few weeks later she emailed again with contact details for a tour guide friend who was able to cover her tours in late summer and autumn – but it was too little, too late as far as we were concerned. I'm sure you know all our guides are freelance, so we couldn't actually fire Ruth, as such. But her name was removed from our list of guides and she won't be called again. Simple as that.'

'What reason did she give for cancelling the tours?'

'That's just it. She didn't give a detailed reason, just a half-hearted apology and some excuse about *personal issues*. Maybe you can enlighten us?'

'I wish,' said Chris. 'But what about that other tour guide you mentioned? The one Ruth said would cover her tours? If you could give me their contact details that would be a big help.'

Monty hummed and hawed, then said he'd need to check with head office before he gave out details. 'Clients always say the guide is the most special part of the tour – and Ruth was one of the stars, which was why it pained us so much to part ways. But unfortunately we've had a couple of cases where clients become a bit obsessed with guides, bombarding them with messages long after the tour is done. Not nutjobs, but they're annoying.'

'That's not really what I'm wanting to hear, Monty.'

'Oh. Sorry. But that's why we're banned from giving contact details.'

Chris sighed. 'Look, I can't get hold of Ruth and her mum's . . . not well. She's in hospital. I'm just trying to find someone who knows where Ruth is.'

'Oh. Sorry. Again. About Ruth's mum. Look, I'll do my best about getting you that other guide's details, the one Ruth recommended. And in the meantime, well, try not to worry. Ruth's a resourceful woman. I'm sure she'll be fine.'

She'll be fine.

If Chris saw those words in a newspaper he'd edit them out. They said nothing, meant nothing, convinced nobody. They were just things people said, words that slipped out without thinking, as useless and irrelevant as a sneeze.

'Did she sound fine when she called you to quit?'

'Oh, we didn't speak,' said Monty. 'That was another thing that annoyed me about the whole thing. She broke the news by email. I'd have expected her to phone me directly with something like that, but no. It was another black mark from me, I'm afraid. I'd offer to send a copy of the email to you – but I delete all unnecessary emails every month so it's long gone.'

'But do you remember the exact date she quit?'

'Not off the top of my head but it was literally the day before she was due to start a tour. Let me see if I can find the tour dates on the system.'

The line flipped to hold music.

Chris waited, desperate for an answer – then realised he could probably find the answer at home. When Ruth received her assignments at the start of the year Maria would highlight the days with bright yellow marker on the kitchen calendar so they'd know exactly where she'd be and when. On the rare occasion a tour was cancelled she'd let them know and Maria would use correction fluid to white-out the boxes and guilt trips to encourage Ruth to come home for a visit instead. She rarely responded as Maria would wish. This year there was a huge block of yellow. Ruth had told them she was taking on more work than usual because she wanted to pay off a big chunk of her mortgage. She'd be gone from March until late September, she'd said, and then was planning to head off travelling as soon as she was done. There had been no word of cancellations.

When Monty came back on the line he said Ruth had been due to start work on Tuesday, March 20th but had emailed to cancel all of her tours the day before. He'd not heard from her since. Chris didn't need to check his calendar to know that Tuesday was two days after his birthday celebrations – when Ruth had told them she was taking an early flight to Spain on the Monday morning to start the tour season. But he now knew that instead of starting her tours that day, she'd emailed Monty to cancel them. But why? And did she even take the flight to Spain? The questions wouldn't stop, made him feel nauseous.

'Does that help, Mr Morrison?'

'Kind of.'

With that Monty ended the conversation, job done.

Chris hung up, then put his foot down and powered his car towards Portobello, Edinburgh's seaside. It was a long time since he'd been there but he didn't need a map or sat nav or a memory, jogged. It was a place of golden beaches and a promenade busy with dogs and bikes and children. It was a place of big skies that framed the hills beneath them. A place of shallow sea and packed pubs. A place where they'd all lived once, in the flat now owned by Ruth. Back then, it had been a place for their family, as they were, as he hoped they always would be. It was a place surrounded by the sea, that held the scent of the water in its bricks and cement and slates. And now, he hoped, it was a place that held answers.

CHAPTER 10

The communal door to Ruth's tenement was wide open when Chris arrived, held in place by a convenient rip in the hall carpet. It was already getting dark outside and any remaining daylight was turned to shadow by the cold, grey concrete of the steps that led to the flat, six floors up.

Chris sighed, started the climb.

It was a classic Scottish tenement, bikes chained to the railings, ash on the stairs, bin bags temporarily dumped on doormats. The weekend would bring the reek of chips and scraps of untouched lettuce by the front door next to bashed polystyrene boxes from the kebab shop.

Chris and Maria had bought the flat when they first got married and lived there until Mikey was twelve and Ruth was seven. For years after that they had rented it to students. When they'd decided to sell it, Ruth had decided to buy it, got her foot on the property ladder thanks to a generous reduction on the price. Needless to say, Mikey hadn't been pleased. But the deal was done and she'd been making a fortune ever since, letting it to tourists and short-term tenants whenever she was out of the country.

Her tour guide work meant she spent the vast majority of her life in hotels, and her obsession with travelling meant she spent most of her free time living out of a rucksack in places with unpronounceable names. She'd only come back to Scotland three or four times a year, and she never stayed long enough to establish any kind of life there. Despite that, she slept in her own flat when she came, ignoring Maria's repeated attempts to have her stay at home with them.

Ruth would refuse and Maria would be loudly offended.

At least she tells us when she's back, Chris would say. *Always.* He clung to facts like those, evidence of a connection not entirely lost. Somewhere in Ruth were the memories of things that always made them laugh, and of the easy silence they used to share when he'd given in to her pleading to go out on the boat, just the two of them. She loved to be the last one in the water and he loved the joy in her face when he was helping her back on to the boat: her wet hands gripping his fingers so tightly it hurt. She always looked so chuffed and so perfectly at home when she had salt water flattening her thick, dark hair and waves beneath her.

Ruth, as she was – in exactly the place she wanted to be.

Was she still? He hoped so – and hoped her tenants could give him the answer.

The first thing he noticed when he reached the top of the stairs was Ruth's nameplate – or the lack of it. Maria had bought a little brass plate when she'd first moved in, sent Chris to get it engraved – but with strict instructions not to write *Ruth* because then people would know she was a woman living on her own and would therefore be more likely to break in to rob and rape her. And so R. *Morrison* it was.

Whoever was living there now had removed it and stuck a piece of blank paper over the four holes where the screws used to be. Chris muted the rush of questions in his head but his body protested, made the hairs on his arms stand on end when he firmly knocked at the door. When he knocked a second time he heard the thud of footsteps but then the neighbour's door opened instead.

'There'll be nobody in, pal.'

The neighbour was wearing a red tracksuit, top and bottoms. The belly in between made Chris think of a Russian doll. He imagined turning him at the waist, round and round until his top half came off and he found a smaller version of the same man inside.

'I've not heard a squeak in there for ages. He comes and goes a lot, that lad. Works away, I think. You a pal of his, are you?'

'No, I'm not,' said Chris. 'This is my daughter's flat. Ruth Morrison. You probably haven't seen her either but she stays here occasionally, when it's not let out.' He pulled out Maria's phone, showed him the photo of the four of them. 'You know her?'

The man glanced at his phone then shook his head.

'But you said it's let at the moment?'

'It's been rented for a good wee while, so it has. Used to change all the time. Current lad looks foreign. Italian, maybe. I've got no problem with that – but he totally blanks me, every bloody time. Rude bastard in my books.'

'How long's he been in?'

The man pulled an exaggerated frown, puffed out a breath that smelled of cheese and onion crisps. 'I couldn't tell you. Maybe since the summer? Not that you'd know he was there. He's quiet. A bit too quiet, know what I mean?'

'You got a phone number for him?'

'Nope.'

'Name?'

'No idea. Try the mail boxes downstairs and you might find a name in there, if that'd help. He's shite at talking but he's maybe got a penpal.'

The man laughed at his own joke. Chris forced a smile then held out his phone again, zoomed in on Ruth's face. 'And you definitely haven't seen my daughter?'

'What's with all the questions, pal?'

Chris held his stare. 'Like I said, I'm just looking for my daughter.'

'Well, you won't find her here.'

'Fine.' He turned and knocked on Ruth's door again, stayed until the neighbour tutted and went back inside.

Chris cursed himself for not bringing his notepad from the car. He'd need to leave a note under Ruth's door with his number, asking her tenants to call. He had to get hold of them.

He started down the stairs, thought about all the times he and Maria had run down these stairs together, heading for the beach. She could take three at once without losing her pace, or her balance. Fair enough, she'd been much younger when they lived there, but she'd never lost her touch. He'd never known her to fall, in all their years together. And he couldn't believe she'd fallen now – or that nobody else was on that street. Somebody must have seen what happened. He'd call Farida for an update when he got back to the car.

But first he needed to check the wooden mail boxes in the hall, as recommended by the Russian doll. Even before he reached the bottom of the stairs he could see they were all stuffed full – and Ruth's was one of the worst.

Chris pulled out the pile of mail, flicked through it. Most of it was glossy flyers from supermarkets and pizza delivery services. There were a few letters but the envelopes addressed to Ruth's flat had names he didn't recognise.

They'd be tenants, past and present – but all the dates were recent, so it was impossible to know which of the names belonged to the person renting the flat now. But he'd track them down. He had to. Ruth was an absent land-lord but surely in nine months she'd have had some contact with them?

He wrote a message on the back of a junk mail envelope then trudged back upstairs to deliver it. If Ruth's tenant didn't respond to his note, he'd come back. Or Farida would.

Job done, he left the building that had once made him feel so instantly at home. Outside, the rain was pouring down. Chris stood beside his locked car, muttering obscenities at the weather while his hands patted pockets but did not find keys. He didn't hear the door of Ruth's tenement's slam shut, or the heavy footsteps approach him from behind. He didn't notice when they stopped, either. But then a hand grabbed his shoulder and forced him to turn – and his eyes were inches from the ruddy face of Billy Mason, Ruth's downstairs neighbour.

'Chris? Glad you're here,' he said. 'We need to talk about Ruth.'

CHAPTER 11

Chris took a step back, tried to escape Billy's unforgettably bad breath.

'Ruth's tenant has fucked up the intercom for the whole building,' he said. 'Excuse my French, but I'm getting chased all day, every day, by folk whingeing about it, and it's driving me scatty. I know I'm the only owner living in the building but that doesn't mean I should be the one who deals with all the crap. It should be shared responsibility – that's what the council says. But if I don't fix problems, nobody else bothers, do they? And why not? Because they know good old Billy will deal with it in the end. Like this intercom issue. The engineer came, did some tests, said the problem was definitely coming from Ruth's flat. So we need in, Chris.'

'Have you tried knocking?'

Billy released a sarcastic laugh and the reek of mouldy potatoes.

'I've been hammering on the door for days – but that tenant of Ruth's is never there or, if he is, he doesn't answer. And before you ask – no, I don't have a number for him. I've got Ruth's number, though. Been calling non-stop for almost a week and getting nowhere fast. It's always switched off. Fat lot of good that is. I call that neglect, so I do, and I'm sure the council would agree. Madeline on floor four thought she heard voices one night and told me to get up there but when I knocked on the door, nobody answered. It's not right, Chris.

'Anyway – it was Madeline that suggested I call your house phone, so that's what I did. Tried about eight Morrisons in the book before I got hold of your Maria, last Friday afternoon. She came round right away, to be fair, and—'

'Maria was here?'

'I just said that, didn't I? On Friday afternoon.'

'And did she get access to the flat?'

'I wish,' said Billy. 'She spent a good wee while knocking on their door herself. I told her not to be daft and just let herself in using the spare keys – the ones your Ruth keeps in that wee security box – but she said she'd have to try to contact the current tenants before she went into the flat, "by law".' He made a face and inverted commas with his fingers when he said that. 'I told her she could go about it however she wanted, but we'd need to get hold of them urgently so the engineer could get inside. In the end she left a note under their door with her name and number, explained an engineer needed access.

'That was when I stepped in and suggested she could go and look for Ruth's tenant at his girlfriend's work, since he never seemed to be at home. Maria said that was a good idea so at that point I told her to speak to Madeline.'

'Sorry – who's Madeline?'

'Floor four, like I said – red door.'

'And she knows Ruth's tenant?'

'She knows everyone,' said Billy. 'She was moaning to me about her buzzer and I was complaining to her about Ruth's tenant not answering his door and Madeline said he was always hanging about at his girlfriend's work – said I should go and hunt him down there. Apparently she's a very nice lassie. More talkative than him, but that wouldn't be hard. Anyway, Madeline told me she'd seen them together on the number 26 bus, heading into town. They get off at the same stop as her and then they walk the same route, up the bridges. Madeline stops at the Royal Mile but I'm sure she said they always kept on walking.'

'Up South Bridge?'

'I'd imagine so, but Madeline would know better. I'm sure she knows exactly where the lassie works. I felt bad, ordering your Maria to trail all the way up there – but I certainly wasn't going to go.'

Chris felt a surge of adrenalin. Farida had said Maria was running on South Bridge shortly before she fell – miles from the starting line of the race.

This would explain why she'd gone there.

But Chris knew Maria wouldn't have gone into the city centre without a specific address in mind. He had to speak to Madeline, get the details.

'Will Madeline be home just now?'

Billy shook his head. 'You're out of luck, pal. She's away to Tenerife. Told me she won't be checking her emails and that, so no point in trying.'

'When's she back?'

'Two weeks. Lucky so-and-so. But what are you wanting from her?'

'More details, so I can head into town myself and find Ruth's tenant.'

'I just told you Madeline spoke to your Maria – can you not ask her?'

Chris opened his mouth to explain, then thought the better of it. 'Aye,' he said, then made his excuses and extracted himself from Billy's grip.

It was dark now, and chilly, but he headed for Portobello beach and walked part of the route the four of them used to do together when the kids were small. Miles of golden sand and an endless sky that was never the same two days running. When Ruth was a toddler she'd ask to sit on Chris's shoulders for the hike. He remembered the way her tiny hands gripped his hair then she'd curl forward over the top of his head, bring her face in line with his – but upside down. She'd smile and he'd smile back, in love. Once her legs got longer she'd race way ahead of them all and usually they'd find her at the far end, lying on her back, smiling to herself as she stared at the sky.

After a while Chris sat down on the sand and picked up a handful in his hands. He let the grains run through his fingers and tried to gather his thoughts.

Finally, he had a logical reason for Maria being in the city centre on Sunday morning. She'd gone to find Ruth's tenant at the place his girlfriend worked – but then what? She obviously hadn't found him if the intercom problem persisted at the flat. And as for the race – the fact she'd been dressed in running gear suggesting she'd intended to compete when she left their house that morning. But something – or someone – had changed her mind.

Chris wondered why Maria hadn't told him about Billy's phone call, or her visit to Ruth's flat. Probably it had seemed unimportant to her at the time, just one more task on a long *To Do* list. But what else had she done that weekend that he didn't know about? Who else had she been spending time with?

For the first time in years, Chris thought about Maria's affair.

They'd rarely spoken about it – and she'd never spoken much about the man she'd turned to when Chris was at his lowest. The stranger who'd held his wife while he was busy falling to pieces.

It had started a few months after That Day; had ended when Maria realised guilt weighed even more heavily than grief. She'd confessed, distraught and ashamed. When he'd asked her *why* she'd said it was hard to love somebody like Chris; somebody with a sadness that would never shift; somebody that she could not fix, regardless of how deeply she loved him. It had hurt to hear it, but Chris had understood, told her he felt the same way about Ruth. He'd saved his daughter's life That Day but the sadness in her lingered on, haunted him.

Anxiety tugged his nerves so he shifted his gaze, watched a black labrador chase a ball into the sea. For a moment it disappeared, lost somewhere between the darkening sky and the water. The dog's owner stood at the shore, called its name over and over until it returned, tail wagging, and soaked her with a shake. Meanwhile, the questions in Chris's head were like the tide; unending.

But if he was patient, if he kept asking, if he maintained even a tiny smidgen of positivity, answers would come. His years as a news reporter had taught him the power of perseverance – but he'd also learned that the story would not end there. Once he'd managed to get all the facts straight, he'd be left with the hardest question of all: the one that usually hurt the most. The why.

High school unleashed a viciousness in Ruth that I'd never known she had. It's all your fault, *she'd say, convinced bullies targeted her because they knew about me. What we shared tainted her; rendered her ugly in the eyes of her peers. I was the reason boys her age kept their distance.* They know, *she'd say, and her face would flush blood-red, her insides burning with the shame of it.*

She wrote of her tormentors in a little diary with a brass lock that was easy to pick and agonising to read: the laughter that day in gym class when one of the big boys pulled down her shorts in front of everyone; the comments she'd overheard in the toilet cubicles at school; the boy who bent over double and pretended to vomit when she asked him to dance at the summer disco.

She told her diary but not her mum and dad, because people said her birth was A Dream Come True for them, and she knew she'd disappoint them if they knew her life was not. Nobody ever mentioned The Dead Sister but Ruth thought being dead was probably worse than being bullied so she kept it to herself.

Her words, handwritten.

She told the truth to her diary but she'd also invent scenes and write them down. She'd imagine what They were saying about her when she was not there. She'd write pages and pages of it, think up vile bombardments of abuse directed at her own back, turned. Then one day her diary suddenly stopped; the day she realised that all those hateful words were not coming from Them at all.

The loathing was within her.

We all know what happened next.

CHAPTER 12

Chris circled the hospital car park twice before he found a space at the far end. He walked slowly towards the main entrance, head spinning, cold afternoon air stinging his cheeks. When he got inside he grabbed tea, chocolate and a little packet of shortbread from a vending machine, then headed for Maria's room.

Hospital life had continued as normal in his absence. Nurses wore squeaky shoes and carried plastic clipboards, cleaners hunched over wheeled buckets and porters with empty beds manoeuvred effortlessly around common obstacles such as crumpled old men in wheelchairs and children with grey skin and little heads that should have hair and grown-up sons slumped in the corridor outside the room where their mother lay, stilled.

'Mikey? Is Mum okay?'

'She's fine.' Mikey sniffed. 'They're just washing her.'

Chris was amazed that the idea of his unconscious wife being given a bed bath offered a sense of comfort. But it did. It was better than being dead.

'You two made any progress?'

'Kind of.'

'Meaning?'

'Ask Sandy.' Mikey started to say something else but stopped when his voice wobbled. He was not one for crying, especially not in public and definitely not in front of his family. *It's learned behaviour*, Maria said. Translation: *it's your fault*.

Chris hunched down beside him, wondered why and when he'd become the kind of dad who could no longer offer comfort to his children. He didn't even have a paper hankie to hand, let alone anything of deeper significance.

He was relieved when the nurse came out and told them they could go back in. She'd changed Maria's sheets; carefully folded the edges, smoothed down the sides, then placed Maria neatly in the middle like an ornament; the subject of a still life on white canvas, framed by the metal bars of a narrow bed.

They'd just sat down on opposite sides of Maria's bed when Sandy pushed open the door, carrying his laptop under his arm. He removed a box of hankies and an uneaten yoghurt from the little table at the end of Maria's bed and brought the computer to life. It was open at Ruth's Facebook account.

'Welcome back,' he said. 'I got your text and I agree – we'll need to track down Ruth's elusive tenant. Shouldn't be too hard, really. But first let's take another look at Ruth's photos on social media. We found a pattern.'

'What is it?'

'Selfies – or rather, the lack of,' said Sandy. 'We tried to find photos that *could* feasibly belong to Ruth. We ruled out the ones with copyright symbols and the ones you found on other people's blogs. There were only a few images left, to be honest – but they all have something in common. There are no selfies, Chris. In fact, Ruth has not posted a single picture of herself on social media for nine months. We trawled through every single social media site she uses regularly and the same pattern is repeated on every one. Photos without faces. Now, Mikey says Ruth has never liked getting her photo taken, and I appreciate that fact, but I think we need to—'

'Can I interrupt?' They both looked over their shoulders. Mikey was sitting with his arms crossed. 'What Sandy's trying to say is that there are no selfies or pictures of Ruth on any of the sites we checked, but – and this for me is key – we only checked the sites we know for sure she's on. I'm way behind with technology but for all we know Ruth's super-active on other sites.'

'*For all we know* is not good enough,' said Sandy. 'We have to work with certainties. The rest is speculation, and speculation is a waste of time.'

Mikey sighed, shook his head.

'Can I continue?'

'Och, you will anyway.'

'Thanks,' said Sandy. He explained that Mikey had sent private messages to a few more people he knew for sure were good friends of Ruth – on- and off-line. He'd also contacted a few names he didn't know but who'd responded frequently to Ruth's old posts. He hadn't detailed what was wrong, just made a joke of the fact they'd lost track of her. *You know Ruth*, he'd said.

But it turned out that they didn't, not really.

The few who had responded already reported similar versions of the same tale. Since mid-March – around nine months ago – Ruth's contact with her friends had been reduced to an absolute minimum, and nobody had actually seen her in person. One couple had sent out wedding invitations in July and got a refusal. An old flatmate from university said she'd organised a September reunion but Ruth had responded in the same way, with no explanation given. It was proof her emails were being read, but didn't prove who was reading them.

'You still with me, Chris?'

'Aye.' Chris sighed then stood up and stretched. His back hurt, and his head. In fact, all of him hurt. 'So what's your conclusion?'

'I wouldn't call it a conclusion. But we do have a few solid facts.'

'Solid sounds good.'

'I wouldn't hold your breath,' said Mikey.

Sandy glared at him, then turned back to Chris. 'First fact – Ruth is not answering any calls or responding to emails. Second fact – some of Ruth's travel photos are not her own. Thirdly – Ruth is not currently working as a tour guide and in fact her company says she didn't work at all this year. Fourth – Ruth hasn't posted any photos of herself on social media during the past nine months and hasn't been tagged in other people's photos either. Fifth – Ruth's definitely not living at her Portobello flat, confirmed by your visit this morning. Put this all together and what have you got? Fact number six – the last time we can be absolutely certain of Ruth's whereabouts was the weekend of your sixtieth birthday, back in March. So far we've not found anybody who can convincingly confirm her presence anywhere else since then. She might be where her photos say; she might not. The reality is this – Ruth's not been *seen* for nine months.'

'Och, here we go.' Mikey scraped back his chair and stood up. 'I've had to listen to this nonsense for hours. You're just looking for a headline, Sandy. You can't help yourself, can you? Just give her time and she'll get in touch.'

'We've already been through this, Mikey. I'm not saying anything has happened to Ruth, okay? But I do think it's time to alert the authorities.'

'Because then you'll have a drama – and a story.'

Sandy glared at him. 'I'll pretend you never said that.'

'I said it, and I meant it. My family is not yours to fuck with. We don't need police. And we certainly don't need newspapers printing Ruth's face everywhere.'

They both went quiet, Sandy rigid on a plastic chair and Mikey standing with his arms crossed on his chest, jaw pulsing. Maria's ventilator puffed, slowly in, slowly out. Chris waited until Mikey's breathing matched the rhythm.

'I'm with Sandy on this one,' he said quietly.

'Surprise, surprise.'

'Och, grow up, Mikey. If nobody on the planet has seen your sister since my birthday dinner then I think we're allowed to be worried, no?'

Mikey sighed. 'Whatever you think.'

'Glad we've got you on side,' said Chris, then glanced at Maria and took a deep breath before he spoke again. 'Okay, first things first: we need to establish who was the last person to see Ruth. I left for Glasgow on the Sunday afternoon, remember?' He glanced at Sandy. 'I had another birthday night out with the boys, stayed over in a shit hotel near Central Station.' He turned back to Mikey. 'But what did you three do at home? And who was the last person to see Ruth?'

Mikey sat down, stared at the floor while he talked. 'Ruth came to mine at night and then we went for some drinks at the Alba. She said she wasn't wanting a late night because she had a super early flight to Spain the next day. But she was still going strong when I left around half–past ten.'

'So you left the pub before her?'

Mikey nodded.

'And how was Ruth planning to get back to her flat?'

'She said she was going to get a taxi.'

'*She said* isn't good enough. So you didn't actually see her get one?'

Mikey shook his head. 'I already told you, I left before her.'

'So you just left here there on her own?'

'Not exactly.'

'Meaning?'

Mikey sighed. 'She'd been talking for a while with a group of guys at the bar – said she knew one of them from school. And before you ask, no, I didn't know them. Anyway, they were getting pretty boozy, making a bit of a scene. I was pissed off Ruth wasn't spending any time with me – so I left.'

'And you thought that was fine, did you? Just abandoning her like that?'

'She's a grown woman, Dad.'

'And steaming drunk, by the sounds of it.'

'It wouldn't be the first time, would it?'

'Aye, but what if it's the last? *Christ.*'

Chris pulled out his phone, hand shaking as he dialled Farida McPherson's number. His head flooded with images he did not want to see. Ruth sprawled face down on some filthy street. The stench of life, lost. Scabby dogs sniffing at her hair, flies settling on the parts still warm. And all the while he'd been toasting his sixtieth with pals in Glasgow, doing absolutely nothing to protect her.

The call was answered quickly. Chris forgot to say hello, tripped over words as he quickly explained his reason for calling. He told Farida about the photos on Ruth's social media. He updated her on the news from Monty at Trobador Tours – the fact that Ruth hadn't led that tour in March, and that she'd cancelled all guiding work for the rest of the year. He told her about Ruth's night out with Mikey, and that she'd stayed at the pub, drunk, with a group of men they didn't know – and the fact that nobody had seen her since that night. Then his voice gave way.

Chris had hoped he wouldn't be taken seriously, that Farida would scoff at his worry, tell him in no uncertain terms that he was getting anxious over nothing. Instead she said she'd be right down, giving credence to Chris's concern and the six words that held within them an ache too great to be ignored.

'I think something's happened to Ruth,' he said.

CHAPTER 13

The chairs in the visitors' room were sitting exactly where they'd left them.

Farida opened her laptop bag and took out a folder, flicked through the papers inside until she found the form she was looking for.

Then the questioning began.

Farida repeated Chris's answers, but slightly paraphrased every single one. She'd have made a terrible journalist. *Just listen to me and write down what I say. That's it. Simple. Easy. Far less irritating.* But no. Farida continued, using a multi-pack pen to write down the basic facts of Ruth's life story in block capital letters. Ruth's age (28), profession (tour guide and landlord), permanent address (good question), distinguishing features (Maria's favourite). The questions went on, the answers a sketched outline of her life.

Farida told Chris that each and every detail was like a breadcrumb of information that might just bring them closer to Tracking Down Your Daughter and Bringing Her Home. It made Ruth sound like a fox, and Chris the hound.

And if she couldn't be traced?

Chris knew the way it worked, didn't need to listen to Farida's interpretation of the process. And he certainly didn't need that leaflet she'd slipped across the table. *When Things Go Wrong: A Guide*. I mean, really?

Really.

He glanced at it, felt sick. Here it was, a neatly arranged list of all the horrendous things that could have happened to Ruth. It didn't seem real, any of it. This was Ruth they were talking about. Ruth, who threw herself off boats and cliffs into the frigid sea, just for the fun of it. Ruth, who'd punched a boy at high school because he'd teased her about a new haircut. Ruth, who'd travelled solo to places most people wouldn't go with an armed guard. Christ, maybe Mikey was right – maybe he was making a drama out of nothing.

Ruth would be fine.

But they all said that, didn't they? Every family he'd ever interviewed for a missing person story deluded themselves in the same way. And every one of their sad tales started just like Ruth's: a missed call, an unanswered text.

Maybe Ruth was too old to be lured; too big be picked up and stuffed into the boot of a car. But she'd always be the baby of the family. She'd always be his only daughter – the one who'd survived and the one he'd vowed to protect.

'Chris? I said – tell me about the last time you saw Ruth.'

When he looked up Farida was staring at him, jaw slowly churning, expressionless mouth wafting peppermint. He'd always wondered if she was a secret smoker, didn't want to ruin the hard-but-healthy image she'd worked so hard to present in the press when she was first appointed. There was interest at the time because she shattered the usual profile, praise from the top because she got the results. She was Syria-born but Glasgow raised, moved to Edinburgh almost twenty years ago to lead an all-male team with twice her experience.

'The last time I saw Ruth was March when she came home as a surprise for my sixtieth birthday. Turned up out of the blue – that's typical Ruth. I was happy to see her – of course I was – but it would have been good to have some notice so I could have changed my other plans. We were together Friday and Saturday; we had a lovely weekend overall. Ruth was on good form, most of the time. She was a bit annoyed with Maria at one point, but overall? Fine.'

'What annoyed her?'

'Och, it was nothing. Maria had organised a special dinner with friends and family on the Saturday. She'd made a video with all our old family photos, showed it on a big screen after we'd eaten. There were loads of Mikey and Ruth when they were little – and they got a lot of laughs. It was hard to believe those two wee scamps on the big screen were the same two people sitting at the top table, all glammed up. They both got a fair ribbing and Ruth got a bit pissed off. But she was fine after a few drinks. She lightened up and laughed it off.'

'And that was the Saturday, yes? So Sunday was the last day you saw her?'

'Aye. I went to Glasgow on the Sunday afternoon. I had another birthday celebration with pals that night. They were coming from far and wide so we all stayed in a hotel and I drove back to Edinburgh on the Monday morning.'

'But what about that Sunday morning with Ruth. How was it?'

'Fine. Ruth came round for lunch, then I packed the car and got ready to go. I gave them all a goodbye hug – and that was the last I saw of her. It was all perfectly normal.'

Chris pictured his last glimpse of them as he'd turned out of the driveway. Ruth and Maria standing at the front door, waving. Mother and daughter, side by side, smiling. Those two faces, framed by those unmistakable thick black curls. Mikey had appeared behind Ruth and Maria just before he lost sight of them, saluting at the car when Chris tooted the horn and turned on to the road.

'As for what happened after that? Speak to Mikey. But I remember Maria telling me she'd got the usual two-line email from Ruth the next day, saying she'd arrived in Spain for her tour. We had no reason to doubt it.'

'But we now know she didn't lead that tour?'

'That's right,' said Chris. 'Christ, we don't even know if she made it home from the pub, never mind all the way to Spain.'

'I'll contact the e-border programme to trace her movements – and I'll get in touch with the airlines,' said Farida. 'Do you have her flight details?'

Chris shook his head. 'Mikey might know.'

'Mikey is your eldest child, correct?'

Chris nodded. 'He's five years older than Ruth.'

'Any other children?'

Chris always struggled with that question. The easy answer was *no* but he could never bring himself to say it. Saying no would be a betrayal of that short life and of the damage its loss had caused them both. Chris and Maria rarely spoke of her but she was always with them: their second baby, Heather, born between Mikey and Ruth. But she'd only lived a week.

'It's just the pair of them,' said Chris. He'd found dozens of ways over the years to answer questions about his family without actually telling the truth.

'How would you describe the relationship between Ruth and Mikey?'

Chris paused, bunched his lips. 'Changeable. Ruth always idolised her big brother so they got on fine when they were small, basically because Ruth did whatever he said. They were always getting up to nonsense. But once they got a wee bit older Mikey convinced himself Ruth was the favourite – and that was when the bickering started. They were always fighting as teenagers. He'd jump on the slightest thing, claim Ruth was always getting her own way.'

'And did she?'

'We treated them the same,' said Chris – but, suddenly, he wasn't sure. Nobody had ever questioned him so directly on it before, except Mikey. He'd been the star attraction right up until the day Heather was born. After her death grief took hold, then frustration when they couldn't get pregnant again as easily as they'd hoped. Mikey had been five by the time Ruth came along, and with her had come hope, renewed. It was logical Mikey wouldn't get so much attention when Ruth was a baby – but after that? It was impossible to measure. Chris had always dismissed Mikey's complaints as sibling rivalry, nothing more. Good parents treated all children equally; that was a given. But maybe, just maybe, that wasn't what they'd done after all.

'And how about their relationship now, as adults?'

'Ruth's not around much.'

'That's not what I asked.'

Chris bunched up his lips. 'They get on fine – always go out for a few drinks when she's back, just the two of them. Same way they did that Sunday.'

Farida nodded. 'Is Mikey still here?'

'He's in Maria's room, with Sandy.'

'You mean Sandy Hamilton?'

'Aye.'

Farida frowned, did nothing to hide her disdain. 'You can tell me what's he's planning once we're done with this. But first, is there anything else you'd like to add about your birthday weekend? You said Ruth was annoyed after that video was shown – but was there anything else? Anything out of character?'

'Och, Ruth was moody on a few other occasions, but that's not unusual.'

Farida paused, looked up. 'Can you elaborate?'

'Not really,' said Chris. 'She's a bit sulky, always has been.'

'So nothing that sparked it that weekend? An argument, maybe?'

'Not that I know of. Ruth and Mikey were nipping each other's heads by the time I left, but that's not unusual, especially when drink's involved. Ruth adores Mikey but she also winds him up better than anyone on earth. He said she was pissing him off at the Alba on the Sunday, but best ask him about that.'

Farida nodded, appeared satisfied. She turned a page, looked up.

'Tell me about Ruth's most recent contact with you.'

Chris pulled out his notepad, found the timeline he'd cobbled together.

'Her last post on social media was that volcano picture I told you about, the one that's copyrighted. From Nicaragua, a few days ago. Her last email to Maria was about ten days ago. Said she was just leaving Costa Rica, heading north. She's not sent a text in ages – she only sends them when she can't get internet. As for phone calls, the last one was a few months ago now, probably around the time she was due to head off travelling. I can't be more specific than that – but I do remember she didn't speak for long. Said she had a sore throat.'

'Was it a video call?'

Chris shook his head. 'She was calling from a payphone, I think.'

'And nobody else has had video contact?'

'Not that I know of. We've tried contacting friends and the tenants at her flat in Portobello, but so far we've not found anyone who's seen or spoken to her more recently than us.'

Farida nodded. 'And you're sure she's not at her flat?'

Chris nodded. 'Positive.'

Farida nodded then put down her pen. Was that it? Chris felt something like relief spread in his chest but it tightened when Farida spoke again.

'Chris – how would you describe *your* relationship with Ruth?'

Chris corked that one with a single word. 'Fine.' Wished he'd said *good*.

Next.

'To the best of your knowledge, is Ruth at risk of harm in any way?'

Chris felt the phrase on his tongue for a while before he answered. *Risk of harm*. It was so polite, so clean, so utterly sterile. 'Of course Ruth's at risk of harm. Everybody is, all the time. That's living, isn't it? Christ, look at Maria.'

'You know that's not what I'm asking.'

Chris stared at the floor, clenched his jaw to stop the words slipping out, same way he'd done every day since That Day. Maria wouldn't want him to drag it up now, would she? And Christ, he didn't want to either.

'Is there something you want to tell me, Mr Morrison?'

If Farida were a dog her ears would have been standing on end, twitching. It was the only thing about the woman that reminded Chris of himself. The ability to spot a line in a story: a tiny chink in somebody else's armour.

'I don't think *want* is the word,' said Chris. 'But I should.' He closed his eyes and for the first time in fifteen years he allowed the full scene to run, both in his head and out of it.

CHAPTER 14

'It happened when Ruth was thirteen,' said Chris, eyes fixed on the floor. 'We were all in Barcelona for a final family holiday before Mikey went to university. We had to drag him along, but he came. We were staying at their Uncle Mateo's flat, same as always. Anyway, I surprised Maria with a special lunch to celebrate our wedding anniversary. Mikey had arranged to spend the afternoon snorkelling with some pals he knew from previous years.

'To be honest, I think Mikey's trip was more about the beer than the marine life, but he was eighteen by that point, so there wasn't much we could do to stop him. Ruth wanted to go with him – she's obsessed with the sea – but Mikey said she couldn't, said he didn't want his wee sister cramping his style.

'Needless to say, Ruth was furious. She stormed off and locked herself in the bathroom for ages. We'd arranged for her to go shopping with a few of her second cousins, but when she finally opened the bathroom door she point-blank refused to go. In the end Mateo offered to stay in and babysit. Maria wasn't keen, given Ruth's behaviour – but

I insisted, convinced her Mateo would be fine. It was only for a few hours, and we weren't going far. And it wasn't like Ruth was a baby, was it? She was almost a woman. But she was so unpredictable when she was in a mood.'

Chris sighed and closed his eyes, wished again that the story of that day ended right there with an expensive lunch, a snorkelling son, a helpful uncle, and a sulking daughter.

'And?'

'In short, Mateo got bored. And when that man gets bored he starts drinking – and when he starts drinking the rest of the world disappears completely. He went out on a bender, left Ruth alone at his flat. Maria knew he couldn't be trusted. She *knew* it. And I did too, if I'm honest. But I was so determined to go for that bloody lunch, as if that actually mattered at all.'

Tears came then. Chris didn't care or try to stop them.

'She sharpened the knife before she did it,' he said. 'That was the first thing we noticed when we got home – the sharpener sitting on the kitchen table. Mateo's brandy bottle was there too, half empty. We assumed he'd drunk it but the doctors told us later that Ruth had very high levels of alcohol in her blood.'

Christ, Ruth's blood.

He stared at his hands, was relieved they couldn't speak. He remembered the way Ruth had struggled under his grip; the crust of red under his fingernails.

'What was Ruth's intention that day?'

'Her intention? Isn't it obvious?'

'With respect, I'd say nothing is obvious in this kind of case.'

Chris sighed. 'The doctors suspected it was a proper . . . attempt as opposed to a cry for help – but Ruth refused to speak about her reasons. In the end a nurse sat me and Maria down in the hospital, handed us a list of *warning behaviours* and asked us to identify which ones applied to Ruth. Only two matched, which meant Ruth was neatly filed as *unlikely to repeat* and sent home.

'Before she got back we searched her room for a letter but found nothing. That's a key indicator, apparently. If there's a letter, it means they really want to . . . end it. Mateo and Mikey swore they hadn't seen or touched a thing while we were at the hospital. We repeatedly asked Ruth what triggered it but she never said much. Told us she didn't fit in, that she felt ugly. Typical teenage stuff.'

'But an extremely atypical reaction, I'm sure you'll agree.'

Chris nodded.

'Did she speak to anyone else? Any professionals?'

'We took her to a couple of different therapists, but she was completely uncooperative and refused to go after a few sessions. Her saving grace was her languages teacher at school. He was young, seemed to have a gift for talking to kids. I don't remember his name but I remember he quit before Ruth's final year, went to do a charity project abroad. She was a bit down when he left, but overall she was much brighter by that stage. More like the Ruth we knew.'

'And now?'

'Now what?'

'Did she seem like herself the last time you saw her?'

'Honestly?' Chris observed the words in his mind before he released them into the world, a crushing acknowledgement of the distance between them. 'These days, I don't think I know her well enough to know.'

Farida looked at him with an expression he could not read. 'Are you worried she's done it again, Chris?'

Chris screwed up his face. Farida had a reputation for being direct, but this was taking the piss. 'I worry about a lot of things, not just . . . that.'

'But you can confirm she's never disappeared before?'

'I wouldn't say Ruth has *disappeared*.'

'No?' Farida handed Chris the completed paperwork, marked a cross in the place he should sign. 'So shall we forget about this?'

Chris hated her. He wanted to grab the form and rip it up or scrunch it into a ball or hold a lighter to the corner and let it burn, watch the flames creep upwards and swallow the blobs of fresh ink and that one word in big black block capitals that should not be written next to Ruth's name and should not be a part of her story or his story or their story. MISSING.

When Ruth left home, I followed.

I mostly watched her from a distance, trying to reinvent herself in places that held no memories of me. For the first time in her life she was Ruth without labels attached. People looked at her with fresh eyes and with interest and when she spoke they listened to her without doubting what she said. Nothing was out of character. Nothing was typical. She could act however she liked and it would be accepted as The Way She Is because nobody knew any different. Nobody could compare it to the Ruth she always had been but no longer wanted to be.

Except me, of course.

Please leave, she said. Then expected me to disappear. She thought that was all it would take, as if I were a curiosity that could be picked up and played with for a while, then discarded when the novelty wore off.

Please, she said, again. Then she cut me out of her life completely and filled the space with vodka swigged from the bottle and fags she rolled herself and drugs that secretly terrified her and boys she didn't really like who had darkening lips and lowering voices and hands fingering the zip on her jeans.

For years, I watched her.

And, for years, she knew but would not turn.

Instead she stared straight ahead, kept her eyes on all the things she could do and buy and be to prove she was happy and successful and someone her parents would be proud of. She convinced herself that this was the life she'd chosen for herself but in fact it was the life the world had chosen for her. You'll fit here, *the world said, and Ruth squeezed herself into a mould so tight there was no room for me or for the memories of the we that we were.*

But fear stalked Ruth almost as closely as I did.

She'd be out drinking cava with the girls and I'd take my chance when she went to the bathroom on her own. She'd be checking her make-up or washing her hands and suddenly she'd sense there was someone else in the room, just as I stepped back into the shadows. Or she'd be sitting on a late train with some boy she'd met in a club and she'd look out of her window and into the window of a passing train and I'd be there. She'd glance back, as though I'd grabbed her long hair and tugged it, reeling her in. Our eyes would meet for a second, maybe two.

Long enough to know she knew.

You might wonder why I just didn't stop her where she was and force her to acknowledge me. It would have been easy enough, even when she studied other people's shoes all day for fear of seeing me; even on the many nights she drank so much and smoked so much she could hardly see herself in the mirror.

But here's the thing.

I wanted Ruth to turn around, not because I forced her to, but because she wanted to. I wanted effort on her part.

I wanted commitment. I wanted her to make a conscious decision to let me back into the life she'd tried to carve me out of. I wanted her to regret ever wanting to do that. I wanted her to look at me and not look away; to hold my gaze and say what I'd always hoped she'd say.

As we are, we are enough.

CHAPTER 15

Once Chris had signed the statement, Farida closed her notepad, then the door. 'We need to talk about your wife, too,' she said. 'Strictly off the record.'

'What's happened?' Chris crossed his arms then read his own body language and immediately changed position. 'Do you know something?'

'I was going to ask you the same thing,' she said, holding his gaze. 'It's clear to me that you're suspicious. You don't believe it was an accident.'

It wasn't a question, but she looked as though she wanted an answer.

'You're right. I think we need to do more digging.'

'Convince me.'

Chris flipped pages in his notepad to distract himself from Farida's eyes.

'First of all, we need to find out who's been making these silent calls to the house. Could it be Ruth? Maybe. And was it Ruth calling Maria's mobile yesterday afternoon? Another maybe. We know from Ruth's neighbour that Maria was going to look for her tenant near the Royal Mile – so could that be why she was there on Sunday morning? Maybe. But *maybe* is not good enough, and you know it. Plus none of it explains why Maria was sprinting down that stinking close at ten a.m. on a Sunday morning when she should have been at the starting line of a race, at the other side of the city. It can't be a coincidence that all this has happened at once, out of nowhere. The silent calls, then Maria's accident, then Ruth going missing. They must be connected.'

'With respect, it hasn't *all happened at once*, Chris. It's true that Ruth has just been registered as missing now, but in reality she's been missing for nine months, hasn't she? It's just that nobody noticed until now.'

Chris met Farida's gaze and held it, knew he was being judged. What kind of dad didn't notice his only daughter was missing for that length of time? Not the kind that knew how to protect his family, that was for sure. And, if that thought was in his own head, he knew it was in Farida McPherson's too.

'What's your theory, Chris?'

'In a nutshell? There was someone else involved in Maria's accident.'

'Who?'

Chris shook his head. 'No idea.'

'Then let's try *why*.'

'Same answer.'

Farida stared at him. 'Has your wife had any disagreements with anyone recently? Problems at work? Is there anyone who'd have a grudge against her?'

He crossed his arms again. 'She's got an inheritance dispute with her brother that's been dragging on for years. He was pissed off that their dad's money was divided into four, so that Mikey and Ruth got the same share he and Maria did. He thought it should have been halved – half for him and the rest divided between Maria and the kids. Needless to say, it's not helping family relations.'

'I assume it's a sizeable inheritance?'

Chris nodded. 'Not enough to quit your job, but enough to make a difference. Ruth does okay for money with her tours but she's mainly paid in tips so it's a bit hit-and-miss. Mikey's always a bit tight. A sum like that would give them both a bit of security, and that's what their grandpa obviously wanted. And the thing is, Mateo's already living off his parents' money. The man's forty-three years old and has never paid a day's rent in his life. He assumed ownership of the family flat in Barcelona well before both parents died, when they moved out of the city, so I don't know why he's complaining. It's just pure greed that's driving him now.'

'Does he have children?'

'Thankfully not. The man can barely look after himself. He's ruled by his demons and by drink. It causes Maria an enormous amount of stress.'

'And you?'

'What about me?'

'How do you feel about Mateo?'

Chris stalled, wished it were appropriate to say *no comment*. Nobody had ever asked him that before, but somehow the answer was right there, waiting.

'Honestly? I suppose I still blame him,' he said.

'For the incident with Ruth?'

'Aye. The tiny part of me that doesn't blame myself blames him. But despite my personal feeling towards the man, I know he'd never do anything to hurt Maria. At the end of the day his sister's all he's got now.'

Farida nodded, appeared satisfied. 'Any other disputes?'

'Not that I know of,' said Chris. 'Maria is very loved.'

'Many victims are.'

'What are you suggesting?'

'The same as you, Chris. You've been in this business long enough to know that most women are attacked by men they already know. In your case the odds are doubled. One family, two women. So, other than this wayward uncle, does Maria have any other family? Males, in particular.'

Chris shook his head. 'Just me and Mikey.'

Farida's eyes were still on him, didn't shift an inch. Chris got the distinct sensation she was trying to catch him out. 'I urge you to think carefully about it. And if there is anyone at all who might hold a grudge – from Maria's present or past – you must let me know. I take your concerns seriously but at this stage neither case is a criminal investigation and therefore I cannot treat them as such. I need something more.'

'What should I do?'

'For both cases, speaking to people is key,' said Farida. 'The last people Maria and Ruth spoke to might have the answers, even if they don't realise it.'

After that Farida talked about contacting friends and followers and hospitals and airlines and banks and mobile phone providers. 'They can provide us with a map of a life,' she said. 'Day by day, sometimes minute by minute.

And, in addition to all of that, we can of course make Interpol aware of Ruth's case – but that doesn't mean a whole lot at this early stage. While Interpol can liaise with the police here and abroad, all responsibility for conducting searches in foreign countries lies with local officers in those locations. In short, if it becomes obvious Ruth is missing abroad, the police in Scotland will not be allowed to participate in any part of the investigation – unless and until they are invited to do so by the police force abroad. You with me?'

'Aye.' Chris sighed. 'Which means nothing will happen until we know for sure which country she's in, right? But, now that we can't trust her photos, I don't have a clue where to look. She could be absolutely anywhere.'

'I can assure you we'll do everything in our power to find her, Chris. And as for Maria . . . have a think about what I said.'

Farida shut her notepad and stood up.

'One last thing. I know Sandy Hamilton is a good friend of yours, and a trusted colleague. But I'd advise you hold off any major newspaper campaigns at this stage. I know that goes against your nature but we need to gather as much information as we can before we go public. And I'm sure you understand why: if there *is* someone else involved in this case and they happen to read the paper, it might give them time to cover their tracks before we reach them.'

'I get that. But Sandy knows what he's doing.' Chris looked over Farida's shoulder when Sandy opened the door to the visitors' room and looked in. 'Speak of the devil.'

Farida nodded to Sandy the same way she would at a crime scene. 'We'll get you an official statement as soon as we're ready,' she said. 'Anything Chris tells you about our conversations is completely off the record. Understood?'

'Perfectly,' said Sandy, almost smiling.

'That'll be a first,' she said. 'Now if you'll excuse me, I'd like to have a word with Mikey before I leave. Assuming he's still here and happy to talk?'

'He will be,' said Chris. 'You'll find him in Maria's room.'

Farida nodded then left.

Sandy placed tea and snacks on the table, then his hand on Chris's shoulder. 'You okay?'

'Not really.'

'Anything I can do apart from keeping you fed and watered?'

'Aye,' said Chris. 'Get Ruth on the front page.'

Sandy sat down, stared at Chris until he looked him in the eye. 'You sure?'

He nodded. 'I understand that in an ideal situation we'd do what Farida suggests and wait for her to finish her investigation – but time is the one thing we don't have. Ruth needs to know about her mum, *now*. She needs to get here, *now*. So we need the front page, *now*.'

'I'll do whatever you think will help. But you know what'll happen if she's on the front, don't you? The press will bombard you, Chris. They'll ask difficult questions. And, if you don't answer, they'll dig until they find them.'

Chris nodded, sinking his head into his hands. 'I'll deal with it.'

'It won't be easy.'

'And this is? Christ.'

'Come on, then,' said Sandy, digging into his jacket pocket for his reporter's pad, ballpoint pen pushed through the metal ring-binding at the top. 'Let's get the damn thing written.'

An hour later the article was complete and the two men exchanged an awkward goodnight hug. Chris went back to Maria's room and found Mikey dozing beside her bed. He woke him up and sent him home to sleep, just before a nurse came in and dimmed the lights.

Chris watched Maria for a while then grabbed a blanket from the wardrobe and turned his chair to face the window. Security lights outside the window illuminated brown grass, a cement path, harled walls, and a sliver of angry sky with clouds so thick it was hard to believe they'd ever shift.

He thought of home, of all the times he and Maria had sat up in bed watching tree branches sway and clouds change position. If they stretched their necks a little they could also see the bench where they went to drink their tea after lunch, and the unintentionally crooked path that led to it. They'd carved it out just after they bought the house, on one of the hottest days ever recorded in Scotland. They'd woken up with the sunrise and taken the kids snorkelling in the still, sparkling water of the bay, then returned home focused and determined, spent the next six hours hunched over the slowly toasting lawn with spades and shovels, cursing and blessing the heat at the same time, stopping every few minutes and rubbing their hands on the backs of their old jeans to dry off the sweat that was making the plastic handles slip under their fingers. Mikey and Ruth played happily on the shady part of the lawn, the garden a novelty after growing up in a flat.

And again Chris asked himself – how did *that* turn into *this?*

Back then Chris had still been a news reporter, good and getting better. Maria was a young, innovative teacher. And Mikey and Ruth? They were immersed in the joy of an uncomplicated life. In fact they all were, for a while.

They'd gone for another snorkel when they finished the path, headed out on the boat until they made it to the reef and could no longer hear voices from the shore. Maria had counted to three and then they'd all leapt, screaming, into the water without wetsuits. They had felt blessed when the water enveloped them, cleaned their sweat-sticky skin, soothed their stinging palms, removed all weight.

Chris turned back to Maria, wishing for weightlessness now. He squeezed her hand then focused his attention on her pulse: the anchor that kept her here.

I'm alive, it said. *I'm alive.*

He followed the rhythm, repeated those two words over and over in his head until there was no room for thoughts of a life without Maria and Ruth in it.

And only then, sleep came.

CHAPTER 16

Sandy pushed open the door of Maria's room with his foot, three steaming coffee cups balanced in his hands. A rolled-up newspaper was tucked under his arm. He handed Chris a coffee. 'Mikey not here yet?'

'I doubt he'll even be awake this early,' said Chris, glancing at his watch. 'Anyway, I'm sure he needs a decent sleep – and to spend time with Rachel.'

'She's not been in to visit yet, has she?'

Chris shook his head. 'Can't say I'm bothered.'

'You still don't get on?'

'Och, same as ever. She's nice enough, just not the kind of girl I'd have pictured Mikey ending up with. But it's Ruth who's got the big issues with her.'

'What about?'

'Jealousy, I think. She always had Mikey to herself and suddenly there was this girl on the scene – dolled up to high heaven, one of the popular ones at school – and Ruth was sidelined. To be fair, Rachel made a really big effort with Ruth when they were teenagers, acted like a big sister in some ways. She'd lend her clothes and teach her how to put on make-up, all that nonsense. It was good of her – and Maria really enjoyed having two girls around the house. But as adults that connection is totally gone. They mostly avoid each other.'

'Can't be easy for Mikey.'

'I don't think life with Rachel is easy, full stop,' said Chris. 'I'm sure that's why he's always working late. Earns peanuts but he's a workaholic.'

'Is he still plugging away with that custom wetsuit idea?'

'Aye.' Chris resisted rolling his eyes. 'He says business is fine. No idea how he makes it work but he's resilient, I'll give him that. Anyway – enough about Mikey. Are you going to let me see that paper?'

Sandy had read the article to Chris before it went to print but it was still a shock to see the words in black and white, telling his own story. He'd sent over several photos of Ruth, some alone, some with the family. The news desk had chosen a picture taken two or three years ago when they were out hiking. Ruth looked young and pretty and healthy and happy. Completely indestructible.

The article was short but to the point, following the same formula as every other story that made it into the paper. There was a general appeal, requesting members of the public to get in touch with any information that could aid their investigation. *If you've seen Ruth Morrison, spoken to Ruth Morrison, or been with Ruth Morrison in the past nine months, get in touch.* After that there was a statement written by Chris and Sandy *on behalf of the family* – a direct plea from Chris to Ruth, explaining again that her mum was unwell and urging her to call or come home.

'Is she on the front for all editions?'

Sandy nodded. 'I insisted.'

'Appreciate it.'

In a few hours Ruth's face would stare out from shelves and racks across the country and then it would be in hands and on trains and left on buses. Ruth's face, stained with coffee and smudged with fingers; ripped and tossed in the bin.

Chris flipped the paper over so he could only see the sports pages on the back. 'You think the UK press will pick up the story?'

'Probably. It's an unusual case. And it won't take them long to realise Ruth's dad is *the* Chris Morrison, sidekick of that old bastard Sandy Hamilton. You've been out of news for a while but they'll remember you.'

'You think they'll remember why I left?'

'Most folk don't know, and unless they dig they won't find details.'

Christ sighed. '*Revealed: Tragic Past of Missing Girl's Dad.*'

'Don't torture yourself.'

'Life is doing a pretty good job of it without my help.'

'True, but complaining about it won't help. Stop wondering what you could have done. Focus on what you can do to make things better, now.'

'Christ, you sound like a therapist.'

'That's exactly who I got it from,' said Sandy.

'You?'

'Saw one for months after Maggie left me for that arse-wipe. Cost a fortune but helped me no end. Think I'd have hated her forever, otherwise.'

Chris looked at Maria, felt an almost imperceptible trace of bitterness raise its head – just for a second.

'Maria had an affair too, you know,' he said. Fourteen years had passed, but it was the first time he'd told anyone. 'I was already teetering on the edge after everything with Ruth – but that's what pushed me over.'

'I had no idea,' said Sandy. 'Who was it?'

'Supply teacher at school. Younger than me, and no doubt refreshingly free of mental health issues. She regretted it, of course, told me she'd just wanted to hold somebody who wasn't in pain.'

'That's original,' said Sandy. 'Maggie said she cheated on me because I'm a selfish twat who never paid her any attention. Either way, it hurts.'

'Aye.'

'Was it Maria who ended the affair?'

Chris nodded. 'As far as I know she's not seen him since.'

'Did you tell Farida?'

'Why would I?'

Sandy widened his eyes. 'He could be your Man With A Grudge, Chris. Teacher or not, he might be a nutcase. And he's also Man With A Motive.'

Chris looked up. 'You think?'

'I wouldn't rule anything out at this stage.'

'Christ.' He picked up the newspaper, stared at Ruth's face on the front. How could this be his family? He loved them, but that wasn't enough, was it? It hadn't been enough to stop That Day, or to cure the scars it had left on them. His eyes were locked on the front page and his hands were gripping newsprint – but his mind was back on that terrace, with the blood of his child on his fingers.

'You know what bothers me the most about That Day? It's the moment *before* Ruth stuck that blade in her arm, knowing how totally hopeless she must have felt to think that was the only way forward. It's one thing to think about it; it's another thing to take a knife and push down, hard enough. I think of That Day and I see Ruth, sitting alone on the terrace, rolling up her sleeves.'

'It wasn't your fault, Chris. And this isn't either.'

'I really wish I could believe that.' He stood up, grabbed his car keys from the table beside Maria's bed. 'I need to find her, Sandy. Will you stay?'

Sandy nodded.

Chris kissed Maria then headed for the car park, mobile phones silent as death in his pocket. He was sick of so many unanswered calls and so many unanswered questions. It was time to find answers for himself.

Ruth finally gave in nine months ago.

It was just past ten on a Sunday and Ruth was in an old pub by the shore, one of those traditional places tourists think are charming until the barmaid calls them a cunt. She was squeezing her way through a group of fat men in football tops when she saw me looking back at her from the other side of the bar. She held my gaze and just like that, the whole world clicked into place.

She was transfixed at first, boozy eyes creeping over every detail of my face. I think she expected to find more flaws than she did. But what she found was the desire of her childhood, still there, thick enough to choke on.

If she'd put down her pint glass and reached into the space between us I'm sure she'd have felt the love there, warm to the touch. There was no distance between us at all, despite the years that had passed and despite her best efforts to flush me out with alcohol and pills and shots of sperm from boys whose names she rarely remembered and who I knew she'd never love the way she'd loved me. She held my gaze and for a moment I was right there with her in her bedroom, chair against the door. I was looking at her and I was home.

But let me get one thing straight.

Home has nothing to do with signing a mortgage agreement or mail boxes in the hall with my name written on all the letters. It has nothing to do with familiarity; knowing exactly what the view from the kitchen will look like in every season or knowing how it smells when you open the door after holidays.

It took me years to realise that kind of home exists only in my head, constructed out of abstract thoughts and ideas and ideals that have no consistency to them. That kind of home is not built to last. That kind of home will change and rot and fall down and be replaced. That kind of home was not the home I felt when I looked Ruth in the eye and she looked back and we both smiled and my whole body turned to love and I wanted to tear myself open and pull her to into the gap; feel her completely inside of me, absorbing every single drop of her. We left the pub and headed for the flat.

Fifteen years after the last time, it was time.

CHAPTER 17

The Alba was a proper pub, a place of polished wood and shiny beer taps and tiny packets of peanuts hanging behind the bar. The low winter sun was pushing stripes through the window, illuminating drips on glasses and crumbs on tables and the glittery decorations hung on the fake Christmas tree by the door.

The man behind the bar nodded to Chris. 'What can I get you?'

He ordered a water, told Ruth's story, got a knowing nod. 'The police have not long been in. I'm assuming it's the same lassie you're talking about?'

'Aye.'

'And you're her dad?'

Chris nodded.

'Then I know your son. Mikey. Comes in here a fair bit. But I wasn't working the night it happened. You'll need to speak with Liz, the owner. She always works a Sunday, rain or shine. Wait and I'll get her.'

The barman disappeared through the back, leaving Chris at the bar with two men who had red faces and zipped-up winter coats. Both were flicking through the papers, occasionally nodding or commenting to their pal.

They'd have seen Ruth's face, maybe sat their pint on it.

Chris had just closed his eyes to escape them when Liz Catto pounded into the bar, a ruler-length of metal bracelets ringing each of her flabby arms. They rattled like a drum roll. 'Leo says you're Mikey Morrison's dad?'

When Chris nodded her smile turned to pity, turning his stomach.

'I know Mikey. Nice lad. Awful to hear his sister's missing.'

'You know her as well?'

'I wouldn't say so,' said Liz. 'I've only met her the once and to be quite frank I only remember her because . . . well, because she was in such a bad state.'

Chris's body tensed. 'You mean drunk?'

'I mean absolutely out of it. I found her in the ladies' loo, crying her eyes out, stinking of vomit. This isn't really that kind of pub, you know? She was apologetic, to be fair, but pretty far gone. God knows how much she'd had.'

'Did she tell you why she was crying?'

'I asked, but she just blamed the drink,' said Liz.

'Do you know who she'd been drinking with? Mikey said she was with a group of men – said she knew one of them from school. You remember them?'

'More or less,' said Liz. 'The pub was busy, but I do remember one group of lads getting a wee bit wild – not regulars – and I think she was with them. But it was so long ago that I don't remember much about them, to be honest.

Just normal-looking lads, maybe a bit older than Ruth. But all very drunk.'

'Do you remember Ruth leaving?'

'Kind of,' said Liz, flushing. 'It was me who called her a taxi.'

Chris's pulse quickened. 'So you saw her leave?'

'Unfortunately not. Once I got her cleaned up I looked for Mikey – thought he'd want to help his sister get home – but there was no sign of him. Ruth wasn't bothered, said she'd nip outside for a fag before the taxi arrived. She said one of the lads she'd been drinking with would wait with her. But next thing I know the taxi driver came in, said he'd been waiting five minutes and nobody had come out. I went out to look but he was right – she'd already left.'

'Was anybody else outside?'

Liz shook her head. 'There was nobody there – and I didn't see that lad inside again either, the one she'd been drinking with.' Liz bit her bottom lip. 'God, I never for a single second imagined anything would happen to her.'

Chris stared straight ahead and clamped his jaw, wished this was just another news story he was reporting on. But that was it confirmed, wasn't it?

Ruth had got blind drunk then left the pub to smoke with an unknown man. Was it someone she knew from school, as Mikey said? Or someone else? Whoever he was, that man was the last person who'd seen her. *Alive.*

Chris's eyes welled up. He headed for the toilet before they spilled over.

The toilets smelled like blocked drains. They had no soap at the sinks, no lock on any of the cubicles and mildly offensive graffiti scrawled into every inch of the walls. Chris checked his phone for calls or texts or emails but there was nothing. He hung over the sink, avoided looking himself in the eyes.

Maria always made a point of acknowledging herself in mirrors. She'd wish herself good morning, give herself a proper smile. On bad days she'd stop and stare deeply into her own face, said it helped her work out what she really felt. *If you don't really look, you don't really see*, she'd say. Exactly, thought Chris, then turned on the hot tap and let it run, willing the steam to block out feelings he could not face. But it couldn't block out the images on the inside.

Ruth, standing with her mum, waving goodbye. Ruth, drunk and distraught in a pub toilet, then leaving to smoke with some unknown man.

Ruth's taxi waiting, but empty.

But what came next?

CHAPTER 18

Chris phoned Farida on the way back to the hospital, leaving a message in a voice that sounded far stronger than he felt. Maria's secret life, exposed. The affair: the potential for a grudge. He also told her he'd spoken to Liz Catto, confirmed Mikey's claim that Ruth had left the pub with a man nobody knew.

He was almost back at the hospital when Farida called back, wondering if this was this a bad time. Of course it bloody was. He pulled over, put the phone on hands-free then reached into the glove box and pulled out his notepad. Out of habit he wrote the date at the top of a clean page, wondering if today would turn into one of those dates he would always remember but wouldn't want to.

'I'll keep this short as I can,' said Farida. 'The good news is, we've obtained key details from Ruth's mobile phone provider. The bad news is that Ruth's device has not been used at all in Latin America. I know you were under the impression she'd been travelling in Mexico and neighbouring countries.'

'You're saying she's not even been?'

'I'm saying her phone hasn't.'

'Christ.' He could tell there was more news coming, knew Farida had paused only to let that first bomb drop to earth. And there it was, ripping up his solid ground, exposing the lies that lay beneath. 'But she's sent texts to Maria from that phone, saying that's where she was. She's been telling us about all those places in her emails. She *must* have been there.'

'With respect, you've previously cast serious doubt on the truthfulness of your daughter given her use of other people's photos on social media. And unfortunately this new information appears to confirm your fears.'

Chris wanted to speak but no sound came.

'We also have information about where the device *has* been used in the nine months since she was last seen. It's been used in Spain, Chris.'

'Spain? When? And where?'

'All over the country, in September. You said Ruth works as a tour guide, correct? That would perhaps explain sporadic use over there.'

'It would – but I already told you that Ruth didn't work any tours at all this year. Remember? Her boss at Trobador Tours said she emailed them the day before her first tour in March, cancelled all the tours she'd been assigned. They said they wouldn't offer her any more work after that.

'Yes, I know that, Chris. But if Ruth is a freelance guide surely it's possible she could have been leading tours for a different company?'

Chris paused. 'I hadn't thought of that,' he said. 'But it makes sense. And that might explain why she left Trobador

130

Tours so abruptly, right? Maybe she was offered tours with a rival company and had to start right away. But why wouldn't she tell us?'

'Not all children talk to their parents about their work.'

'True,' said Chris, felt a stab of guilt when he turned it on his head – not all parents asked their children about their jobs. He thought back to their conversations during his birthday weekend – had he asked her how work was? No. He'd shown no interest in her job for years, so why would she bother telling him she was changing companies? In fact – had he asked her anything about herself at all? He felt hurt she didn't share details of her life with him, but, sitting there in the car, he realised the fault lay with him. He rarely asked.

'So what now? If we know she's in Spain, or has been at some point, will you contact the police there? Should I go? Or maybe Mikey, since he speaks the language? But . . . no . . . we can't go while Maria's in hospital. But if she wakes up and finds out something's happened to Ruth . . . Christ, I can't think straight.'

'At this stage I don't advise you travel abroad,' said Farida. 'In fact, I'm starting to suspect the answer to Ruth's disappearance lies a lot closer to home.'

Chris flushed, her words a finger pointing at him down the phone line. 'What do you mean?'

'Meaning I've got one final detail from Ruth's mobile phone provider – and I'm afraid this one doesn't match with anything we've discussed so far. Ruth's phone is not in constant use but they're able to trace its location whenever it's been switched on. And, Chris – Ruth's phone is currently in Edinburgh.'

Another bomb dropped.

'But why wouldn't she tell us she was here?'

'Her *phone* is here,' said Farida. 'That doesn't prove Ruth is.'

'Then who's been using it?'

The question hung in the air, tempting Chris to think the unthinkable.

'Chris? I know this news may give you some hope, but be aware that, even if we find Ruth, she has the right to refuse contact. We can't force families back together, however much it may hurt the people involved.'

'Finding her . . .' Chris closed his eyes, blinked instead of saying the next word. *Alive.* He couldn't say it, for fear of its opposite. 'Finding her is enough.'

'We'll do our best,' she said, softening. 'For your part, I'd suggest you focus on connections in Spain. Anyone else Ruth might have seen in Spain if she was working there on the dates I mentioned? It's vital we get a more recent sighting than March. Did you say Maria's brother still lives in Barcelona?'

Chris felt his jaw tighten. 'Aye, Mateo still lives there.'

'Is there any chance Ruth would go to visit him?'

Chris thought again about the city skyline topped with a clear blue sky, the way the sun had bounced off the sharpened tip of the knife. He remembered the muffled roar of a plane passing overhead, wondered again what his life had looked like from above that day. Him, hunched over Ruth, hands slippery with her blood.

132

'Chris? I asked if Ruth would have visited him?'

'Doubt it. She's not been there since . . . That Day.'

'You know that for sure?'

'She wouldn't go back there. She's not spoken to him in fifteen years.'

'I still recommend you call him. You have a number?'

'No. Not here,' said Chris. 'I'll be able to find one at home.'

'Let me know as soon as you've spoken to him. And good luck.'

'It'll take more than that,' said Chris, then hung up.

He sent a text message to Sandy, asking for an update on Maria and telling him he'd be gone a little longer. Then he turned the car around and, for the first time since the accident, he headed for home.

CHAPTER 19

The first thing Chris saw when he unlocked their front door was Maria's winter coat hanging on the banister. He caught the scent of her and felt her absence. So this was how it felt to leave the house as two and come back home as one. He'd asked the question often enough when he was a reporter, knew the way tragedy crept into ordinary moments and smashes them to pieces. And time and again, when he'd asked which part was the most difficult to deal with, husbands and wives and parents had given him the same sad answer.

The first homecoming.

In hospital he looked at Maria and saw only the shell of her. She was a photo, a still life, sheet music. But home was the opposite of all of that. Home didn't modify its behaviour Given The Circumstances. Here he was immersed in the world they'd created together, was clearly half of something. He cringed, knowing Maria would tut and roll her eyes. *I'm half of nothing*, she'd say.

He'd loaded the car on Friday after lunch – almost five days ago now – then given Maria a goodbye kiss while she was sweeping up leaves in the back garden. Chris now knew that at some point that afternoon Billy Mason had called her about gaining access to Ruth's flat and she'd gone round to knock on the door and try speaking to the tenants. Later that same night she'd texted Chris to tell him about another silent call. Sunday was the day she'd tried but failed to find Ruth's tenant – or his girlfriend – and it was the day of the race she hadn't run; the day her head was smashed open on stone steps.

But what about Saturday? Had she gone anywhere? Who with? Was any of it linked to Ruth's disappearance? *Speak to people*, Farida had said, and that was what he intended to do. He had to ask difficult questions to get to the truth.

And he'd start with Maria's brother, Mateo.

Chris was halfway up the stairs to the office when he noticed a flash of red on the hall table, coming from Maria's old answerphone. He went back downstairs, felt a surge of adrenalin when he read the digital display. Two new messages. He pressed play, held his breath, wished he could turn down the volume of his heartbeat as the first message started playing. It had been received on Sunday morning from a withheld number. Beep, static, beep. It lasted two seconds, maybe three. He played it again. Beep, static, beep. He sighed, then played the next one. Again, the phone number was withheld but the answer machine told him the second message was left on Sunday evening.

Beep, static, then a voice.

The caller was a man.

His words were muffled. Chris listened over and over until he was sure what was said. Four words, then the caller sighed and hung up the phone.

Soy yo, he said. A few breaths and then two more words. *Lo siento.*

It's me, in Spanish. And then? *I'm sorry.*

Was it Mateo? He'd soon find out.

He found Maria's old address book in the top drawer of the office desk. The digital age had made it redundant but she held on to it regardless. Chris sat down and thumbed through the pages until he found the number he was looking for. Mateo's mobile. Chris clenched his jaw when the phone started ringing. How long had it been? *Long.* He flipped through the address book to distract himself, had just finished the F section when the call was finally answered.

'*Si? Quien es?* Yes? Who is it?'

The voice was different from how Chris remembered, but the sharp accent was unchanged. And the slur was there. Chris remembered the reek of alcohol that coated every word, from good morning onwards.

'It's Chris.' He swallowed hard, pushed out the words. 'Maria's Chris.'

The silence that followed was uncomfortable but not unexpected. Chris could hear a bird singing in the background, imagined the sad little budgies Mateo used to hang on his balcony. *Nature in a cage*, Maria would say. He could hear traffic, too, remembered the hum of the city that was always there, a choir of metal and oil and fire that formed the baseline for every other sound.

When they visited Barcelona Chris would go out on to the terrace as soon as he woke up, enjoy the shock of cold terracotta tiles on the soles of his feet. He'd hear birdsong and neighbours hoisting up their metal window blinds and Maria making coffee in the kitchen. But beneath all of that was that hum. It was like the sea in some ways: the rush of it, wave after wave; an endless presence that permeated everything.

'It's been a while, Chris.'

'Fifteen years,' he said.

'Are you well?'

Chris had practised answers in his head before he dialled, debated the best way to explain the reason for his call. But when it was time to speak, all ideas fled from his exhausted brain. 'Maria's had an accident,' he said.

'What kind of accident?'

'Running.'

'Is it bad?'

'She's in a coma.'

'But . . .' Mateo paused, then cleared his throat. 'Will she be okay?'

'We don't know what'll happen.'

Even the birds seemed to sense a change in mood. Chris waited, heard Mateo take a few deep breaths. He wondered if he was alone, if he was looking at that photo in the hall, of him and Maria as children; and if he'd ever replaced the photo of Ruth that she'd ripped to pieces before they left, That Day.

'That's not everything, Mateo. Tell me, have you seen Ruth recently?'

'Depends if you think fifteen years ago is recent.'

'Is that a no?'

'What do you think?'

Chris swallowed a sigh. He refused to be riled – or at least, refused to show Mateo he still had that power over him. 'So she's not visited you?'

'Why are you asking this?'

'Because Ruth is missing,' said Chris.

He wondered how Mateo pictured her, if he ever wondered who she'd grown up to be. She'd have been thirteen when he last saw her. Chris told him about Ruth's disappearance, left spaces big enough for questions or offers of support. But none came. Mateo just sighed, muttered a few words in Spanish.

'The thing is, Mateo . . . the police say she's been in Barcelona.'

'And?'

'*And?*' Rage blazed in his chest. 'And since you're also in Barcelona I want to know if she'd been in touch. You're my only contact there.'

'The word is *family*.'

'You seem to forget that when it suits you. *Have you seen Ruth or not?*'

'I already said no.'

'You're sure?'

'How many times do I have to say it?

'She's not emailed or—'

'*No*, Chris.'

'Come on, Mateo. I'm desperate. I wouldn't contact you otherwise.'

'I'm touched by your honesty,' said Mateo. 'And it seems Maria's true to her word too. She can certainly keep a secret, my big sister.'

'What secret? What are you talking about?'

'She really hasn't told you, has she?' Mateo laughed then, the sound it a slap in Chris's face. 'Even if Ruth had come looking for me in Barcelona, she wouldn't have found me. I left almost a year ago – and it was all Maria's idea. She thought I'd behave better if she could keep a closer eye on me – managed to book me an all-inclusive stay at Scotland's grimmest rehab clinic.'

Chris was stunned and instantly, achingly sad. Everywhere he looked, he found deceit. Was anyone in the family capable of telling the truth?

'But why wouldn't Maria tell me?'

'Knew it would upset you, I imagine.'

'You've got that one right,' said Chris. 'So where exactly are you?

'Just outside Glasgow.'

'You're kidding.'

'I wish I was.'

'Christ.'

'I know how you feel.'

'Is it permanent?'

Mateo sighed. 'Some questions have no answer.'

'Well, I've got one more for you. Was it you who called the house on Sunday? There's a message on the answerphone, in Spanish.'

'It's not from me. I've not called Maria in weeks, and she's not called me. She usually visits once a month but she's been too busy, she said.' Mateo sighed but when he spoke again his voice was softer. 'Can I come and see her?'

'I'd rather you didn't.'

'Surely it's my right.'

'You lost that right fifteen years ago.'

'You'll never let it go, will you?'

'Got that one right,' said Chris, then hung up.

His heart was pounding. He dropped his head into his hands, tried to slow the swirl of questions in his brain. Why hadn't Maria told him Mateo was in Glasgow? He wondered what excuses she'd invented when she went to visit him. He felt sick at the thought of it, hated the fact there were parts of her life that he knew nothing about; that she'd kept deliberately from him.

And if the answerphone message wasn't from Mateo, who was it from?

It's me, the man had said. This wasn't a wrong number.

Chris had come home for answers and, already, one thing was absolutely certain. Maria's story and Ruth's story were strung together by the same thing.

Lies.

Ruth was excited on the way home, but by the time we reached the flat her mood had slumped. She got nervous. She got paranoid. She got her bag of tobacco and spent the next hour in a fug of dirty fag reek, trying to deny the fact she was happy to see me, determined to convince both of us our urges were imagined or immoral. You're still a freak, she said, and I said nothing.

When she got bored with tobacco she opened a crap bottle of red wine and drank the whole thing, slowly, as if she wanted to delay the part that came next.

It came, of course.

Ruth's bedroom smelled of hairspray and the floor between us was littered with tags snipped off new clothes that I could tell she'd bought with me in mind. She'd made an effort, done her best to tighten the parts that now sagged. When she was a teenager all of her was tight. Now everything was fatter, fuller. Now her hips whispered suggestions of childbirth. Her body did not fit so perfectly with mine as I remembered.

We had let ourselves go.

I wondered how we would be if we'd been together these past fifteen years; if we'd have perfectly adopted the tiny gestures and expressions of the other; if we'd be exactly as I'd always hoped. As it was, we were not.

I looked at her in that room, her grown-up body pushed into clothes that did not fit, and, just for a moment, I doubted. Maybe Ruth had been right all along. Maybe we weren't worth the wait.

But there was only one way to find out.

I downed the dregs of the wine and then I was on her, covering every inch of her skin with mine, and feeling her body give in to a force that was stronger than both of us. Suddenly nothing and nobody and nowhere else mattered at all.

Stay, she said.

In the space between one breath and the next Ruth sealed her fate, and mine. It's funny how one night in your life can shape all the days that follow.

CHAPTER 20

Chris showered then went through to their room and lay down on Maria's side of the bed, shivering when the bare parts of him touched the cold sheets. He wished he could roll over and feel her warmth, then be accused of stealing it.

And what would *he* accuse *her* of?

His mind replayed the answerphone message. *It's me. I'm sorry.*

He couldn't bear to think about it. He looked for distraction and found it when he opened the wardrobe and pictured it without Maria's clothes.

It made him think about the day he and his mother had packed up his dad's stuff to take to the charity shop, both of them sitting awkwardly on the bedroom carpet, a mound of clothes between them as their fingers poked into the pockets of limp trousers and jackets. It was all receipts and pennies and hard hankies, nothing that sparked a decent memory. Chris was disappointed; he had half-hoped they'd find something that would make his mum say *ha!* then laugh and launch into one of her zig-zagging memories about one of their holidays in the caravan.

He'd never known her to be so silent, and told her as much.

Aye, she said. *But I've never known so much pain, son.*

The doorbell interrupted the memory. Chris was half-way down the stairs when he noticed feet on the step. Women's boots, framed by the glass-panelled door. He stopped, suddenly nervous. Could it be Ruth? She'd lost her key years back and never replaced it, always rang the bell when she arrived. His legs felt unsteady and he took the remaining stairs slowly. He was three from the bottom when the woman's face came into view – and the photographer behind her.

Reporters.

He hesitated then opened the door, gave them an answer before they had time to ask a single question. 'Everything I want to say, I've said to the police already – and to Sandy Hamilton. I know you're only doing your job, and I've been in your shoes. But I'd ask you to leave me in peace.'

It was only then that he realised he was still in his dressing gown. He stepped back, was closing the door when the woman threw out a question that seemed to jam it open. 'Just one question, Mr Morrison – we understand there are currently two ongoing police investigations – one regarding your wife and the other regarding your daughter. But can you confirm there was a police investigation following the sudden death of your first daughter, Heather?'

Time stood still, and Chris with it.

He'd done dozens of door-knocks like this one during his career – creeping around, ringing doorbells, hoping he'd find a grief inside that was big enough to fill a front page but small enough to fit within quote marks.

The flash from the camera stunned him and he stumbled when he stepped back into the hall, slamming the door behind him. He turned the lock, twice, then picked his way back upstairs. The first room he reached was the office so he went in, sat down and closed his eyes. His pulse thumped in his fingertips. When he eventually opened his eyes he was staring at the open page of Maria's address book, and the fat tears that fell left a dull stain on the paper.

He flicked through the remaining pages to distract himself, not sure who he was looking for or what he thought they could tell him. It was only when he reached the U section that he slowed his pace. Maria had made a special sub-section called *University and Beyond* and underneath that heading was a list of names and places linked to Mikey's and Ruth's time as students. The number for the residential halls, the name and address of Mikey's best friend up in Nethy Bridge. There were numerous entries tracking the different Edinburgh addresses where Mikey had lived before he and Rachel had bought their house.

But Ruth was a different story.

She'd never shared a flat again after university. In fact, she'd rarely stayed anywhere for more than a few months at a time – and wherever she was, it tended to be as far away from him and Maria as possible. But why?

Chris was never sure if Ruth was just restless, or running away.

When the doorbell rang again he stayed where he was, questions racing in his head. It rang again, was ignored again. After a long silence Chris got dressed and crept downstairs, felt relief flood through him when he saw the doorstep was empty. He went to the kitchen and made himself a cheese and pickle sandwich which he wolfed down. He'd started making another one when the doorbell rang yet again – and it wasn't until he was halfway along the hall that he noticed muddy green wellies planted on the front doorstep. It would be Jim from next door, a well-meaning pain in the arse.

Jim nodded to him through the glass, taking a few steps back as if he expected Chris to burst right through the door instead of unlocking it.

'I'm just getting ready to leave, Jim.' Chris nodded towards the hall clock. 'Hospital.' His throat closed, chopped off all verbs and description. He wished he hadn't said anything at all.

Jim bowed his head as if he were already at Maria's funeral. 'I heard about what happened,' he said. 'It was on the radio.'

'Right.'

'I'm . . . sorry.'

'Thanks.'

'Wishing her a speedy recovery.'

Chris nodded, looking over Jim's shoulder towards his house. He could see a Christmas tree in Jim's bay window, was relieved he and Maria hadn't yet put up their decorations. Jim's garden overlooked theirs and he spent most of his life stooped over with his hands in the earth, planting and taking away, over and over. There was no sign of photographers there, but there were places to hide.

'I should really get going.'

'I won't keep you, don't worry.' Jim held his hands up. 'I just wanted to tell you I'm thinking about you and your family. And to let you know I spoke to that young police officer again last night, same one who was here on Friday. Nice lassie. I explained about Maria's situation, told her the place was now lying empty, asked them to keep an eye on your house. I mean, it's an easy target, isn't it? Especially since that lad knows the lay of your land already.'

Chris frowned. 'You've lost me, Jim. What lad?'

'The one who was snooping around at the back of your house on Friday night. Did Maria not mention it?'

'Not a word,' said Chris and again his mind was dragged back to Maria's affair; to the man she'd met in secret so many years before. 'Was it Maria who called the police?'

'No, it was me,' said Jim. 'I was putting out the bins and I saw him heading towards your back door, sniffing around that wee path at the side where you keep the spare keys hidden for me when you're on holiday. Skinny, scruffy wee beard, hood up. I didn't think Maria was home. I'd waved to her on Friday afternoon when she was leaving in the car – but I must have missed her coming back. So when I saw that lad snooping around I called the police before I'd even rung your doorbell. I think Maria got a fright when the officer knocked your door, but I was there to help explain. Maria didn't seem very worried, but we talked about it again a few days later. Sunday morning, in fact. Before . . .'

Chris didn't hear what was said after that word. *Before*.

He wrapped his lips around his teeth and clamped down. Was this how it would be now? His life, a before and an after. A wife who became a was, and a daughter, disappeared.

'What time was it?'

Jim stopped mid-sentence, his mind lodged in an entirely different conversation. 'When?'

'Maria, when you saw her on Sunday morning. What time was it?'

Jim clicked his tongue, as if to trigger the memory. 'Must have been . . . just after eight? Or maybe just before. I always make a pot of tea at that time, you see, after I've checked the greenhouse. I saw Maria and invited her over for a cuppa but she was in a rush and couldn't come. Said she had to go and collect her number for the race then quickly go to meet somebody in the city centre before the race started. She's always so busy, your Maria. Such a shame she's—'

'Aye,' said Chris, cutting him off. He could not stand pity, and Maria couldn't either. But if Jim was right about the time, it would help him map her day. If Maria had left the house at eight she'd have had two hours to collect her number, find Ruth's tenant at his girlfriend's work, then get back to the starting line before the race started. Maria was such a precise planner. It was hard to believe she'd just lost track of time – unless she'd met somebody else as well.

'Did Maria say who she was meeting?'

Jim shook his head. 'Not that I remember. But the other lass left at the same time, so she might know. Or maybe they were heading to town together?'

'What other lass?'

'Blonde. Glasses. Looks a bit posh.'

'Rachel? Mikey's wife?'

'You know better than I do. They don't visit much, do they?'

'Did she say why she was here?'

'I didn't ask.'

'Thanks, Jim,' said Chris, then locked the front door and headed back upstairs, mind jammed with questions. He was stunned that Mikey hadn't mentioned the fact Rachel and Maria had been together on the morning of the accident. And why had Maria not told him about the intruder in their garden when she texted on Friday? Just when a few of his theories had started hardening into certainties – why Maria was in town, and when – more questions had started flooding in.

He went back to their bedroom, packed pyjamas and underwear and a razor and enough clothes to last until the weekend. Then he headed to Mikey's old room. He'd grab a few of his old T-shirts from the wardrobe, just in case.

But when he stepped into the gloom of the landing he noticed the light was already on in Mikey's room. Chris stopped, body tense, adrenalin like a wasp in his veins.

The door was almost closed but Chris could see the corner of that old Mexican rug on the floor, partially covered by a soft-edged, dark shape Chris couldn't identify from where he stood. He forced himself closer, was a few steps from Mikey's room when the door slammed shut, the crash of wood on wood only just covering the sound of the shout he released and tried to recapture in the same instant. He inched back across the landing, feeling calmer as he gulped in the familiar smell of his and Maria's room. His heart and thoughts slowed, made space for logic. It would be the wind that had slammed the door. In fact, it slammed every single time that window was left open, even a tiny bit – which was precisely why they always kept it locked unless someone was staying. When the kids were wee, the slamming doors had driven him and Maria mad during the summer months. Chris would curse that bloody door then joke that the shock of the slam had shaved another year off his life. Maria would whoop the same way she did when she was watching an exciting tennis rally on TV, then laugh and say it was a good security measure. An intruder alarm, of sorts. *If Mikey's out and that door suddenly slams, we know what it means, don't we?*

Aye, Maria. We do.

It means someone's been in there recently and left the window open.

Or it means there's someone in the house.

CHAPTER 21

Mikey's room was in chaos, but Chris's eyes were immediately drawn to a stubbed-out cigarette on the windowsill, surrounded by scattered ash and the curled scraps of a photograph, burned black until it was impossible to make out the image. He tapped the tip of the fag and thought he felt a trace of warmth – or was it just his body heat? He wasn't sure.

He left the cigarette where he'd found it and turned to examine the rest of the room, heart thundering.

The place had been ransacked – cupboards had been emptied, shelves cleared, drawers pulled open and their contents tossed on to the floor or the bed. Mikey had taken most of his childhood things when he'd left home, but Rachel had branded it as junk and sent it back. And so his old room had become a room of relics. Chris stepped around his prized *Beano* comic collection, picked up his red director's chair and an old photo album with a broken spine. The album was open and Chris recognised all of the images – him and Maria clinking glasses over a massive paella dish, Mikey and Ruth doing handstands in their underpants at the beach, and the four of them together beside a Barcelona street performer who got abusive and threw grapes at them for only leaving one euro.

Opposite was a photo Mikey had stuck on his mirror years ago: him and his pals from the football team, when they were fourteen or so. Mikey looked chuffed to bits with the captain's band on his arm – and his hands held high in the air, gripping the league cup.

Rachel was in the photo too, standing sullenly with a group of excessively preened girls behind Mikey and the other players. Blonde, skinny, too much make-up, too few clothes. Her mouth was pulled tight, as though she'd just inhaled a fart – but Chris had quickly realised it was her standard expression. She looked just the same these days, despite the fact two decades had passed.

They'd both been part of the popular crowd at school – Mikey with the football lads and Rachel with the squealing girls that trailed after them – but they didn't officially get together until Mikey was eighteen, the summer before he started university – and not long after they'd come home from Barcelona for the last time. He'd spent the rest of the summer working at one of the local bottling factories and charmed Rachel over a conveyer belt loaded with cheap vodka. By the time the summer ended Mikey had carved out a distance between him and his troubled little sister that no amount of sibling adoration could bridge. Age had started to matter – or that was his excuse at the time.

But now, Chris wondered if it was more than that. Maybe it was a defence mechanism. Maybe Mikey had pushed Ruth away to avoid facing the agonising fact that he hadn't protected her either.

Chris sighed and turned his attention back to the photo.

Ruth was there too, of course, standing on the sidelines with him and Maria. She'd have been eight or nine years old. She'd wanted to pose with the football team but Mikey said she couldn't. Little sisters were not allowed, and that was that. The image wasn't good enough quality to show the gloss of tears on Ruth's eyes or the fury that had stained her cheeks, as though she was burning red on the inside. But Chris remembered it well. She'd curled her hands into tight little fists when he'd tried to link fingers and lead her off the pitch.

His heart stung at the memory of it; that first rejection.

It was the only photo on that page – but it was obvious the one below it had been removed, leaving a white rectangle on a yellowing background. Was this the picture that had been burned? It must be. Chris turned back to the window, was sweeping the scraps of that photo into his hand when the scent of tobacco reached him through the open window. He sat the scraps of the photo on Mikey's desk, further opened the sash-and-case window and scanned every corner of the garden. The leafless trees that backed the lawn shivered, trunks grey as the sky. There was no blue and there was nobody there. He reached again for the scraps of that photo, held them up to the window for better light.

But then it came.

Furniture, bumped. Stairs, creaking. Footsteps, approaching. *Christ.*

Chris quickly moved behind the door, looking for something he could use to protect himself, but finding nothing. When the door was pushed open the air in the room changed, smelled suddenly of washing powder he didn't recognise. Someone came in. They were inches apart but the bedroom door stood between them. Every few seconds the person on the other side of the door sniffed the way the children did when they'd been crying a lot; sniffs that would catch in the throat and slice breaths into a hiccup.

Chris resisted the temptation to close his eyes. Fear hardened his veins, gave them sharp edges. He had to take control before panic took him. He had to face this.

When he moved, the other person turned. Their eyes met at exactly the same time, then didn't look away. Chris tried to speak but could not.

But one word filled the space between them.

Dad.

CHAPTER 22

Chris and Mikey stood face to face, awkward and silent in his old bedroom like strangers at the start of a really shit party.

'What the hell's going on, Mikey?'

Mikey clamped his teeth together, sealing his lips. This was how he'd always dealt – or failed to deal – with difficult emotions. He'd done the same thing since he was a toddler. Maria was the only one who'd ever managed to coax him out of it. Chris tried again.

'Is it something to do with your mum?'

Mikey shook his head.

'You and Rachel?'

He said nothing.

'Is it something to do with Ruth?' Chris stepped back after he'd said it, his natural defences sensing that the answer would cause him damage.

Mikey nodded. 'I've been looking for my old mobile phone,' he said. 'I got an upgrade just after Easter and Mum said she'd keep my old handset in case any of us ever needed a spare. I assumed she'd keep it in here, but . . .'

'Why do you need the phone? And how is it connected to Ruth?'

Mikey cleared a space on the bed and slumped down, motioning for Chris to sit beside him. 'I've been keeping something from you. From everyone.' He shut his eyes. 'Something Ruth told me, the last time I saw her.'

'The night she went missing?'

'Aye. She sent me a text, that night after the pub.' Mikey kept his eyes shut but the tears came anyway. 'She said she was going to disappear, Dad.'

'*Disappear*?' Chris stood up, felt suddenly nauseous. He held the door, felt his pulse racing through his fingertips. 'What do you mean, disappear?'

'That's what Ruth said. *I'm going to disappear for a while.* Totally casual, like it was a normal thing to say. Said she had to sort stuff out.'

'What stuff?'

'I don't know.'

'Christ.' He walked to the window and stared out. He saw clouds change position, a bird land on their roof, life continuing as normal on the other side of the glass. When he turned back to Mikey he ignored the tears, and his own.

'Why haven't you mentioned this until now? I can't understand it. Your sister is *missing*, Mikey. Or had you not realised that?'

'Ruth asked me not to tell you and Mum.'

'And what about the police? Did she ask you not to tell them either?' Chris pulled out his phone, scrolled through his recent calls list. 'I'm calling Farida – since I'm assuming you didn't mention it to her yesterday? Christ, this could be vital. But one thing before I call – I assume you've still got that text from Ruth?'

Mikey shook his head. 'That's why I'm here, looking for that phone.'

'And it's not here?'

'I've been looking for it all morning, going through all the junk in my room, and there's no trace of it here. You'll just have to take my word for it.'

Chris shook his head then turned back to the window. He tried to think straight, but couldn't. All he could think of was Mateo drinking, Ruth bleeding, Maria running, Mikey crying. And all of them, lying. Panic clawed at his chest.

He scooped up the scraps of the burned photo, held it out to Mikey. 'And what's this about?'

'What is it ?'

'Used to be a photo. Someone burned it.'

'Wasn't me.'

'Then who the hell was it?'

'I'm not to blame for everything, Dad.'

'Och, don't start with that,' said Chris. 'You need to tell me everything – absolutely every detail of what happened after I left that Sunday afternoon.'

Mikey nodded, took a few noisy breaths. 'I left the house not long after you did. Mum and Ruth started one of their arguments and I couldn't be bothered getting involved. I headed back to mine, told Ruth to come later.'

'What were they arguing about?'

Mikey shrugged. 'Ruth just said that Mum was doing her head in, asking lots of questions. She was still wound up when she got to mine, got stuck into the beers and then made some snide comment about Rachel's outfit. You can imagine how that went down. I thought a few pints at the Alba would help calm her down but then she started on me. It was just the usual brother and sister stuff, made worse by the fact we were both steaming drunk. Anyway, she eventually apologised for being an arse and went to get a round in – but then she got talking to that guy I told you about. I got tired of waiting. I told her I was heading to the casino, asked if she wanted to come. She'd just bought a drink, said she'd maybe come later. So, I left. And that was the last I saw of her.'

'I still can't believe you left her there,' said Chris.

Mikey scowled at him. 'Do you blame me for this, Dad? Do you?'

'Can we please just focus on Ruth?' Chris stared at Mikey until he looked away. 'Appreciated. Now tell me about the man Ruth was talking to.'

'I don't know any more than I did the other day. There was a bunch of guys at the bar, pretty rowdy, but she said she knew one them from school.'

'And you definitely didn't recognise him?'

'Definitely,' said Mikey. 'Ruth was five years below me, Dad.'

'You remember what he looked like, at least?'

'Just . . . normal. About my height, dark hair . . . nothing that stood out.'

'But you think there's a chance Ruth went home with him?'

'It's possible, I suppose.'

'And when did you get home from the casino?'

'I've no idea, but it was getting light,' said Mikey. 'I didn't notice the text from Ruth until the next day. My phone was on silent all night. But she'd sent it the night before – around half-eleven or something.' Mikey looked suddenly confused, narrowed his eyes. 'But thinking about it now – maybe when she said *disappear* she just meant she was going back to her flat after the Alba and wasn't coming to the casino. Maybe we're reading too much into it.'

'You really believe that? After everything that's happened?' Chris shook his head. 'Now – tell me why you've lied about this text until now.'

'I haven't lied.'

'You've kept a secret. Means the same in my book.'

'That's not fair.'

'What is? Now tell me why you kept it to yourself.'

'Ruth asked me to. That's it.' His voice was waterlogged. 'It's nothing sinister, Dad. And you know what? I nearly told Mum the next day – but then Ruth posted some photos on Facebook and I assumed everything was fine. I just forgot about it after that, dismissed it as Ruth being boozy and dramatic.'

'Tell me something,' said Chris. 'Did you reply to that text?'

Mikey nodded. 'I replied as soon as I read it, said she could rely on me.'

'Do you remember your exact words?'

'Word,' said Mikey. 'I wrote *contigo*. It means *with you*, in Spanish.'

'I know what it means.'

'It's always been our way of signing off, instead of saying lots of love or anything like that. It's like a code word between us, I suppose.'

'And did Ruth reply to the text?'

'No.'

'And has she been back in touch with you since?'

'Not since that day, no.'

'And have you been worried?'

'Not really.'

'Not really, or not at all? You're telling me Ruth sent a text saying she wanted to disappear – and hasn't been in contact with you since. Correct?'

'But she was in touch with Mum.'

'I'm asking about contact with *you*,' said Chris. 'I know texts have been sent to your mum from Ruth's number several times since her disappearance. But that doesn't mean Ruth wrote them. You understand what I'm saying?'

Mikey flushed.

'So let me ask the question again. Given the state your sister was in that night; given the nature of Ruth's text; given the lack of contact since that text; and most of all given the fact that you're fully aware of what Ruth did to herself That Day in Barcelona – you're telling me you've not been worried?'

Mikey glared at Chris but, if he was trying to look strong, he failed. The beard was a cheap disguise, couldn't hide the face of a wee boy who didn't want to feel the way he felt. 'I was no more worried than normal,' he said.

'Christ. And what does Rachel make of it?'

'I didn't tell her.'

'Why not?'

Mikey shrugged. 'No reason. I just didn't.'

'You *just didn't*? Brilliant answer, Mikey. Well done.' Chris wondered again why Mikey hadn't mentioned the fact Rachel had been with Maria the morning of her accident. He must know, so why not tell him? He wanted to ask but didn't, knowing he'd doubt the answer. 'Did you tell anyone else?'

Mikey shook his head. 'If I got stressed out every time Ruth went AWOL I'd drive myself mad. We all would. She buggers off whenever and wherever she wants, but she always comes back, eventually. *Always*. Right, Dad?'

Chris stared at Mikey, wishing for two things. First of all, he wished that he could answer that question, and with a positive. It was his job to reassure.

Second wish – that he didn't doubt Mikey's sincerity.

Christ, he couldn't bear all this deception. He stormed downstairs to the kitchen, flicked on the kettle, made tea. It was something to do, a way to bring normality into the room. He phoned Farida, cursed her when it went to voicemail. He left a short message with all updates from Mateo, Jim and the house answerphone. Finally, he told her about Mikey's text from Ruth and urged her to come as soon as possible so they could speak face to face.

Then he sat at the kitchen table, drained and desperate.

He watched vapour rise from his mug, then swirl and disappear. He wished that word would too. It was so alien, so final.

And now, it was Ruth's.

Disappear.

When she woke up the next morning Ruth saw my clothes beside the bed and vomited. I understood. She'd spent the last fifteen years convincing herself she was better off without me; filling herself with tiny pieces of other people in the hope they'd fill the space she'd carved out between us. Fifteen years of running from her parents so they would never get close enough to ask the question she feared most; would never be disappointed that she wasn't who they thought. Fifteen years of never settling anywhere or with anyone for the same reason.

Fifteen years of never stopping, an endless flurry of doing and buying and having and smoking and drinking and going and coming and searching outside of herself for the next distraction because if she had stopped and looked inside she would have found the love for me there. Still, silenced, stagnating.

I was a scab that should not have been picked.

And so she bled. But just tears, this time.

I let it happen, watched her purge regrets and thought about the way we cry the same tears whether we're happy or sad, joyful or grieving. Our bodies don't care if we've lost a sister or severed a limb or won a marathon. Someone once told me tears contain a natural painkiller so in theory, the longer you cry, the better you should feel. It didn't seem to work like that with Ruth.

It was as though she'd forced open an old tap that had been sealed shut for years and then couldn't switch it off. This was not the pain of one day. This was the pain of all of her days since That Day. Blood on fingers, the revulsion of it.

And me?

My fifteen years had been made of waiting.

I had not moved on. I had not healed. I had not realised with hindsight that Ruth and I were a bad idea after all. I had not forgotten how bewildering it felt to be so very loved and then so deeply despised.

I got dressed and forced Ruth to open her eyes, see what she was losing before I left for good. When she looked up I expected loathing, but instead I found longing. Her face told the story she couldn't bear to tell out loud.

She wanted me in the flesh, on her flesh.

And, just like that, I knew I had her hooked.

CHAPTER 23

Chris flicked on the radio as he drove back to the hospital, switching it straight back off when Ruth's name was mentioned on the afternoon news bulletin. He'd overheard a report on a local station earlier which openly linked Maria and Ruth's cases, treating his crumbling world like an on-air Cluedo game. And who was the wicked culprit? Someone they both knew, in a rage, with a grudge.

It was shockingly bad reporting. Once this was all over he'd get the Press Complaints Commission on to them and shut down the whole bloody station.

But that word lingered in his head, the same one Farida had asked him to think about. *Grudge.* Who in the world might hold one so strong they'd want to harm both Maria and Ruth? He thought again of Maria's affair, the lover she'd left behind. He thought too of the answerphone message at home, in Spanish.

It's me. I'm sorry.

But for what?

His mind kept dragging him to the most painful answers and when he tried to think of something else his brain played the conversations with Mikey on repeat. Chris had demanded he stay until Farida called back, but Mikey had insisted it was a waste of time. The tension between them was unbearable and eventually Mikey had made a crap excuse about an emergency at work and fled.

Chris desperately wanted to believe Mikey was being honest, but it was like wanting to love somebody. Wanting wasn't enough, meant nothing.

He lowered the window and kept it wide open even once the rain came on. When it got heavy he turned the wipers and heater to their highest settings, and for a little while managed to distract himself with the sound of water and air, Nature pushed around by Man. Then a light flashed on the dashboard, warned him he was low on fuel. He followed signs for a service station, had just joined a long queue for the petrol pumps when his phone rang. It was Farida.

'Chris? I just got your voicemail – and yes, I'll definitely need to speak with Mikey again.' She paused, cleared her throat. 'I also have some news.'

Chris noted the absence of the word *good* or *bad*. Just news. And in his experience that usually meant the latter. When someone had good news they advertised the fact, spoke with urgency, were keen to share. Bad news was always delivered at a slower pace, as if to weaken the strength of the blow.

'Go on,' he said, hoping he sounded calm.

'We've gained access to Ruth's bank account, based on the details you provided us. First question – are you sure this is her only UK account?'

'It's the one she's always used,' said Chris. 'Why?'

'I ask because there has only been one transaction on this account since Ruth was last seen – a transfer of £8,000 at the end of April into a personal account belonging to someone called Javi Fernandez. Mean anything to you?'

'Javi Fernandez?' Chris scanned his brain, found no trace of a memory. 'Never heard of him. And you said Ruth transferred all her money to him?'

'Not all of it, no. But £8,000 is a significant amount.'

'And do you have anything on him?' Chris had so many questions on his tongue he felt like he might choke. 'I mean, is this Javi character known to the police?'

'You know I can't reveal that kind of information,' said Farida. 'But if I thought Javi Fernandez were a threat to your daughter I'd inform you. As it stands I can offer you no information at all on the recipient of Ruth's money.'

'But you *have* heard of him?'

'Repetition will get you nowhere. I wonder if you can tell me about Ruth's spending habits? Are you surprised by the lack of activity on her UK account? One simple and obvious explanation is that Ruth has been using a foreign bank account – has she ever used one?'

'She always told us she didn't,' said Chris. 'But that doesn't mean she was actually telling us the truth, does it? It's not unusual for Ruth's account to be static for part of the year – she spends nothing at all when she's on tour. Her salary goes into the bank but her tips are cash in hand. That's what she spends when she's travelling. As far as I'm aware she'd withdraw cash or swipe with her regular UK bank card if she was here. Are you positive it's not been used over these last few weeks, when her UK phone's been used here?'

'Actually, I was just coming to that,' said Farida. 'I got a call this afternoon from a colleague in the fraud department. The thing is – Ruth's name came up as part of a totally different investigation. Somebody attempted to use her bank card last week, in Edinburgh. They failed, then fled the store. And, since Ruth is now registered as missing and her account has been blocked, the case ended up on his desk.'

'Do you know who tried to use it?'

'We have identified a suspect, yes.'

'And it wasn't Ruth?'

'I'm afraid not, Chris. Off the record – the suspect is male.'

'Christ.' He closed his eyes, wished it made a difference. 'You think it could be the same man Ruth transferred cash to? This Javi Fernandez?'

'It's certainly a consideration,' she said. 'But until the investigation is complete we won't be able to confirm the identity of the suspect.'

'Can you tell me more details of what actually happened?'

'Not at this stage. You'll appreciate this is a criminal investigation and this is very sensitive information. We can't release any detail that could potentially reach suspects and allow them to cover their tracks.'

'But surely I'm not a suspect, Farida?'

Farida started to speak, then hesitated. For a few seconds too long, the line between them went silent. 'We have to keep an open mind, Mr Morrison,' she said. 'But I will tell you this – we have several witness statements from staff and customers which will help us identify the suspect. The shop didn't have security cameras but there are several public CCTV units installed in the vicinity so we've got officers analysing footage as we speak. I'm confident we're closing in on him.'

'And does all of this change your focus?'

'In what sense?'

'I mean – is this still primarily a missing person investigation?' Even as he said it, Chris knew this was not really the question he wanted to ask – and, as if she sensed it, Farida fobbed him off with an answer that said nothing either.

But really, he didn't need to hear the word to know it was on both of their minds. *Ruth, disappeared.* Delete a few letters and what did you get? *Ruth, dead.*

CHAPTER 24

It only took a minute to fill the petrol tank but when Chris went inside to pay the queue snaked right around the extensive chocolate bar display and reached the fridges at the back. Chris took his place at the end of the line, studied the vacuum-packed bacon and lumps of square sausage – anything to keep his eyes away from the newspaper stand. He had his debit card ready when he reached the front but instead of a quick swipe and a smiling thank you he got a sigh, then tuts and mutters from customers waiting behind him. His card was rejected. He tried again, mind leaping immediately to the conversation with Farida, to the man who tried and failed to use Ruth's card; whose account was full of Ruth's money. His card was rejected a second time – then a third.

The cashier sighed. 'You not got cash, pal? There are folk waiting.'

Chris nodded, made a show of searching his pockets and wallet for money. He eventually found two grimy ten-ners tucked behind his loyalty cards and had just got back to his car when his phone started ringing.

It was Liz Catto, calling from the Alba.

She told him she'd just been having a chat with Leo and it turned out Wee Mary the Cleaner told Leo that someone left their mobile phone in the pub toilets the night Ruth went missing – and Liz wondered if it might have been Ruth, after she spewed. Wee Mary said some guy had been in to collect it finally – but if Chris wanted to speak to Wee Mary for more details she'd be there for half an hour and then she was off until Friday and would be looking after her mother up in the Highlands where, Liz emphasised, Wee Mary would have no signal.

Chris quickly called Sandy to make sure there was no change at the hospital then turned the car and sped back towards the Alba.

When he arrived at the pub, Wee Mary was waiting outside the entrance, as wide as she was tall. They sat on a wooden bench outside and when the barman came out Chris ordered an espresso. She pulled out a vape cigarette and refused his offer of a drink, insisted she wouldn't be staying long.

'Liz says you found my daughter's phone,' he said.

'Trust Liz. That's not what I said.' Wee Mary rolled her eyes. 'Leo told me that Liz was talking to you because your daughter had gone missing and that she hadn't been seen since the night the girl spewed on the new carpet – and that Liz thought the girl that spewed was your daughter.

'I then said to Leo that the day I cleaned up the spew was the same day I found a phone in the ladies' loo. It was a Monday morning – they're always the worst. Anyway, I almost chucked out the phone with the paper towels, but then it started ringing. Just about gave me a heart attack, so it did. I answered it and a lassie told me it was hers, asked if I could keep it safe. Said she'd send her friend in to collect it so I put it behind the bar with a note for Leo. I'd totally forgotten about it by the time her pal eventually came in for it, weeks later.'

'What pal?'

'Some skinny wee bugger wrapped up like hell had frozen over and he was stuck in the middle of it. You should've seen him – ski jacket, hood up, sunglasses, the works. He had a wee shaved head underneath, right enough, so he might have been chilly without it. But still. Anyway, I came in at eight a.m. as usual, was just polishing the bar when there's a knock on the door and I open it and he's standing there mumbling, saying he's here for that lassie's phone. The one who spewed on the new carpet, he said. Now maybe I should have asked more questions but I remembered the lassie calling, so I found the phone where I'd left it and handed it over, got back to work.'

'And when did this happen?'

Wee Mary bunched up her lips. 'Hard to say, but I'd guess it was in April some time or maybe early May – whenever we had that good stretch of sunshine. Remember? Proper tops-off weather. Whole town smelled of barbecue smoke and burnt sausages. Anyway, that's why I remember your daughter's pal, turning up like he expected a snowstorm.'

'I don't suppose you got his name?'

Wee Mary shook her head.

'Did he have a local accent?'

'Not sure. He barely said a word.'

'You remember what he looked like?'

'He had his hood up, so I couldn't really see his face.'

'Did you see where he went once he left here?'

'Nope.'

Chris tried to stay calm. He'd hoped for a few more certainties. But at least he knew one thing for sure: this was the man he needed to find. Was it the same man Mikey had seen Ruth talking to that night – some old friend from school? Whoever it was, if he'd collected Ruth's phone in April or May then it was vital to find him. If he'd returned the phone to Ruth, he was definitely the last person to see her.

And if he hadn't returned it to Ruth, why not?

The answer was on the tip of his tongue, daring him to say it out loud. But he swallowed it instead, washed it down with the bitter dregs of his espresso.

'Anything else at all that you think could be useful?'

She shook her head. 'And before I go – I want you to be totally clear it's Liz who seems to think that mobile belongs to your daughter, not me. I'm sure your daughter wasn't the only person drunk enough to leave their phone in the toilets that night – and if the phone's not hers then that oddball man isn't anything to do with her either. All of this might come to nothing.'

'It's definitely not nothing,' Chris said, then turned and scanned the wall of the pub, searching for security cameras. His heart leapt when he saw one above an upstairs window. 'You think Liz would let me see the CCTV?'

'They're fake,' said Mary, frowning as if was her fault. Then she leaned in, whispered, 'I think they get a discount on the insurance if they nail the cameras to the wall, but they don't do a thing. Sorry about that, pal.'

'Not your fault,' he said, smiling, but cursing Liz in his head.

When Mary left, Chris went to pay, was embarrassed when his card was rejected again. He made the gesture of checking his wallet for change, knowing fine he didn't have a penny on him after paying for the petrol. Liz leaned across the bar, put her hands on Chris's wallet. 'On the house,' she said. 'It's the least I can do, given the circumstances. Wishing you all the best.'

Chris hated her pity, but thanked her and left.

He called his bank on the drive back to hospital. Four automated menus later he was speaking to Victoria, a real person diligently reading from a script. Yes, it was okay to call him Chris and yes, he was happy to hold the line while she investigated the problem even though beeps on the line told him someone else was trying to call.

She said she wouldn't be a minute but she was more like seven; said she was sorry to tell him the account had been emptied out but she didn't sound as though she cared at all; and she said yes, she was totally sure.

'That's impossible,' said Chris. 'I had nearly £5,000 in that account. A few direct debits will have gone out this week, but there's no way I've spent anything like that amount. Can you run me through the last payments?'

Yes, she could.

Victoria's voice was cheerful as she ran through the most recent transactions on his and Maria's joint account. Yes, she could repeat that. The last transaction was a transfer of £4,000, made on Sunday – the same day as Maria's accident.

Did Victoria have the name of the recipient?

Yes, she did. But could he just hold the line for a few minutes?

Chris waited, half-expecting to hear that same name again, the man Farida had told him about. Javi Fernandez had swiped most of Ruth's money and maybe now he was going for Chris and Maria's as well. But who was he? What was his motive? Possibilities swarmed his brain, none of them innocent.

But his mind went completely blank when Victoria came back on the line, told him who'd received his cash. Her answer just created another question; exposed yet another chunk of life hidden from him by the people he loved the most. According to the information the bank held on its system, the money from his account had been transferred into a UK account, held by Mr M. Hidalgo.

M. Hidalgo, otherwise known as Mikey.

Chris ignored the honks of horns behind him when he braked suddenly and turned into a residential street. He ignored the stares of two smoking mums standing by the swings when he abandoned his car on double yellow lines in front of a children's play park. His legs almost gave way when he got out. There it was again, that familiar burning in his chest, the creep of acid under his skin. He steadied himself on the bonnet then started walking, as slowly as he could. Slow your step and you're taking back control, Chris. Slow your step and you're putting a distance between you and the panic. Slow your step and your breath will take the hint. Right? Well, not today.

Today panic came, and stayed.

This was the reason the news editor had shunted him to the features department, convinced he'd lost his edge. This was the reason he'd lied to Ruth and Mikey when they'd ask why he wasn't at work and why for months he'd been too frightened to move further than the back garden. It was the reason he'd lock himself in the en suite at home and let the shower run for far longer than necessary, just so Maria wouldn't hear the sobs that fear forced out of him. It was the reason he slept with a nightlight, and that was the reason Mikey had stopped believing he was actually a superhero. It was the reason Ruth had used her pocket money to buy him a new packet of pens and a reporter's pad and it was the reason she'd written a note on the first page telling him he was the best dad and the best journalist in the whole world and should write more stories to help people and then said *PS I'm sorry I worried you so much, Dad* and *PPS I promise never ever to frighten you again.*

By the time he got back to his car his heart rate was almost back to normal and the swings were occupied by teenagers emptying a bottle of vodka into cans of Coke, then into their bellies. They all laughed when one of the girls shouted at Chris, told him he was a shite driver. He heard but paid no attention.

As he drove back to the hospital a song came on the radio, one that Maria used to have on her favourite mixtape. He turned it up, thought of her face when she sang in the car with the kids in the back, the way they always laughed when she struggled to reach the high part of the chorus. Fear whispered in his ear, told him those days were long gone. Ruth was a corpse. Maria was a cripple. And Mikey? He was alive, aye, but he was a bloody liar. Christ, they all were.

Just how many secrets could one family keep?

And so we became Us again; but, with us, came lies.

Ruth had always told mistruths in letters home. The only difference now was the method. Letters needed stamps and stamps tied Ruth to a place where we'd too easily be found. So she replaced her pen with pixels, her paper with a screen, and her words with images she knew would please but give nothing away.

It was surprisingly easy to maintain the illusion of her life continuing as normal, without any trace of me in it. We spent hours, sometimes, creating emails and social media posts, constructing yet another travel adventure for Ruth that nobody had any reason to doubt. The truth of the matter was this – most people didn't actually care for any longer than the one second it took them to click a thumbs-up icon.

And so we convinced the world Ruth was on the other side of it.

She even managed the occasional phone call when her parents demanded it. I'd sit with her, monitoring every word, whispering threats in her ear every time they asked a question I didn't want her to answer. She'd sit with her head in her hands, trying to remember how the Ruth they remembered would have reacted to things they said; how the Ruth they remembered would have laughed; who the Ruth they remembered actually was.

It was tough, but so was she.

If ever she started feeling lost or sad or homesick, whenever she cried, I'd make sure I was right there with her, sharpening the claws of her demons, reminding her that this was what we'd dreamed of. Me and Ruth, together.

But what do you do when everything you've always wanted is suddenly within reach?

I'll tell you what you do. You reassess. You question. You reflect. Then maybe, just maybe, you start to wish you'd dreamed of something else.

CHAPTER 25

Sandy was sitting in the pink chair when Chris got back, holding the newspaper in the air with both hands like an ancient navigator studying his map.

Chris snatched it from him, then stuffed it on to the top shelf of the wardrobe and shut the door. 'Sorry, pal, but from now on the paper's to be stored under strict instructions. Keep out of reach of paranoid relatives.'

'Fair enough.'

Chris looked at Maria, thought she looked paler. 'Any change here?'

'Just the sheets,' said Sandy, then looked at Chris with an expression usually reserved for death knocks. He stood up, pointed to the chair.

'Sit down, Chris. Please. You look awful.'

'I'm fine.'

'Did you eat anything at lunch?' Sandy reached out, touched his hand. 'You're shaking.'

'I said I'm fine.'

'Has something happened?'

'Some*one*,' said Chris, then he told Sandy the little he knew about Javi Fernandez – and what he suspected. He talked about the transfer from Ruth's bank account and the fraudulent attempt to use her card this week. He reeled off Liz and Wee Mary's story about the lost mobile – and the man who collected it.

'You're losing me, Chris,' said Sandy. 'There are too many phones in the picture for my liking. So first of all we have *Maria's* phone, with the silent voicemail left on Monday. For the record, my contact is still trying to trace that, but no luck so far. What next? Two calls to *your landline* on Sunday, and one answerphone message, in Spanish. Then there's that text from Ruth – sent to *Mikey's* old phone, which is now lost somewhere at your house? And now we've got *Ruth's* mobile lost at the pub and then collected by a stranger?'

'Aye,' said Chris. 'We're in the age of digital footprints, Sandy, but they're leading us nowhere fast, are they? We don't even know if the phone left in the Alba toilets belongs to Ruth. So that's the first thing we need to confirm.

'I'll ask Farida to have another look at Ruth's phone records. If there's an incoming call on the same day and same time that Wee Mary says the lost phone rang in the toilets, then that would confirm it belongs to Ruth.

'Second – if it *is* Ruth's phone then we need to identify who made the call that Wee Mary answered. If we call back and they answer, we've got our man. If they don't, we can use the number to track them down. All of that *should* tell us who Ruth was with and where she was the morning after the Alba.'

'And what's your theory?' Sandy asked. 'At first glance it seems obvious she went home with that man from the pub, the one Mikey said was an old school friend. But now we've got this bizarre connection to Javi Fernandez, whoever he is. You think she was with him?'

'Anything is possible,' said Chris. 'There's obviously some kind of relationship between Ruth and Javi if she's transferred all that money to his account. But whether she went home with him that night, and whether it was the same person who collected the lost phone? No idea. We'd be guessing. But a key point is this – Wee Mary says the phone was collected weeks after we thought Ruth had left the country, so the man who collected her phone must know where Ruth was at that time – and hopefully he'll know where she is now. Confirming that man's identity is absolutely key.'

Sandy nodded. 'Have you told Farida what Wee Mary told you?'

'I'm just about to – and I'll ask for those phone records too,' said Chris. 'In the meantime – could you ask the news desk to search the digital archives for any mention of Javi Fernandez? For all we know, he's already in our files.'

'Consider it done,' said Sandy.

Chris reached for his laptop. 'I'll see if there's any trace of him on the internet. There can't be too many men by that name in this part of the world so between us we should be able to track him down.'

'Excellent idea. How about I leave you with Maria for a while? I'll go work in the visitors' room and we can reconvene in, say, half an hour?'

'Wait. Before you go. There's something else.' Chris glanced at Maria, sighed. 'I've been having issues using the joint account that Maria and I share. My debit card's been rejected twice today already. So I phoned the bank and asked them to check the balance. Turns out it's been emptied as well, Sandy.'

Sandy stopped, turned to face Chris. 'Emptied?'

Chris nodded. 'The girl told me almost £4,000 left the account on Sunday morning, by bank transfer.'

'To Javi Fernandez?'

'Worse.' Chris bit down on his bottom lip, closed his eyes until the threat of tears had passed. 'The money went to M. Hidalgo, a.k.a. your best pal Mikey. He has to use his full name for legal stuff. Michael Morrison Hidalgo. Maria and Ruth do the same. It's a Spanish thing. Kids take both names, and the mother's surname goes second.'

'Have you asked Mikey about it?'

'I would if he'd answer the bloody phone.'

'And I suppose you haven't told Farida about this either?'

'Not yet.'

'You planning to?'

'I'll do what I feel is right.'

'That doesn't really answer my question.'

'I know that.' Chris turned away from Sandy and looked out of the window. Daylight was fading fast and he could tell it would rain soon, probably stay all night. But none of it made the slightest difference. Chris turned back to Sandy, feigned brightness he didn't feel. 'I'm sure there's a logical explanation.'

Sandy sighed. 'You couldn't sound less convinced if you tried. How about telling me what you're really thinking?'

Chris held his eyes shut, as if such a simple gesture could ever numb the force of a fear he knew would grow and grow, without limits. Panic was silent torture; like internal bleeding, imperceptible from the outside. And what was he frightened of right now? His own doubts and suspicions; the dread that Mikey had done something that every single one of them would wish he hadn't.

He had no idea how much time had passed before Sandy spoke again, but when he did there was a softness in his voice that he rarely exposed.

'Breathe, Chris. It'll pass.'

Chris nodded.

'Tell you what, I'll work in here. It'll be just like old times.'

The room was quiet as the two men worked, bent over glowing screens at the end of Maria's bed. The plan was simple – they'd each search for the name 'Javi Fernandez' then compare notes at the end, see where it took them.

Chris started by scrolling through Ruth's extensive list of Facebook friends, looking for anyone called Javi and all men who used a nickname instead of their real name. He repeated the search on Instagram, on Twitter, on Pinterest, and the rest. Ruth had hundreds of followers on each – but none of them was called Javi Fernandez.

After that he did a general internet search. At first he just typed in 'Javi Fernandez' but the search engine produced dozens of answers, forced him to be more specific. He added the word 'Barcelona', then 'Edinburgh', then Ruth's name, then Mikey's name. All of it produced too many answers.

He repeated the checks looking only at images, made himself dizzy peering at tiny faces of strangers on the screen. He stood up, rubbing his eyes.

'I'm getting nowhere, Sandy. I need to get out, get some air.'

'By air do you mean tobacco?'

'I wish. But the last thing I need right now is a fine for breaking smoking laws.' He glanced at Maria's stilled, sticky mouth, remembering how it had felt to kiss her. She was the only smoker he'd ever kissed more than once. He had picked up the habit a few weeks after she quit, told her he missed the taste of her mouth in the morning. 'I'll have a walk around the car park and then I'll try phoning Mikey again, ask him about that transfer from Maria's bank account.'

'Where is he, anyway?'

'At the office. Some kind of emergency at work.'

Sandy looked at Chris, brow furrowed. 'An emergency worse than this?'

Chris sighed. 'Give him a break.' He felt a twinge of guilt, remembering how he'd thought Mikey's excuse was lame too.

'A break is *precisely* what Mikey needs to give to *you*. All I'm saying is that it would be a big help to have someone else here. I'll help as much as I can – and I'm happy to be here – but the lad needs to get his priorities straight. And God knows why Maria's been giving him all that cash, but we need to know.'

'He'll get back when he can,' said Chris.

'He should be here now. Is there anyone else who can come and help out in the meantime? Friends, neighbours – or what about Rachel?'

'Maybe. I don't know. It depends.'

Depends. That word corked the conversation. If he'd been brave enough to finish the sentence he'd have said it depended on how long Maria was confined to hospital, and it depended on what state she was in when she left – alive, dead, or somewhere in between. He stood up, grabbed his jacket and wallet. 'Time for fresh air,' he said. 'I'll grab us some snacks in the canteen on my way back in.'

'Thanks,' said Sandy. 'But before you leave – aren't you going to ask what I discovered about Javi Fernandez while you were playing about on Facebook?'

'You've got something else?'

'A little sprinkling of gold dust.' Sandy smiled. 'Now sit back down.'

CHAPTER 26

The photo had been taken on a phone, and a crap phone by the looks of it. Without zoom, all the faces were too small. With zoom, details were pixelated or blurred. Sandy had searched through all the other images on the blog, but they were all arty shots or selfies of the blogger, a retired cardiologist who lived in the San Diego area of California and called himself Man With A Heart. His travel blog was *navel-gazing bollocks* according to Sandy but it contained the two words both of them had been searching for. Javi Fernandez.

'He and his wife always travelled independently, until . . .' Sandy glanced at Chris, then Maria, then back to Chris. His expression softened. 'Until she died, unfortunately. He says that on her deathbed she urged him to keep travelling on his own, and he promised he would. Went to Portugal solo, got depressed. So he joined a group tour for the first time in his life. This blog describes . . . let me see . . . *one man's adventure into the world of group travel*, whatever the hell that means. It's mildly amusing in parts, to be fair, but not as funny as he thinks.'

'And where does Javi Fernandez come into it?' Chris was speed-reading the blog, taking none of it on board. 'Is he retired too?'

'Far from it. The name appears in a post he wrote in September when he was touring northern Spain. Javi was the tour director, Chris.'

'He does the same job as Ruth?'

'Exactly. Now, Man With A Heart says Javi is, and I quote, *an inspiring leader with endless enthusiasm*. And that's not all. He says *Javi is a true professional who sets the gold standard for group travel. And . . .*' Sandy looked at Chris with the same expression he wore when he was about to break an exclusive at the paper '. . . *Javi sets the gold standard for Trobador Tours.*'

'Christ.'

'I thought you'd say that.'

'This must be the guide Ruth recommended to her boss – the one who was going to do her autumn tours – though God knows why she's transferred all of her cash to his account. If we can't find Ruth, we need to get hold of this Javi character, get the answers from him.'

'Exactly,' said Sandy. 'First of all, call Trobador again, insist they give us contact details for him. I've already emailed Man With A Heart asking for the same thing. Told him I'd toured with Javi a few months ago but lost his details and was desperate to get in touch.'

'Good job.'

'Not until it produces results.'

'It will. We're getting closer.'

Chris went to the corridor to phone Trobador Tours, left a message when the call switched to Monty's voicemail. He tried to sound calm, felt anything but. First, he said that he needed confirmation that Javi Fernandez was the guide who'd taken on Ruth's tours the previous summer – on her recommendation. And secondly, he wanted Javi's contact details. If data protection prevented Monty from giving answers, Chris assured him that the police investigating Ruth's disappearance would be in touch.

When he got back to the room he and Sandy sat in silence, staring at the photo on the blog. It showed a group of around twenty-five healthy-looking retirees standing at the edge of a vineyard with smiles and intertwined arms. There were two younger men in the photo – a stocky one wearing a flat cap whom Chris guessed was the farmer. The other had a little beard but was looking to one side when the photo was taken, as if he was distracted by something off-screen.

Chris stared at the man they both guessed was Javi Fernandez, wondered if he was the one person who could quickly and painlessly give them the answer they needed. *Ruth is here. She's safe. She'll soon be on her way home.*

And then?

Then Javi could explain why Ruth's money was in his account.

CHAPTER 27

The hospital canteen was almost full when Chris got there but a stout lady with a thick web of freckles and a broken foot moved along one seat to make room at one of the big tables that seated eight. 'Warmed it for you,' she said.

'That's service,' said the man next to her, a young lad with a look of delighted surprise, like toddlers at Christmas. He was probably on drugs.

Chris thanked her and sat down with his plate of lasagne, wishing they'd leave. He called Mikey's mobile while he ate, hoping he'd tut and provide a logical reason for that money being transferred into his account. When he didn't answer, Chris called Rachel's phone, in case they were together.

He wasn't surprised Rachel hadn't been in to visit – their relationship was one of good manners and polite greetings and it would be awkward for all of them if she tried to pretend it was anything else. But, knowing that Rachel had been with Maria the morning of the accident, he'd have expected some contact. He wondered again why they'd been together – and why nobody had told him.

Rachel's 'Hello?' was cheerless, came with an air of accusation and a question mark attached. Chris said his name then switched his identity to *Mikey's dad* when she didn't respond. 'Give me a minute,' she said. 'I know it's late but I'm still at work.'

He'd never quite understood what Rachel did for a living; he'd asked her so many times it was now too embarrassing to ask for any more detail. Something connected to digital design. She always looked distinctly chuffed when she announced her nonsensical job title but Chris could never remember what it was and still had no clue what her role actually involved.

When she spoke again Chris heard the rumble of traffic in the background and from time to time the beep of people passing a security door. He heard the flick of a lighter too, wondered if there was anyone in the family who didn't secretly smoke. 'I'm sorry about Maria,' she said. 'And, just so you know, I'm planning to come in for a visit but I thought I'd wait, give you some family time first – just you, Mikey and Ruth. But I'll be there in a flash if you need me, okay? It breaks my heart to think of her. Is there any improvement?'

'No. She's just the same,' he said, then wondered how many weeks or months he'd be giving that same answer; how long it would be until people stopped asking, or asked only to be polite, knowing the answer wouldn't change.

'Give her my best,' said Rachel, and Chris said he would. He couldn't stand such clichéd phrases but they were typical of Rachel. He'd almost wept at her wedding vows, not because of the beauty but because she appeared to have copied and pasted together twee phrases from pastel-coloured wedding cards.

'I understand you were with Maria on Sunday morning.' Chris paused, leaving room for a response. When he'd started at the paper Sandy had taught him the value of silence, said that in many cases silence was more useful than a question. People couldn't ignore it, felt an urge to break it and fill it with words. But not Rachel.

He tried another trick – use questions to present facts, incite a response.

'A neighbour said he saw you at the house?'

'I was looking for Mikey,' she said.

'Mikey?'

'I assumed that was where he'd gone when he left on Saturday night, so when Maria told me she'd not seen him . . .' Rachel paused, then exhaled noisily. Chris could tell she was blowing out smoke. She coughed before she spoke again. 'I got a bit upset so Maria invited me in for a drink. I had the car so I was only going to stay for one but . . . anyway . . . you can imagine how that went. Three gins later Maria said I could stay, sleep in Mikey's old room. So that's what I did. I left around eight on Sunday morning, same time Maria left for the race. She had to go to town before it started, which was why we left so early.'

'Can I stop you there for a second? I'm totally lost. How come you didn't know where Mikey was?'

'Maria didn't tell you?'

'Tell me what?'

For a few seconds the only sounds between them were mechanical. Engines and sirens and doors, opening and closing. There was nothing soft, nothing that soothed or sympathised. When Rachel spoke again her voice was different, stripped of colour. 'I've got some news,' she said.

CHAPTER 28

Rachel explained the breakdown of her world in three minutes flat, and without any audible trace of grief. After fifteen years together she and Mikey had split up. It had been on the cards for a while but finally happened on Saturday. He'd left and she hadn't seen him since. She'd gone to see Maria on Saturday night, hoping she'd find him there – but didn't. Maria had offered her a sympathetic ear and generous pourings of gin – then a place to sleep it off. The only bed already made up was in Mikey's room but she'd taken it, seen it as a final farewell. And yes, it was Rachel who'd burned the wedding photo that Chris had seen on the windowsill. At least that explained why Jim had seen her on Sunday morning when Maria was leaving for the race. But the reasons for their separation? There were lots, she said, then suggested Chris should ask Mikey to explain. She said the same when Chris asked her about the transfer of cash from his and Maria's joint account into Mikey's. Her only comment was that Mikey was a disaster with money. But for details, she'd insisted he ask Mikey.

And he would, if Mikey would answer the bloody phone.

Mikey, the adored first child then idolised big brother to Ruth. Mikey, with the beautiful wife and the cool job. Mikey, the resilient one, the stable one, the one who just got on with things and rarely complained.

Mikey, an even bigger liar than the rest of them.

Chris couldn't remember the last time he'd asked how things were between Mikey and Rachel. Probably it was before they were married. People stopped asking after that, didn't they? At least, Chris did. He had no qualms asking his few unmarried friends how they were getting on with their partners and usually they were fairly honest, happy to whinge if required, to be vaguely doubtful or utterly pessimistic about the future, to feel unsatisfied, to be pissed off, to want more sex or more freedom and less commitment and a life that felt like their own, that allowed them to live as they pleased. But for some reason he acted as if life was rosy once people he knew got married. He'd ask indirect questions and receive indirect answers. *How's married life treating you? How's the family doing?* It felt more intrusive somehow, asking if a marriage was working.

Still, he was amazed Mikey hadn't mentioned it.

He tried calling his mobile a few more times then gave up and headed back to Maria's room. The door was open when he got there and Sandy's telephone voice wafted up the corridor from the visitors' room. Knowing Sandy, he'd have tracked down a complete stranger in ten minutes flat. Javi Fernandez, identified and charmed and heading in for an exclusive interview.

And here was Chris, unable to track down his own bloody children.

He sat down, tried calling Trobador Tours on the off-chance Monty had popped back to the office and got his message. It was still ringing when the door was opened by a nurse he'd never seen before, carrying an oversized yellow envelope. She started to speak, then hushed herself when Chris pointed to the phone at his ear. She sat it on the table and Chris partially tore it open with his free hand – enough to see the card inside. It said Get Well Soon along the top and beneath was a photograph of bright yellow sunflowers in a field. Chris was trying to manoeuvre the card out of the envelope when Monty's voicemail started playing, demanding he speak after the beep.

But his mind stayed with the sunflower image while he spoke.

It reminded Chris of that road trip the four of them did, the year Mikey turned ten. They'd flown to Barcelona then hired a camper van, spent a month driving the back roads between there and Cadiz, snaking between olive and almond groves and orange plantations and endless fields of sunflowers. The kids had liked the sunflowers the best, demanding Chris stop the van so they could climb the fence and get their photo taken in the middle of it all, a sea of yellow. They'd stood on their tiptoes with their arms clamped to their sides and their necks stretched tall, faces pointing the same way as the flowers while Maria explained the young plants were clever enough to turn on their stalks and follow the sun. Wherever there was light, they'd find it and face it.

And it's all down to teamwork, she said, laughing at their wowed faces when she explained that the head of each big flower was in fact made up from hundreds of tiny blooms, coming together to make one. Their response was a bombardment of hows and whys and whens.

Maria's answer was simple. *Nature just knows*, she said.

When they'd stopped again on the drive home the kids had stayed in the car, staring in disbelief at charred heads drooping over grey necks, flowers sucked dry by the sun that had given them life. Maria had explained that this was the key part of the process; that the seeds could only be harvested once the head was dry. *From death springs life*, she'd said. The kids had cried all the same.

Chris finished his message to Monty then put down his phone and tugged the Get Well card again, trying to release it from the envelope. The nurse put down a chart she was checking and helped him pull it free.

'Lovely,' she said. 'It'll brighten up the room, won't it?'

'Aye,' said Chris.

'Shame he couldn't stay longer, isn't it?'

'Who?'

'The man who brought it.'

'What man? Who was it?' Chris opened the card. There was only one word and it was printed; totally impersonal. But he recognised its significance.

Contigo.

With you, in Spanish. Maria always used that word in cards and letters instead of *lots of love* and its equivalents. Mateo did the same, and both the kids. It was the same word Mikey had texted to Ruth after she'd said she was going to disappear.

'*Christ.*' Chris jumped up. 'Who brought this?'

'A chap in his thirties or forties, big smile, needed a shave,' said the nurse. 'He was only in for five minutes – just when you and the other gentleman had popped out. Said he was sorry he missed you.'

'When did he leave?'

'Just this minute,' she said. 'Said something about a bus.'

Chris ran, dodging a bed left in the corridor and a bucket on wheels and a toddler chased by an old lady. He ran downstairs and through the queue of people lining up at reception and past a man with a drip and he weaved between parked and moving traffic in the car park and he kept going until he could see the bus stop in the darkness ahead – and saw for sure it was empty.

Christ.

For a moment he stopped to catch his breath, scanned the sprawling car park and the woodland garden and the dozens of cars queued up on the bottleneck exit road. Then he ran, heading for the bus at the front of the queue.

It wasn't hard to see the faces of the passengers inside the lit interior of the bus. Chris became at once the watcher and the watched as he walked slowly up and down the pavement beside the vehicle. After that he went on to the road, followed the white line so he could see the passengers sitting on the other side. A few passing cars moved to avoid him, honking their horns, and when he reached the front he could see the driver's irate face in the big wing mirror. He knocked at the glass door, pleading to be let in, but the driver shook his head. Instead he pointed to the pavement then mouthed at Chris, told him to get off the bloody road.

When the bus moved off Chris continued his checks, car by car. The first was being edged jerkily forward by a teenage boy while his mother beamed at him from the passenger seat. There was nobody in the back. The next car was driven by an old man with a navy polo shirt, a beer belly so big it looked like it might jam the steering wheel. The next was a young man in a tracksuit looking into the rear-view mirror at a little baby in the back.

He saw every kind of person, but nobody he recognised.

When he got back to the front door of the hospital he waited there, a breathless sentry, the echo of his efforts pulsing throughout his body. He kept his eyes on the road, scanning every car that passed. But there was nothing, nobody. He jumped when Sandy appeared beside him and touched him arm.

'What's going on, Chris? The nurses said you shot off.'

'We can't leave Maria alone,' he said. 'A man was here. Maybe Mikey. Maybe Mateo. Maybe Javi Fernandez, for all we know. But whoever it was, they left a card, with a note in Spanish. Then fled.'

'Fled? Why?'

'Christ only knows, Sandy. But I don't like it. First I get these Spanish messages on the answerphone at home, now this. It must be connected.'

He scanned the car park one last time, then motioned for Sandy to go back inside. They walked through the main doors to reception and past the chip-scented canteen and the gift shop and along that carpeted corridor to intensive care and into the room where Maria lay with that sunflower card by her side.

And that little word. *Contigo*.

Ruth's moods fluctuated during the weeks that followed.

On social media she was Living The Dream, just not hers. But was she living hers with me, locked up in a flat that I could not convince her to leave?

There were days she looked at me with love but I knew Ruth was still scared of commitment. She was still frightened to give herself to me fully. She wanted to see me from time to time; wanted a few intense hours and then back to a life like everybody else's. She wanted only the best parts of me. She wanted the door to be left open so she could back out and leave whenever she wanted.

As the weeks went on she spent more and more time without me, more time asleep, more time losing herself in wine. Then one day she woke up and called her mum and dad's landline but when the answerphone came on she hung up without saying a word. Still, I heard her message, loud and clear.

She missed them.

I knew if anything could lure Ruth away from me, it was her mum and dad. They'd convince her I was a bad idea, that what we were was not worth it. Their shadow grew longer and darker as the days went on, stalked Ruth almost as closely as I had done. She dreaded disappointing them; knew it would sicken them to know about me, about desires she'd hidden but still held so tightly.

She was convinced her future could go one of two ways – with me but without her parents, or the opposite. With both, she'd be forced to accept pain and turmoil in one part of her life in exchange for peace and love in the other.

No matter what I offered her, I couldn't make the missing part go away.

I'd never be worth more to Ruth than an easy silence with her dad; a knowing smile from her mum. I asked Ruth if I could ever be part of that and she laughed, said her parents wouldn't be seen dead in public with someone like me.

And what about you, Ruth? What about you?

She didn't give me an answer. But, in her silence, I found mine.

CHAPTER 29

Chris moved the sunflowers card from the bedside cabinet to the windowsill while he made yet another round of calls, hoping to get Ruth or Mikey or Rachel or Mateo or anyone at all who could answer any of his questions. But all he got was the same old voicemail messages and instructions to speak after the beep. He stuffed his phone into his pocket, sank his head into his hands.

'I'm not sure how much more of this I can handle.'

'More than you think,' said Sandy, laying a hand on his shoulder. 'But you need to stop assuming the worst.'

'The worst is already happening.'

Sandy sighed. 'Would you publish that? Would you? No. Not on my shift you wouldn't. I know you're suffering, Chris, but please, you need to focus on facts. Evidence. Definites. The rest is speculation, and that means it's bullshit.'

'Eloquently said.'

'Eloquence is my forte,' said Sandy. 'Now if you'll spare me a few minutes of your time I've got some updates on our old pal Javi Fernandez.'

'Already?'

Sandy nodded. 'I think our pal Man With A Heart is also Man With A Social Media Addiction. Tells me he's rarely offline. Anyway, he was more than delighted to give me Javi's email address – and the details of his Instagram account. I've held off writing an email – thought we should do that together – but I've been looking through his photos online.'

'And?'

'Come and see for yourself.' Sandy opened a window on his laptop and started scrolling through hundreds of images. 'Quite a few of them are images of Spain, like these ones – street scenes, bar life, skyline panoramas, that kind of thing. But there are photos of tour groups too, twenty happy retirees decked out with Trobador Tours name tags – so it's definitely the right person.'

'Are there any photos of Javi?'

'It's hard to say for sure because obviously we don't know what he looks like. But the only photos with faces are the old folk and people in the background of street scenes. He's clearly not one for selfies. And before you ask, there are no photos of Ruth either. But I might have found something interesting. Let's see what you make of it.'

He scrolled up the page until he reached the most recent photo uploaded to Javi's account. It had been posted a week ago and showed two pairs of feet resting on a black rock, pointing skywards. It had clearly been taken by someone lying down. The colours and position of the trainers they were wearing suggested it was a woman and a man on their backs, side by side. Beyond their feet a hill sloped downwards to a place where grey clouds blurred with the horizon then merged with the sea.

'Innocent enough,' said Sandy. 'But look at the hashtags.'

And there it was.

#LoveEdinburgh #DecemberRain #FourSeasonsOneDay

Chris looked at Sandy, eyes wide. 'Javi Fernandez was in Edinburgh? Last week? Christ. And you think that's Ruth with him?'

Sandy held up his hands. 'Impossible to know,' he said. 'I certainly think it's worth investigating further. But if he took that photo last week there's definitely a chance he's still here now. If he's with Ruth, all the better. And if he's not, there's still a chance he'll know where she is.'

'You got a phone number?'

'Just an email.'

'I'll send one right now. I'm still hoping to hear back from Ruth's tour boss and hopefully get a phone number – but email's fine for now.'

Chris pulled out his phone, got Sandy to dictate the email address. Then he stared at the flashing cursor, fingers an inch from the keyboard. 'I'm not sure how to approach this, Sandy. Should I mention what's happened to Maria?'

'I wouldn't at this stage – we know he's a good tour guide but we don't know if we can trust him, Chris. Just say you're Ruth's dad and that you believe he knows her – and you really need her to get in touch. That's enough.'

Chris nodded. 'I'll give him all of our contact numbers. And I'll send an email from Maria's email account as backup.

At least we can be sure one of the two will definitely get through. Should we contact him via Instagram too?'

'Can't do any harm, I suppose.'

Chris sent the email from his account then switched phones, writing the same message in Maria's email account. 'Can you give me Javi's email again?'

Sandy read it out, slowly. 'Y-O-S-O-Y-J-A . . .'

Chris stopped listening after he'd typed the third letter. He didn't need to. Javi Fernandez's full email address appeared on a dropdown menu, along with several other suggested contacts already stored in the memory of Maria's email account.

This could mean only one thing.

Maria and Javi had already been in contact.

Thoughts flew so fast they blurred. Chris's eyes did the same, stinging as tears threatened to block his view. But it was right there in black and white, the one thing he'd been looking for since he first heard that man's name.

'Chris? You okay? You found something?'

'Aye,' said Chris, then handed Maria's phone to Sandy. 'A connection.'

CHAPTER 30

'Sorry,' said Chris. '*Sorry*. That's all it says.'

His eyes flitted between that one word and the name in the *From* box. *Javi Fernandez*. A quick search in Maria's inbox had produced one email between Javi and Maria, confirming beyond any doubt that they knew each other.

The email was sent from Javi to Maria – on Sunday.

Chris had overlooked that message during his previous searches – along with hundreds of others in Maria's email account. Ruth had been his only focus, and that was the only name he'd searched for in her inbox. Maria had lots of Spanish contacts so Javi Fernandez could have been anyone – an old friend, a work colleague, a cousin. But now Chris knew for sure he was someone else altogether. He was definitely part of Ruth's life – and it seemed he was part of Maria's too. *Sorry*, he said in the email, and nothing more. And the subject? *Me and Ruth*. But that wasn't even the worst of it. Chris handed Maria's phone to Sandy. 'Check the time.'

Sandy peered at the screen, used two fingers to zoom in. He looked confused for a few moments – and then he turned to Chris, eyes wide. 'Javi sent this email on Sunday morning, not long after Maria had her accident.'

'Exactly,' said Chris. 'So this tells us various things. Number one: the subject of the email confirms that Javi and Ruth are together. Number two: Javi knows Maria well enough to have her email address. Number three: the fact that he's apologising suggests to me there's been previous contact of some kind, and that it's upset or annoyed Maria. And number four? I'm almost certain now that it was Javi Fernandez who left the apology on the answerphone at home. It's too much of a coincidence otherwise. Christ, who is he? And why does he have Maria's email address and home phone number?'

'Calm down, Chris. Don't close your mind to the alternatives,' said Sandy. 'We need to look for facts, not speculate. Now, apart from Rachel, do we know *for certain* who Maria met on Sunday morning, before her accident?

'Not for certain, no,' said Chris. 'And my theory is losing strength by the minute. I'd thought Maria went to town to find the girlfriend of Ruth's tenant so she could get permission for the intercom engineer to enter the flat. But the intercom isn't fixed, which suggests Maria didn't find her. And if she didn't find her, why did she spend so long in town, knowing she'd miss the race?'

Sandy nodded to the mobile phone, still open at the email that Javi Fernandez had sent to Maria. 'Could she have been meeting this chap as well? If he's sending her emails, there *must* have been some previous contact.'

Chris nodded. 'I was wondering that. But how can we find out for sure?'

Sandy pursed his lips and leaned back in his chair, hands clasped behind his head. His thinking pose. Chris knew it well, trusted it. And so he waited.

'Her purse,' said Sandy.

'Sorry?'

'Check Maria's purse for receipts. You can check your joint account transactions for times and places she's swiped a payment – but receipts might tell us where and when she used cash. If there's a receipt for food or drink we should be able to work out if she was alone or not. It won't tell us *who* she was with, but it's a start. And it's more useful than sitting here speculating.'

'You're a genius.' Chris went to the wardrobe and pulled out Maria's running jacket. It barely weighed a thing. He hadn't noticed her purse when he was looking for her phone but it had to be there. He opened all the pockets, found spare contact lenses, chewing gum, hankies and a packet of paracetamol. But no purse. He asked Sandy to do the same in case he's somehow missed it.

Sandy checked, then shook his head. 'There's nothing there,' he said. 'Phone Farida, ask if they collected her purse from the scene of the accident. Or if it's been handed in since. Either way, you'll need to cancel all her cards.'

'Aye, except for the joint account,' said Chris, sighing. 'It's been drained already, hasn't it? All our money's in Mikey's account.

For a moment Chris and Sandy looked at each other, then they looked at Maria. 'I know what you're thinking, Sandy but don't say it. Please.'

Sandy nodded.

'Let's get on with practical stuff, eh? I'll phone Farida, see if they've got Maria's purse. And I'll ask if she can possibly use the CCTV to track where Maria went *before* the accident. I'll also double-check Maria's phone for other emails between her and Javi – although I'm quite sure there's only one.'

'She might have deleted the others.'

Chris sighed. 'Aye. But why bother? What's the big bloody secret?'

'It might not be anything sinister.'

'You think? Ruth's disappeared. Maria's half-dead. Javi is our one solid link to them both, Sandy.'

'Calm down, Chris. We still don't know he's done anything wrong.'

'No? So why is he apologising?'

Sandy's silence said everything.

Chris couldn't bear it. He left Sandy and headed for the Fresh Air Zone. The rain was lashing down but he didn't care. Christ, the weather was the one thing in life that was behaving as it should. He sat on a damp bench and dropped his head back, raindrops pinching his cheeks like needles. He thought about the time he and Ruth were caught in a summer storm when they were out snorkelling. They'd taken a deep breath then dived down together, then they'd turned and watched the surface of the agitated sea shiver and dance above them.

Ruth had been amazed the water was so still underneath, where they were.

For a few moments Chris managed to keep his mind there, in the silence and stillness of that shared moment. But like their held breaths back then, it couldn't last. Questions starting creeping back into his head and his eyes pushed out salty tears that blended with the rain and trickled towards his ears.

He eventually found the strength to call Farida, nearly threw his phone in the bin when the ringing switched to voicemail. Story of his bloody life. His voice wobbled but he left a brief message explaining that Maria's purse was missing. Then he hung up and went back inside, both drenched and drained.

When he got back to Maria's room Sandy stood up and pulled on his jacket, said he needed a shower and his own bed and promised he'd be back in the morning. They shared a slapping hug, and then Chris was on his own.

Chris sat for hours, staring at Maria's bed, watching her chest rise and fall with each puff of the ventilator. He didn't look up when nurses came in to check Maria's blood pressure or when the cleaner came in to empty the bin.

But although his eyes were on Maria, his mind was on Javi Fernandez.

Ruth had sent this man nearly all of her money shortly after she went missing – and now perhaps he had her bank card, and her phone, collected from the Alba. He had sent apologies to Maria's email address and home phone number *after the fall* – a fall Chris struggled to believe was an accident. Javi was the one solid connection between the two women Chris loved the most. One had disappeared and the other had been left for dead. Why?

Chris thought of Mikey and Mateo too, and of the lies that been told to him by his family. It was incomprehensible, all of it. He didn't know who to trust or where his loyalty lay. He closed his eyes, blocked Maria from view.

Of all people, he couldn't bear to think of her deceiving him.

When a nurse dimmed the lights he laid his head on Maria's bed and tried to rest. It was only nine p.m. but he felt exhausted. Dreams came, soothed him for an hour or so. But then a familiar voice woke him; broke the silence and with it, the little peace that remained in him. Farida McPherson sat down, said the four words she'd come all this way to say.

We've found a body.

CHAPTER 31

Chris accelerated when he saw the helicopter, driving much faster than he should. Drystone dykes lined both sides of the road and the tall trees on the skyline looked black in the winter night, as if they'd been scribbled on to the landscape with charcoal. The road was icy and Chris skidded slightly on the final bend, passing a sign declaring *Brewster Bay Welcomes Careful Drivers*, then drove between old wooden boats hauled up from the harbour, dumped on dry land and planted with flowers.

Chris glanced at them as he passed, thought of funerals.

Brewster Bay was all slate roofs and smoking chimneys, built on a pinkie of land poking into the freezing North Sea. A sandy beach stretched for miles on one side while sandstone cliffs loomed over the other, their walls a giant, jagged honeycomb. There was no reason to visit except for the views, and few people did. It wasn't a place people passed through or found by accident or went on a whim. It took effort to get there. Determination. Chris had been before, but only as a news reporter, and only for one kind of story. Suicides.

He signalled and turned down the narrow side street that led to the harbour, but didn't get as far as he'd hoped.

A strip of plastic police tape had been pulled across the entrance to the harbour and a police patrol car was parked on the other side, its headlights illuminating the scene. An officer was standing at the edge of the harbour, peering down into the dark water. He was a big man, beer belly sticking out like a pillow tucked under his black uniform. He glanced up when Chris got out of the car.

'Harbour's closed,' said the officer. 'Police incident.'

Chris felt sick at the sound of those two words. *Police incident.* But that was all it was for most people, wasn't it? He'd seen it before; knew that soon enough people would be lured in by the pulse of a blue light, the wail of sirens, the thunder of rotor blades cutting through night skies. There would be nervous laughs and whispers when the forensics team arrived, started unloading equipment most people only saw on TV. Onlookers would huddle together on the other side of sagging police tape, watch somebody else's life go wrong, from a distance. So far the only spectators were police and the press, the ones who knew what was coming. But the key question remained unanswered.

Who?

We've found a body, Farida had said.

Chris had written and talked about bodies hundreds of times in the newsroom and out in the city, working on crime stories. But until that moment he'd never truly felt their weight.

He parked the car as close to the harbour as he could then got out and walked. A group of teenagers were perched on the wide windowsills of the old fishermen's cottages, eating chips out of white paper.

Further on, a few punters stood outside the doors of the local hotel, smoking, drinking, not working or worried about the sight of another helicopter. Chris strode on, eyes straight ahead. When he saw the press pack gathering at the headland he stopped, pulled up the hood on his hiking jacket. He didn't want to be seen, didn't want them to know why he'd come. Farida had been very clear: there was *absolutely no evidence* the body was Ruth or Mikey – *so far* – but, given the press interest in his family's story, she was worried connections would be made. She'd wanted Chris to hear it from her first, to avoid Unnecessary Suffering. Was suffering ever necessary?

Apparently so.

Needless to say, he'd come here against her advice.

Chris kept walking until he felt the thud of the rotors.

When he looked skywards he could just make out the search and rescue team crouched in the open doorway of the helicopter – two figures in green jumpsuits and helmets, clutching the sides as waves smashed off the rocks beneath them, shooting foam high into the air. Then one of the men eased himself out of the door, became a stilled pendulum. Chris had seen this kind of recovery simulated at air shows. He knew the dangers – crew members losing consciousness on spinning cables, or smashing into the ground if the winch malfunctioned. They could be thrown against rocks if the helicopter was moved by bad weather or poor piloting; be dragged along underneath if engine failure forced it to land.

But this was more than just a display to wow the crowds, a checklist of potential dangers. This was one man, risking his life in the darkness to save one already lost. It didn't matter how hard he worked or how well he did his job or how much he wished they'd got there sooner. The best he could do was deliver a corpse.

And then it came.

The body spun gently as it was hoisted slowly skywards, partially covered by a dark tarpaulin. Chris wondered what was left of it, pictured lumps of human-shaped flesh, burst and leaking like ripe fruit thrown on the floor. Skin and blood and a smile and a voice that used to belong be somebody's daughter or wife or son or brother or mum or friend or neighbour. It stopped five feet from the helicopter and for a moment life and death hung together in the searchlight, stilled.

Chris wanted to look away but could not. He thought of the moment just after the Ruth was born – the midwife holding a clamp in one hand and fierce-looking scissors in the other, asking if he'd do the honours. He'd been amazed at the sight of it, a bloody lifeline connecting Maria to this little human made from pieces of them. That was love, right there at the end of the cord.

It was the only birth he'd witnessed. Mikey was their first baby but he'd missed his birth by a few minutes for various work-related reasons that he'd regretted and felt the need to justify ever since. He was at the hospital for Heather's, but had fainted in the operating theatre when doctors opted for an emergency C-section. Still, the moment he became a dad he'd instantly become every cliché he'd sworn he wouldn't. He made all sorts of vows to himself and to Maria and to that wriggling child that fitted so snugly into his arms. He used words like promise and love and protect and always. He would whisper to Mikey when Maria was asleep, gaze with a lump in his throat at the face that made him feel such peace and such fear at the same time. It terrified him, to love so deeply. He'd seen too many times how often and how easily loss stained lives.

And then it happened to them, with Heather. The police had asked questions, were satisfied with the answers. Doctors called it a sudden death, friends called it tragic, and for once Chris found no words at all. He carried the weight of his lost daughter with him, always. He could not endure it again.

But here it was once more, within touching distance.

One final effort and the rescue crew pulled up death, packed it away – and soon enough the press pack did the same. Chris had kept his distance but he recognised a few people by their coats and the way they stood. The photographers had already turned away from the sky, were packing up tripods and filters. He could see one of the lads he'd trained, separating himself from the other reporters and heading off in the direction of the hotel. He'd be looking for quotes but not many, knowing they'd probably never be used. If the death was a suicide the story would be short and discreet, a personal tragedy reduced to three lines and topped with the line that gave it all away. *No suspicious circumstances.*

Murders were different; gave reporters a licence to question anybody they wanted, gave readers a hunger for facts.

Everyone was greedy, wanted their fill. Chris had spent days sometimes following murder investigations, interviewing neighbours and bus drivers and pub staff and dog-walkers and anybody else who was willing to share a memory of the killer or the killed, sometimes both.

Was someone to blame for what had happened here, today?

The press pack didn't think so.

They'd already split, and most were heading back to their cars. Whether it was a tip-off or intuition, they all agreed: this is not worth our time.

Chris watched the horizon, tracking the helicopter as it disappeared into the night. He could hear it long after he could see it, turned a few times and stared at empty sky as he walked back to his car. He could still hear it when he turned on the engine and turned up the radio and he could hear it above the sound of traffic on the motorway. He could still hear when he was standing alone at the hospital doors with a cup of vending machine coffee he hadn't touched, and he could hear it when he arrived back at Maria's room.

He could still hear it when he bent down to kiss Maria, wishing with all the strength in him that she would not wake up to this; to the ache and the horror of it.

Loss, right there at the end of a cord.

Killing Ruth was always part of the plan.

I'd spent years of my life imagining it, that moment when I'd open her up, bring her insides to the outside. All it took was a sharp edge, pushed down hard enough. That's it. I pictured her body from the inside, imagined the tip easing through her outer layer, past skin and fat and blood and bone and muscle, pushing through all the tiny pieces of Ruth that had always held her together.

In.

And out.

I marvelled at the strength of that sleek silver tip. This was Ruth, smeared on metal. Every drop of blood exposed the pathetic fragility of human existence. It seemed too easy, somehow. Was that really all it took to take a life?

In. Out.

I'd expected more drama. More struggle. Ruth was still hanging on, but only just. I felt no sorrow, no regret, no desire to change anything at all.

In. Out.

You may wonder why I had to take it to such extremes but that only serves to show that you don't know Ruth at all. The way I saw it, it was my life or hers.

And I chose mine.

CHAPTER 32

Chris woke up, startled, when his phone beeped. He grabbed it off the bedside table, heart thundering – then sinking just as quickly. It was just Sandy, saying he was on his way. Chris sighed and slumped back into his chair, neck and back stiff and sore. Early morning sun streaked through the slatted blinds, the window smudged with condensation. He pulled his chair closer to Maria's bed and laid his head as close to hers as he could, wishing the movement of her machine-powered breath would dislodge the image of that helicopter from his brain; the way it raised and carried off the corpse.

Farida had assured him she'd call as soon as she had an update on the Brewster Bay body. In the meantime, she suggested Chris continue his attempts to contact Ruth and Mikey. He'd been calling Rachel too, in case Mikey had been in touch with her – and Mateo to quiz him about the sunflower card.

So far none of his calls – or questions – had been answered.

Farida had encouraged him to try video calls with Ruth and Mikey, stressing the importance of obtaining *live images* of both. Live images? The moment she said it, Chris thought of the opposite.

He'd just about got used to Ruth and Mateo not answering – but Mikey? There had been no contact at all since their tense discussion at the house yesterday lunchtime. Mikey had been upset when he left, supposedly to deal with some emergency at work – but Christ, what kind of emergency lasted this long? He knew from experience that Mikey had a tendency to shut down when he was under pressure, but this was taking the piss.

But there was one explanation, wasn't there? Mikey, Brewster Bay, the body and that bloody chopper. Chris felt sick at the thought of it, needed air.

He left Maria's room and went to the Fresh Air Zone, welcoming the sensation of daylight instead of strip-light on his skin. The cool air calmed him, helped him think more logically. If Mikey wouldn't answer his mobile phone, he could try him at work. *Christ.* Why hadn't he thought of that earlier?

He did a quick internet search for the Mikey's co-working office and dialled the general number. No answer. Too early perhaps; it wasn't even eight in the morning. He then searched Mikey's business website for an alternative contact but the page wouldn't load. After that he scoured his mobile phone contact list to see if he had a number for Mikey's business partner, Carmen – but he didn't.

He sat for a few more minutes, wishing desperately for an ordinary morning, then headed back inside. He found Sandy standing by the window in Maria's room, holding two coffees. He handed one to Chris.

'You get any sleep?'

Chris shook his head. 'Can't stop thinking about that bloody chopper.'

'You should have phoned me,' said Sandy. 'I could have gone with you. In fact, I could have gone *instead* of you. I couldn't believe it when I woke up this morning and read your text message. I knew I shouldn't have left you.'

'You needed to rest,' said Chris. 'And anyway, you're here now. Any updates from the news desk this morning?

Sandy nodded. 'I spoke to Tash on the way here – she was covering the nightshift. There's nothing new on Brewster Bay so far but I do have something to keep your mind busy.' He drained his coffee then perched on the windowsill beside the sunflower card. 'An email came in late last night from someone called Max McAndrew. Saw our article, claims to know Ruth from years back, wants to speak to you in person. Name ring any bells?'

'I think I'd remember a name like that,' said Chris. 'Maria would be the one to ask, really. But . . . anyway, what's he saying? Has he seen Ruth?'

'Claims he saw her the night she disappeared.'

Chris's mouth went dry. '*Christ*. Do you think it's the lad from the Alba? The one Ruth smoked with? Where did he see her?'

'You'll need to ask him that yourself,' said Sandy. 'I'm just passing on the message from the news desk. Says he'll be in all morning. Oh, and one last thing. He's not spoken to the police yet. Says he wanted to talk to you first.'

'So Farida doesn't know?'

'No – but I'd suggest we tell her, asap. I'm sure this boy's got his reasons but Farida needs the full picture. Won't do anyone any good to conceal the fact there's been a sighting. Especially on the day she went missing.'

'I'm with you on that,' said Chris.

They went to the canteen for more coffee and a quick breakfast then Chris headed back to the Fresh Air Zone and dialled Max McAndrew's number. He took a while to answer, said, 'You're who?' as though he'd just woken up.

'Ruth Morrison's dad.'

'Jesus. Right. One second.' Music was switched off then he heard the clink of glass and a tap being run. Footsteps, a yawn, and then Max came back on the line. Chris wondered why a working-age man wasn't up and active on a weekday morning, had assassinated his character before they'd even begun.

'Mr Morrison?'

'You can call me Chris. But first tell me something. Have we met?'

'Doubt it.'

'And how do you know my daughter?'

'From school.'

'Which one?'

'Hartfield Academy.'

'And you're in regular contact with Ruth?'

'God, no. I never saw her again after school and didn't expect to. But when I clocked her face in the Alba that night I knew it was her, right away. She's changed a lot, but I could still tell. I think she recognised me too, but she avoided making eye contact until I went right up to her, bought her a drink.'

'And this was definitely the night she went missing? Sunday, March 18th?'

'Definitely. I remember because it's my mum's birthday. She'd have been sixty-four. She died when I was wee but I always celebrate it on her behalf.'

Chris's heart squirmed. He'd always done the same, but had never told anyone he did it. He'd celebrated his mum's birthday alone for thirty years – and marked the birth and death of their second baby for almost the same length of time. It never got any easier. He'd couldn't bear adding any other names to that list.

'How long did you and Ruth talk?'

'Long enough to tank two bottles of wine. Last I saw of her was when we went outside for a fag and—'

'*Christ.* So it *was* you. You're the last person who saw Ruth.'

'I am?'

'Aye. So what happened when you went outside the Alba?'

'I went in for a kiss and she legged it.'

'And then?'

'And then nothing, I'm afraid. I haven't heard a squeak from her since, but when I saw the appeal in the paper I knew I had to get in touch.'

'Did you see Ruth get into a taxi?'

'No. But she was planning to get one.'

Chris sighed. 'Did she seem in good spirits?'

'She was pretty drunk, if that's what you're asking. As for her mood – there were flashes of the Ruth I remembered. We laughed a bit, ripped the piss out of each other, same way we used to at school. Well, before she decided to become a carbon copy of all other girls in her year and ignore the geeks, a.k.a. me. She never seemed to realise we all liked her because she *wasn't* like them. I tried to explain that to her at the Alba, actually. Probably wasn't at my most eloquent after so much bevvy, but, knowing Ruth, she wouldn't have believed me anyway. But it was good to see her, both of us freed at last from the cursed teenage angst. I think we're both late bloomers, me and Ruth.'

'And you've never seen her since school?'

'Never. Once Ruth got sucked into all that bitchy nonsense I was out of the picture. She was dead-set on being accepted by the cool girls even though it was obviously just a big act. Never saw her again – until that night at the Alba.'

'And you said she fled after you tried to kiss her?' Chris hoped his voice sounded less accusing than his thoughts. 'So was she your girlfriend at school?'

'No, no – people thought she was and used to tease her about it, but we were just really good friends. God knows why I tried to kiss her that night – I suppose I was just drunk and happy to see her. I always thought we were soulmates, in a way, but it wasn't romantic – more like Geeks United. That's why I was so upset when she got herself all these fake pals and cut me out of her life.

'Anyway, I'm straying from the point. You were asking about the Alba, not a full life analysis. In short, Ruth was cheery at the start of the night and was happy to see me, but later on she went a bit . . . quiet. Bit tearful. When I asked her about it she said she was leaving early the next morning for a job in Spain, wasn't looking forward to it. Apart from that, I don't recall much else. God, I'm afraid I'm not helping much, Mr Morrison.'

'It's all useful,' said Chris. 'Can I ask what you did after the pub?'

'Me and some of the lads ended up at the casino. New one, stays open twenty-four hours. One of those things that seems like a good idea at the time.'

'Aye, I think Ruth's brother ended up there too.'

'He tried to.'

'Meaning?'

'Meaning they wouldn't let him in,' said Max. 'He left the Alba before us but he was still outside the casino when we arrived. Last I saw of him, he was ranting at one of the bouncers while his poor girlfriend tried to calm him down.'

'His girlfriend?'

'Blonde girl, looks a bit posh.'

'That'll be his wife, then.'

'Poor woman,' said Max. 'No offence, but he was being an arse.'

'And you're totally sure it was Ruth's brother?'

'Totally.'

Chris thanked him – then suggested Max should speak to the police as soon as they'd finished their call. Max assured him he would, then hung up.

Chris called Rachel after that, left a message when it switched to voicemail. He tried to keep his voice calm and free from accusation as he explained about the call from Max, then asked her to call back when she could. She'd need to speak to Farida as well, but Chris wanted to talk to her first.

'Everything helps,' he said, then hung up.

Mikey hadn't mentioned the fact that Rachel was with him and Ruth the night she disappeared – and neither had Rachel, for that matter. And there was still the lingering question of why Rachel was with Maria, at their house, on the morning of her accident.

Why so many lies?

By omission this time, but they were lies just the same.

He tried calling Mikey's office one more time, then gave up. He went back inside and grabbed his car keys, thanked Sandy for offering to stay with Maria.

If Mikey was at work, Chris would find him there.

And, if not, where was he? His marriage was broken, his mum was dying, his sister had disappeared. And meanwhile, Mikey had cleared out his parents' bank account. Chris wondered suddenly if it was him who'd brought the sunflower card to Maria, not Mateo. And with that thought of flowers came the memory of that body, hanging from a cord. The sound of the helicopter would not shift, stalked his every thought.

Chris put his foot down, chased answers instead.

CHAPTER 33

The sign hung above the glass doors read 'MINE: Makers in Edinburgh'. Chris pushed the buzzer then peered into the co-working office Mikey and his business partner Carmen used as the headquarters for their wetsuit company.

The office was located on the ground floor of an old factory near the Leith docks on a street Chris had visited a few times as a junior reporter. In those days it had been a place of drugs, prostitution and the occasional murder, the neighbourhood he'd drive out to on a quiet news day and know for sure he'd come back with a decent story. Now the factories were home to hipsters and the whole place reeked of freshly roasted coffee and gentrification.

After a few more buzzes the door was answered by a girl with an Italian accent and the face of an elf. She led him to reception, asked him to wait while she fetched someone who could help. Chris thanked her and looked around. He'd let his imagination conjure up happy endings on the way here, picturing himself walking in and seeing Mikey right there, eyes smiling as he chatted on his mobile phone. When he saw Chris he'd leap up and laugh as he handed over the handset, saying at last the words Chris was so desperate to hear. *It's Ruth.*

Chris scanned rows of desks while he waited but the place was vast and there was no sign of Mikey. The back wall was decorated with an oversized photo showing the factory as it used to be – rows of ferocious metal machines that almost touched the ceiling, frowning workers like ants at the controls. Now it was all exposed brick and unpainted timber and glass walls and indoor plants that needed watering. The roar and clunk of heavy metal machines was replaced by the gentle tap of fingers on laptop keys.

He had just turned back towards reception when a man with a goatee beard cleared his throat then asked how he could help. His face lit up when Chris mentioned Wow Wetsuits and said he was Mikey's dad. 'Of course I know Mikey. Everybody does,' he said. 'But he stopped coming here months ago.'

'Really? I thought he and Carmen were really settled here.'

'They were but . . . look, maybe I should get Carmen, let her explain.'

The receptionist led Chris into a glass-walled meeting room that smelled vaguely of microwave dinners, said he'd fetch her. Chris sat down on a yellow chair and waited, tried to keep his mind away from Brewster Bay, and the body.

He stood up when Carmen tapped on the open door. As ever, she looked as though she'd been peeled out of a surfing magazine. Her hair was deliberately messy and her skin looked smooth and healthy even under strip-lighting. She was the kind of woman who'd look elegant wearing her dad's old jeans.

Chris held out a hand, was impressed by how firmly she shook it. He apologised for bothering her at work, then explained the situation with Ruth and Maria – and what had happened at Brewster Bay the previous night. 'The thing is, nobody's heard a thing from Mikey since yesterday lunchtime,' he said. 'He was with me at my house, then he said there was some kind of emergency at work. That's why I'm here.'

Carmen looked at him wordlessly, then closed the door.

'First up,' she said, 'I want to say I'm really sorry to hear about Mikey's mum, and about Ruth. And as for Mikey. . .' She sighed, and Chris knew no good news was coming. 'He wasn't here yesterday. And actually, I've not seen or heard from him in months.'

Chris stepped away from her, his body tense. 'But what about the business?'

Another sigh. 'We folded. Months ago.'

'You're kidding.'

'Wish I was.'

'But why would Mikey not tell me?'

'Your guess is as good as mine,' she said. 'I'm still here because I'm working on a few freelancing projects. Web design, that kind of thing. I'm not sure what Mikey's been doing for work since we split, but he's not here.'

'So where is he? *Christ*. He went AWOL yesterday claiming he had a work emergency, and I've not seen him since. You're *sure* he's not been here?'

Carmen shook her head. 'If it's any consolation, he did this kind of thing with me a fair bit before the business eventually went bust. He'd disappear for a couple of days sometimes – no calls, no emails. Then he'd roll up at the office as if nothing had happened. To be honest, I think he's stressed and has no idea how to handle it, so he runs away. That might sound harsh, but it's how I see it. And obviously it wasn't ideal when we were trying to run a business together.'

Chris sighed. 'You mind talking me through what happened, Carmen?'

'There's not that much to tell. We didn't sell enough wetsuits, plain and simple. Tried to sell off all remaining stock at the end of the summer and could barely even get shot of that. We were both gutted, obviously, but it just wasn't working. Not just the business – me and Mikey had a few . . . disagreements too.'

'What about?'

'Lots of things – but mainly the best way to run a business. Mikey is fantastically creative but he's not so great with the money side of things. He wouldn't listen, ending up spending profits we hadn't yet made. When we did our taxes in March it became obvious how much sales had slowed but instead of putting our heads together he got distant, seemed really distracted all the time. It was better for both of us to call it a day. I'm sorry you've had to hear it from me.'

'Me too,' said Chris. 'You know what Mikey's been doing since then?'

'Workwise? No idea. He said he's still waiting to inherit some money from his grandpa, might use that to do something totally new. But he's been saying that for years and the money has never appeared. He talked about moving abroad at one point, using his Spanish. Maybe setting up a dive school. But I've no idea if he's made any progress with any of his ideas. Like I said, we've not spoken in months.'

Chris sighed. 'And I don't suppose you've heard anything from Ruth in the past few months? I seem to remember you and her get on pretty well.'

'We do, aye. Or did.' Carmen flushed. 'But it's ages since I saw her.'

'Join the club,' said Chris, sensing another door closing. 'But do you remember roughly when it was? And where? Sorry to ask so many questions, but it would make a huge difference if there were a sighting after March 18th.'

'Actually, let me check something.' She pulled out her phone and started scrolling through her calendar, frowning. 'You remember my mum had treatment for her breast cancer last year? Well, she had a few follow-up appointments in Glasgow this spring and I took her through in my car. It was near Easter time – I remember because, every time we went, the receptionist offered us a wee chocolate egg and we ate them while we waited. Not exactly promoting good health, is it? Anyway, the point is, that's where I saw Ruth.'

'In Glasgow? At a clinic?'

Carmen nodded.

'And when exactly was this?'

Carmen nodded to her phone and tutted. 'I was hoping I'd have the dates marked in my calendar, but I don't,' she said. 'I think I maybe deleted them after we'd been. They're not exactly days I want to remember forever.

'But if my memory's right I went to that clinic three times with my mum – in March, in April and in May. I honestly can't remember which month I saw Ruth but it was one day we were running late, had about eighteen seconds to spare before my mum lost her appointment. I saw Ruth on the way in. I couldn't stop but I shouted to her, asked if she wanted to go for coffee once I dropped off my mum. She said no; said she was just waiting for someone and would be leaving any minute. She was gone by the time I came out.'

'And you're sure it was her?'

'Positive. She was quite far away but I know the way she holds herself – and anyway, she wouldn't have answered if it wasn't Ruth, would she?'

'True,' said Chris. 'And she said she was waiting for someone?'

Carmen nodded. 'The clinic is in the arse end of nowhere so there's no other reason for anyone to be there. You've either got an appointment or you're with someone who has. It's not exactly a place for passing trade.'

'And Ruth didn't say who she was waiting for?'

'Afraid not.'

'You remember the name of the clinic?'

Carmen was shaking her head before he'd finished asking the question. 'My mum directed me,' she said. 'I couldn't even tell you the neighbourhood. All I know is that it was private and had nicer toilets than most five-star hotels.'

'Any chance you can call your mum? See if she remembers the dates of her appointment and the clinic name? It could be a big step forward for us.'

Carmen looked down at her phone again, kept staring even once the screen went to sleep and turned black. After a while she started shaking her head. 'Mum died. Last month. Turns out it spread to her liver.'

Chris clenched his jaw, but left space for a cliché to pass. 'I'm so sorry.'

'Thanks.' Carmen slipped her phone into her back pocket. 'Listen – I'll try to get the clinic name and mum's treatment dates from my sister. She's working nights this week so she'll be sleeping just now. But I'll try to get hold of her tonight – and don't worry, I'll let you know as soon as I do.'

'Great, thank you – and will you speak to the police?'

'You think it'll help?'

'Definitely,' said Chris. 'You might be the last person who saw Ruth.'

Carmen gave Chris her number and offered him an awkward goodbye hug before he left. He only realised how much his hands were trembling once he was on the street, trying to call Farida. He stopped, took a deep breath, tried to calm himself. This was potentially the first positive sighting of Ruth. He knew Farida would need dates – but Ruth had been seen, alive, in Glasgow. That was enough. He'd come here to find Mikey but instead he'd found a glimmer, almost imperceptible, of something he hadn't felt in days. Hope.

CHAPTER 34

When he left Carmen, Chris headed back towards the hospital. The city was awake now, and lights from cars and cafés and Christmas decorations brightened the thick gloom of a Scottish winter's morning.

Hope did the same job. He'd still not managed to get hold of Farida but in the meantime he let his mind enjoy this new image of Ruth that his mind now held. His daughter, alive, waving at Carmen. Questions followed, of course. Who was she waiting for at that private clinic? And then the usual ones – why she still hadn't answered his calls; why the photos on social media suggested she was on the other side of the world. Not an hour from here, in bloody Glasgow.

He stopped at traffic lights, saw a sign for the motorway. For a moment he was tempted to take the turning, drive west and scour the streets of Glasgow until he found her. But it would be time wasted. Instead he signalled left, stared at the ordinary lives passing through his own while he waited for the lights to change.

And then he saw it, felt it. Another sign of hope.

He pulled over, got out, ran towards a restaurant that was painted red and gold. Its shutters were down, but there, in the window, was a poster.

It showed the silhouette of the Edinburgh skyline. Beneath it was an image of runners, numbers pinned to their tops. And, under their feet, details of the event – a 10km, for charity, last Sunday. *Runners wishing to register should call the number given below, and ask for Deborah Stewart.*

This was the race Maria should have run.

He pulled out his phone and dialled, kicking himself for not thinking of this before. Deborah Stewart answered quickly and said *good morning* as if she meant it. Then Chris told his story and she made sympathetic noises, told him she'd be happy to help. Fifteen minutes later he was there.

Deborah was sitting on the bench outside the sports centre when Chris arrived, dressed in a green hooded top and leggings, which should have detracted from her elegance but did not. Her hair was long and grey and scooped up into a bun which she tightened as Chris approached, forcing a smile.

'Mr Morrison?'

'Aye,' said Chris. 'Thanks for meeting me so quickly.'

'No bother.' She smiled and seemed to mean it. 'Now, come on inside.'

The sports centre smelled of chlorine and Deep Heat rub, had a soundtrack that blended trainers squeaking on linoleum with the rhythmic thump of dance music. Deborah talked as they walked, explaining that she'd run eighteen marathons since she retired and would have signed up for more if her knees hadn't objected. And so she'd joined the organising committee of various race events instead – including the 10km Maria was supposed to have run on Sunday.

Her main job was organising the registration process, which involved a variety of tasks – including giving out numbers on the morning of the race.

She paused at an open door, motioning for Chris to enter an office that was smaller than the bathroom at home. There were two desks inside, one a chaos of bulging paper files, the other almost bare apart from a closed laptop and a framed photo of a little girl with a big dog.

Deborah sat at the messy desk and told Chris to pull up a chair.

She glanced at the stacks of folders then gave a slight shrug and started flicking through them. 'The surname is Morrison, you said? They should be in alphabetical order, so it shouldn't take us too long to find your wife.'

Chris offered to help but the idea was waved away.

He was nervous, wasn't sure what answer he hoped to find. If Maria had come here to collect her number on the morning of the race, then it made even less sense that she'd ended up where she had. And if she hadn't come at all? He wasn't sure what that meant. Both answers would create more questions, but at least he could map her day more accurately once he knew for sure.

'Bingo.' Deborah waved a tatty red file in the air. 'The L to N surnames, all forty-seven of them. Let's see how many Morrisons were signed up to run.'

She pulled out a stack of printed pages then licked the end of her thumb, started flicking through them. 'Magnusson, Martins, Martinez, Michaels, Mitchell . . . here we go. Morrison.' Deborah pursed her lips, shook her head slowly. 'Not finding her. It's Maria, you said?'

'Aye,' said Chris. 'She must be there. She signed up months ago.'

More licking of thumbs, more flicking of pages. 'Still not seeing her.'

'Tell, you what – try the H surnames. Her full name is Maria Elena Morrison Hidalgo. She never goes by Hidalgo but sometimes in official documents they take that one since it's at the end. It's her maiden name.'

A minute or so of paper shuffling later, Deborah nodded. 'Got her,' she said. 'Under H, like you said. So that means she definitely registered for the race and she definitely came here on Sunday to collect her number.'

'How long would that take?'

'To collect her number? Five minutes, maximum, for a race like this.'

'So if she left our house at eight a.m. like my neighbour says, she'd have had loads of time to spare,' said Chris. 'How far is South Bridge from here?'

'Walking? Half an hour. Running, fifteen minutes.'

Chris nodded, brain whirring.

If Maria could reach town in fifteen minutes, she would've had more than ninety minutes time to find the place she was looking for, then get back in time for the race. And if she'd collected her number she'd obviously intended to run.

Maybe if he followed her footsteps he'd find out why she hadn't.

Chris stood up, held out a hand. 'You've been very helpful.'

'Not at all,' she said. 'But listen – I would like to double-check one last thing before you go. If you'll give me one minute more?'

She left the room than reappeared, slightly out of breath, with yet more folders. Chris stayed on his feet, felt his nerves slowly tighten as Deborah flicked between one page and the next, silently mouthing words. He was about to make his excuses when Deborah waved a page in the air and smiled.

'Number nine,' she said.

'Sorry?'

'That's the locker allocated to your wife before the race.' Deborah stood up, nodded towards the door. 'Shall we see if she left anything behind?'

Deborah led Chris back downstairs and found the janitor in an office too small for the three of them to stand in at once. He spun his office chair to face the door then pushed off with both feet, rolling slowly towards the doorway. His breath carried the scent of penny sweets; his skin the scars of acne.

Deborah explained, was listened to, then the janitor took a set of keys off his belt and opened a metal cupboard behind him. Inside were hundreds of keys, all tagged. They were hung neatly in rows under labelled hooks. The janitor clicked his tongue as he scanned them, eyes narrowed,

bony fingers fidgeting until he found the one he was looking for. He picked it off, held it up, nodded.

'That's the one,' he said, then explained that particular
set of lockers was close to the weights room. 'If you start
seeing beefcakes you've gone too far,' he said, then directed
them towards a set of double doors painted red.

The only sound in the corridor was the clank of metal
weights on metal supports and the groans and puffs of the
people who were trying to lift them. It was a place for men
with fat biceps and skinny legs. Maria could have outrun
the lot of them without breaking a sweat. If she'd bloody
run, that was.

'I think you better be the one who opens it,' said Deborah.

She was standing next to a row of lockers with narrow
white doors. A few had stickers on them, stuck on at jaunty
angles for maximum effect. Others had graffiti scratched
into the plastic coating. A few had home-made nameplates.
Keys dangled from some of the locks. Deborah handed him
the key from the janitor, tapped the door of the locker at
the far end.

'This one,' she said.

Chris stepped forward, feeling a rush of adrenalin when
he pushed the key into the lock and heard it click. He
glanced at Deborah, got a nod, then pulled open the door.
The main part of the locker was empty apart from a little ball of paper. He reached in and picked it up, started
to unfold it then quickly realised was stuck tight with old
chewing gum. He left it where he'd found it then stood
on tiptoes. And then he saw it. Right at the back, Maria's

purse. *Christ*. So it hadn't been stolen or lost. It was right here, exactly where Maria had left it.

He thought of Mikey, felt relief and guilt in equal measure. Yes, he had their money – but he didn't have her purse.

Chris forced those thoughts aside, pulled Maria's purse out of its hiding place then opened it to show Deborah the old passport photo of himself, tucked behind dirty plastic.

'It's definitely hers,' said Chris.

'Then I'm glad I could help with something,' she said.

When Deborah left, Chris sat on a bench outside the weights room and squeezed Maria's purse in his hand. It was so familiar to him, but he wasn't sure he'd ever actually held it in his own hands before. He knew the zip was tricky. He knew she kept her cards and receipts separately; knew that when he looked under the loyalty cards he'd find a spare tenner and a piece of paper on which she'd written her all of her PIN codes, disguised as names and phone numbers.

But there was another piece of paper there too, folded into a tight square.

His hands trembled as he opened it. He recognised Maria's handwriting but the numbers she'd written meant nothing to him. *0615*. It was probably another PIN number or a password but there were no other clues on the page.

Chris put it back where he'd found it then started unfolding receipts, just like Sandy had suggested. There was one from the petrol station, one from a pharmacy, one from a clothes shop where she'd gone for a refund. There was nothing there that suggested she'd been with anyone else; nothing that suggested she'd had anything other than an ordinary weekend. What had he hoped for? He wasn't sure, but he felt like an intruder raiding his own house.

There were no receipts from the day of the accident – but if she'd left her purse behind, it was yet another sign that she'd intended to return to the sports centre and run the race – but that something or someone had stopped her.

It made sense that she'd gone to find Ruth's tenant or his girlfriend – but if she'd found them and got permission to enter the flat, Billy would have known.

The only other certainty about Maria's morning was the fact she'd received that email from Javi Fernandez shortly after the accident.

Me and Ruth, he wrote. Then, *Sorry*.

But for what?

Chris left the sports centre and started walking the route Maria would have taken, wondering what words she'd have written in reply if she had not fallen; if she were not now fighting for life.

But she's not dead, Chris. Nobody is dead.

He repeated the words over and over as he walked. He steps were strong but a single word trailed behind, ready to trip him up like loose laces.

Yet.

Ruth's body started to break down more quickly than I'd imagined. I'd try not to look at her but my eyes were drawn towards the decay, would swoop down and pick greedily over every inch of her, searching for scraps of a life now over; anxiously awaiting the moment there would be no trace left at all.

It was strange to look at Ruth and know she would not look back at me, ever; to touch her lips and know I'd never hear her voice again. I cut off her hair, pulled it into one big ponytail and chopped through it with the scissors from the kitchen drawer. It weighed nothing, the very deadest part of Ruth.

When I left the flat I wondered if I'd carry the scent of her with me, no matter how many times I scrubbed myself in the shower or how many miles I put between me and the home that was hers for so long but where, finally, I'd stripped life from her. The moment I stepped outside I expected the worst, imagined a hand on my arm and voice telling me, We know. We all know.

But it never came. Edinburgh paid me no attention at all.

I was just a customer, a client, a tourist, a passenger, a runner, an unshaven man taking a stroll on a Sunday, a pedestrian paused at traffic lights, a kind but quiet boyfriend going to a harbour pub early one morning to collect a mobile phone left in the toilet by his drunken girlfriend.

It was strange, at first, to spend whole days without Ruth; to learn to live the ordinary parts of life alone. Still, she was useful for paying the bills.

I drained her savings then used her contacts to get work as a tour guide in early autumn, spent my life with people who knew nothing of my past and had no reason to ask. Ruth always said the truth would catch up with me in the end.

But now? She said nothing.

Finally, and forever this time, Ruth said nothing.

CHAPTER 35

Chris reached South Bridge in half an hour, as Deborah predicted – and he was sure Maria would have run it in half that time. But where had she gone next? That's what he hoped to find out – but he'd have to be patient. South Bridge was lined with shops and cafes and bars but many were still closed so, for the moment, Chris kept walking, towards the place that Maria had been found.

He paused when he reached the crossroads with the Royal Mile, knew that beyond the majestic townhouses to his right stood Edinburgh's mountain, Arthur's Seat. On a morning like this its craggy peak would already be dotted with hikers and dogs and, no doubt, tourists wearing the wrong shoes. It was a day of blue skies and shimmering dew on the boggy ground, a day when the mighty crags in front of it would glow like red embers. In the Old Town the streets smelled like baking biscuits – in reality the aroma of roasting malt from the whisky distillery. But it was as distinctive to Edinburgh city centre as the castle on the rock. These were the things that usually made him feel at home.

Today they did not.

He kept going, calling Farida as he walked.

'Chris? I got your message about the purse, and about the sighting of Ruth in Glasgow. Was about to call. We'll need dates, and the name of the clinic where she was seen. One thing that wasn't clear – who was it that saw Ruth?'

'Her name's Carmen. She's Mikey's business partner.'

Farida started to speak, then paused. Chris could almost hear the cogs turning. 'And she hadn't mentioned this sighting to Mikey?'

'Apparently not.'

'I assume you haven't heard from him yet? I've been trying to get him on the phone but he's a hard man to get hold of, isn't he? It shouldn't take long, but I'd really like more detail about that text he received from Ruth.'

'He's not answering my calls either.' Chris wasn't sure what to say; didn't know how many of his fears he could bear to say out loud. 'He's resting, I think.'

'I know you're worried,' said Farida. 'But please get him to call me when you see him. In the meantime I wanted to let you know the airline has finally responded. Ruth completed an online check-in for a flight to Barcelona at six-thirty that Monday morning – but she definitely didn't board.'

'Could she have caught a later flight?'

'She didn't,' said Farida. 'We've also obtained data from the e-borders programme confirming that Ruth did not leave the country that day. We're still waiting for details of other dates when she may or may not have left the country – and where she went. Initially we'll focus on Spain, since we know her mobile was used there in the autumn. I'll keep you informed. And . . . I'm sorry, Chris.'

'Aye,' he said. 'Me too.'

But there it was, the lie that started all of this. Ruth hadn't taken the flight.

Chris thought of all the emails and photos she'd sent since then. Had she really been lying all that time? He wondered where she'd gone instead and where she was now. And then his mind took him to a place he hoped she'd never been and would never go. Brewster Bay.

'Any word on . . . the body?'

'We'll contact you if and when required, Chris.'

He knew what that meant.

It meant a body in a fridge, the bashed bits hidden with make-up. It meant a sheet pulled back like a wedding veil and a kiss, maybe, if the face was the one he didn't want to see. Then they'd slide the body back into a freezer alone until it was ready to be burned. *I'm sorry for your loss*, they'd say.

Enough, Chris. Enough.

He sharpened his elbows and pushed through an American tour group who were gawking at a street performer, blocking half the Royal Mile. He turned right to escape them, felt a sting in his chest as he stepped onto Cockburn Street.

He stopped and lit a cigarette, staring downhill. It was one of his favourite streets in Edinburgh, was elegant without being pretentious. He loved the cobbled road, the colourfully painted shop fronts, the absolute lack of symmetry when he cast his eyes over the rooftops. There were slated spires and sandstone crows-steps and, as ever in Edinburgh, row after row of chimney pots. The street curved like a gently bent branch as it climbed towards the Royal Mile.

He'd walked up and down it a thousand times when he was a student and a news reporter, but he'd never known the detailed history of it until he went on one of Ruth's walking tours, back in the days when she saw the tour guiding work as something to fill in the space between graduating and finding a real job. She'd gathered the group in front of a church on the Royal Mile, told them Cockburn Street was created when the steeple collapsed and smashed through the tenement in front. Probably a tour guide tale, but she told it well.

It had been strange for him and Maria to see Ruth in that role: as someone people listened to and believed; a person who was invited to the pub afterwards so people could buy her a drink and slip her a tip when she stood up and said she really had to be going. Later Maria told him she'd never felt so proud of Ruth, that she'd wished the tour group had known she was the guide's mum. But Ruth hadn't said anything, so Maria hadn't either.

Chris had told her not to worry about it, said he was sure Ruth knew she was proud of her. It was obvious, right? He hoped so. All those years of silent assuming and now maybe her chance to say it out loud was over.

He stubbed out his cigarette and started walking downhill to the place Cockburn Street connected with Fleshmarket Close. Ruth had told the group it was the butchers' area of the old market. But the history meant nothing to Chris any more. Now, this was The Place Where Maria Was Found.

The close was split in two by Cockburn Street. On his left-hand side, heading uphill, was a short, sloping section that led directly to the Royal Mile. Looking right, the lower end of the close had several sets of stone steps that sliced between tenement buildings. Maria had been found about halfway down.

He walked down the first set of steps and glanced into a takeaway, saw greasy meat on a spit, bright red chicken in a glass case, a chef with his back turned. The air reeked of oil, chips in gas form. This was a place of torn crisp packets swirling on the ground and catching in drains, a place of fat black flies padding through splatters of vomit, of metal shutters rattling on closed shops.

But this was the place.

'Gonnae let me past, pal? Ta.'

Chris looked up, met the eyes of a boy with a beard and a hooded top and bright red trainers. Chris watched him go, wondered how many feet had passed over this same stretch of steps since they'd brought in the power-hose to clean off Maria's blood. That was the part most people didn't know about or think about, but he'd seen it. He'd been there, watched the remains of people splatter on the wellies of the clean-up crew.

He knelt down and touched the steps, was glad it had been raining.

It was impossible to believe she'd just fallen.

Perhaps Maria had just got distracted. But maybe – just maybe – there had been someone else there behind her, in pursuit. Before she'd hung up, Farida said she'd call him once they'd further analysed the CCTV, but Chris knew from experience that the task could take days. He'd done a feature about it for the paper once, spent a shift in the police CCTV room with a team of officers trained to see things most people couldn't. There were dozens of screens, a wall of moving images Chris struggled to watch without feeling nauseous.

But things could be missed, and often were.

The CCTV had shown Maria on South Bridge and that was where Ruth's tenant's girlfriend worked. Chris didn't have a specific address but it was such a busy street that *someone* must have seen Maria on Sunday morning before she turned around and started running; before she diverted down the close; before she ended up on the ground, body leaking life.

Someone.

But who?

Chris knew the most effective way to get an answer. He started walking, mind focused, hands clenched into fists. It was time to start knocking on doors.

CHAPTER 36

The rain had just started when Chris got back to the cross-roads of the Royal Mile and the bridges, his view dotted by a scattering of hoods and umbrellas. He'd already been into all the shops and pubs at the top end of Cockburn Street – and the ones on Fleshmarket Close. Now it was time to scour South Bridge.

This was the where Maria had come looking for Ruth's tenant, or his girlfriend. Chris had no address so he'd walk the length of it, ask the same questions in every single business he passed. He wanted to speak to the person or people who'd found Maria – and anyone else who'd seen or spoken to her before she fell. Where was she and when, and who was she with?

He needed to know.

But from now on he'd introduce himself as a news reporter, rather than Maria's husband. He could tell he'd been judged by the people he'd spoken to so far and couldn't be bothered justifying his reasons for being there.

Why was he out on the street instead of in hospital, sitting by his wife's bedside? Because he was sick of lies. Because the only way he'd find truth was hunting it down by himself.

And so he began.

The squat woman working the till in a tat-filled tourist shop struggled to hear him over the bagpipe music blasting out of amplifiers by the door. She cupped her ear and glanced at the picture of Maria, said she barely remembered her own face these days let alone anybody else's. And anyway, she didn't like news reporters very much so she'd rather not speak, thank you very much.

He asked people waiting in a bakery queue but none of them had seen anything or cared – and the hair-netted staff gave the same response.

The cut-price pharmacy was empty apart from an American tourist asking for directions and the best place to buy whisky. The pharmacist put on her glasses when she looked at Chris's photo, then started nodding. She said Maria hadn't been into her shop, bless her, but a few of the customers had been talking about what happened and from what they'd heard the police were starting to think it was suspicious because the woman's daughter had gone missing the same week. The pharmacist said it would be someone in their family that's behind it and the tourist said it always was, wasn't it? Then they both nodded with a certainty that made Chris want to be sick and to leave immediately.

He turned back when he reached the festival theatre that marked the end of South Bridge, then crossed the road and started making his way back towards the Royal Mile, door by door. He smiled faintly when he went into a florist and saw white calla lilies on display. It was Maria's favourite flower. She'd insisted on having them as part of her wedding bouquet despite her father's insistence that they were for funerals. Chris went in, questioned the florist, got another no, felt suddenly nauseous. He kept walking. The next business was an estate agent's, the one after that a pub with a mobility scooter parked outside the main door, the next one a mini-supermarket loaded with dusty bottles of crap wine. He went in shop after shop after shop, and was almost at the Royal Mile when a dog ran across his path, closely followed by a woman pushing a double buggy, closely followed by a little boy in school uniform with a backpack almost as big as he was.

The little boy stopped when he saw Chris, stared, until his mother roared at him, said Santa wouldn't come if he made them miss the bloody bus. He offered a smile to Chris before he left, got one in return. Maria said the smiles of children were like hammers to the knee: it was almost impossible not to smile back. And so there Chris was, smiling at the turned back of a stranger's child, when suddenly he saw traces of his own, strung up and lifeless in Edinburgh city centre.

Summer came and went. Autumn arrived.

I had a new job and new friends, lived a life that looked normal from the outside. In reality I was always waiting for someone to notice Ruth's absence and start asking uncomfortable questions. Still, nobody did. It saddened but did not surprise me to realise Ruth was so forgettable. It stunned but did not sadden me to realise she was forgettable even to me. But here's the truth of it: there were many days when I forgot about her completely. Like the day I met Anna.

I was drinking whisky alone in a classic Edinburgh pub with tiles on the floor and a curved wooden bar with smudged brass trims and a doorway filled with smokers. There was always noise and the threat of a fight and a queue to be served. I'd just paid the barman and stepped back when a girl squeezed into the space I'd left at the bar. She was holding an empty glass and her hand was tattooed with tiny swallows and she was far too beautiful to be talking to me.

I felt awkward and ugly and drank too fast, hoped something would take her attention away from me. Nothing did. She ordered a vermouth with ice that had melted by the time one of her colleagues from the coffee shop where she worked reached over my shoulder and squeezed her arm, said he was sorry to interrupt but they were leaving.

She stayed, and we stayed, long after the owner slammed shut the till, said it was time to drink up, then pointed to the laminated poster stuck beside the door, requesting we go home to bed quietly.

We exchanged looks then numbers but when she stepped in for a kiss I flinched, tugging myself out of the embrace before my body dared fill the space between us. She let me go, then took a half-step towards me, moving so close I could feel her breath on my face. I noticed a small scar on one side of her nose where I imagined a piercing had been. It gave me a glimpse of an unknown past, of a girl I knew nothing about, of moments in her life that I would never be a part of. I wondered what history she saw in my face.

I said nothing for far too long, and eventually she started to laugh.

'We'll do this again,' she said, then kissed me on both cheeks and left.

When I got back to the flat that night I ran my fingertips over my face, hoping to trace the soft wetness of her kiss, but found only stubble, crisp and dry as burnt grass. I got undressed and pulled back the cover, saw the little that remained of Ruth. Both Ruth and the memory of her were stilled, silenced.

And, best of all, they hadn't stirred all night.

CHAPTER 37

Chris pushed open the door of the charity shop, relieved to see there were no other customers. An assistant holding a variety of mismatched yellow jumpers looked up and smiled, telling Chris to ask if he needed help.

'My daughter . . .' he said, then turned to the window display.

He reached out and touched a green dress hanging on a mannequin. A twist of tatty silver Christmas tinsel was draped around it like a cheap feather boa. The dress had been a little too wide for Ruth, but Maria had discreetly pinned it in place before Mikey's wedding and she'd looked gorgeous.

'Beautiful, isn't it? Spanish brand, apparently.' The woman dumped the new stock behind the till, approached him. 'It's for your daughter, you said?'

'No,' he said. 'It belongs to her.'

It was then that he noticed a distinctive purple running top, tagged and hanging from a rail of other people's sports clothes. There was no doubt this was Ruth's. She'd had it for years. He picked it off the rail and held it to his face, wishing it still held the scent of her. Ruth, locked into the fibres.

'This is my daughter's as well. Who brought them in?'

The woman looked a little disgusted, but smiled. 'I don't really deal with donations,' she said. 'I'll get the manager if you like? If something's been handed in by mistake maybe she can help. I just work the till.'

She took a note of Chris's name, asked him to watch the shop then disappeared through the back. Chris studied the accessories section while he waited, saw a scarf they'd bought for Ruth when they visited Lisbon last year.

Behind him a door squeaked, a throat was cleared.

When he turned he was greeted with a gentle smile from a woman who looked as if she belonged in a folk band. 'Mr Morrison? I'm Tina. Shop manager and general dogsbody.' She glanced at the running top in Chris's hands. 'Maureen said you've seen some of your daughter's clothes on display?

Chris nodded. 'I need to know who handed this stuff in,' he said. 'They belong to my daughter and she's . . . missing. Has been for months.'

Tina winced, fiddled with her name tag. 'Missing, as in . . . ?'

'Disappeared. Officially. I can get the investigating police officer to give you a call if you that'll help?' Chris pulled out his wallet, showed her Farida's business card. Tina peered at it, eyes narrowed. 'I know you must get a lot of donations, but if you've got any recollection at all of the person who handed in these clothes it would be a huge help to me.'

'I'll do what I can,' she said. 'And I do remember him, actually. He—'

'It was a man?' *Christ*. The hope of the morning was snuffed out. 'You know his name? What he looks like? And do you remember when he was here, even a rough idea? Anything you remember, please tell me.'

Tina's cheeks flushed. 'Shall we talk through the back?'

Chris followed her through to the back office and down a steep set of stairs to the windowless basement room where all donations were sorted.

'Everything that comes in is numbered,' she explained. 'We attach a label detailing the week number and bag number so we can keep track of how many donations we're receiving. We never know what we're going to get so we always keep back a few star items to put out during quiet weeks – things that will catch the eye, ones that will be suitable for the window display.'

'Like Ruth's green dress.'

Tina nodded, led him to a rail at the back of the basement. 'This is the star items rail – and if I'm not mistaken there are a few more Spanish ones in here, left by the same man.'

She pushed a wedding dress and a yellow leather jacket to one side and pulled out a pair of skinny jeans with a red and yellow stripe down both outside seams. They were definitely Ruth's, bought during one of the Boxing Day sales purely because the stripe looked vaguely like the Catalonian flag. She'd worn them to the New Year party they always held at the house and got into a messy political argument with one of Maria's friends when he said it looked more like the Spanish flag. She'd vowed never to wear them again and, knowing Ruth, she probably hadn't.

'Are they familiar?' Tina asked gently.

Chris nodded.

'In that case . . .' she shifted a crate of shoes then hunched down and opened a safe built into the wall '. . . there's one more thing I need to show you.'

When she stood up again her fist was clenched, and when she opened it Chris knew for sure something had happened to Ruth. She wasn't one for jewellery but she'd always worn it, didn't even take it off in the sea. Chris wasn't one for jewellery either, but even in the gloom of that basement he recognised the little silver butterfly that hung from the silver chain; remembered the way Maria had smiled when she'd first picked it up from a street market at the Edinburgh Festival. *Made with heart by hand*, the vendor had told them, then handed them a business card that bore the same slogan. Maria was sold, explained they were buying it for their daughter before she left home for university. They'd declined when he offered to engrave it for them but an idea had come to Maria during lunch and she'd gone back, said yes. Chris reached for the butterfly, gently turned it in his fingers until he could make out the word Maria had chosen; the word she wanted Ruth to carry with her when they were apart.

That word, again.

Contigo.

'We found this in the pocket of a coat he handed in,' said Tina. 'When we find valuables in unexpected places we hold on to them for a few months, in case it was a mistake. Especially something with an engraving. Take it, please.'

Chris gently passed the fleshy part of his thumb over the word, felt its delicate contours against his skin. *Contigo.* There was absolutely no doubt this was the necklace Maria had bought for Ruth. It was unique, impossible to copy.

'When was all of this handed in?'

Tina pulled a paper label towards her, narrowed her eyes as she read it. 'Week 36, so that would be the end of September, start of October. I only remember him because he brought so much stuff. Eight or nine bags. I expected it to be rubbish, dumped straight in the rags bin. Usually when people are so generous it means an old relative has died and we get the spoils from the full house clearance. Whole wardrobes stuffed into bin bags without a second glance or the vague consideration that perhaps we don't want their grandpa's stinky old cardigan with all the dirty hankies stuffed in its pockets. That's what I expected when I saw that man come in here. He arrived in a taxi, brought a whole carload in. But it was all stuff we could sell. Good condition, well-known brands, recently washed and—'

'Can I stop you there? What did he look like?'

Tina cocked her head to one side as if to shake free a memory. 'Just very ordinary, really. Quite nice-looking – though he looked like he needed to shave. He was wearing baggy jeans and a hoody, nothing that would stop traffic.'

Chris pulled out his phone and showed her the photo from Man With A Heart's blog.

'This him?'

Tina squinted. 'Maybe? But I couldn't be sure.'

Chris sighed, stuffed the phone in his pocket. 'Did he ever come back?'

'The next day,' said Tina. 'He brought the same amount of stuff again so I went out to thank him personally for his generosity. And that was when he told me about his girlfriend.'

'What did he say? Christ, it must be Ruth.'

Tina looked away, studying the cuff of her blouse. 'He said all the clothes belonged to her,' she said. 'I made some terrible joke about the size of her wardrobe then realised right away that I'd put my foot in it. He looked very . . . delicate, all of a sudden. I should have kept my big mouth shut.'

'Did he tell you her name?'

Tina shook her head.

'You're sure? Could you ask the other staff, see if they remember?'

'He definitely didn't mention a name. My goodness, the poor man could barely speak.' She sighed, looked up. 'He didn't tell me details, not really, but from what he said I certainly got the impression that . . . his girlfriend had died.'

Chris's heart felt as though it was being squeezed in a vice.

He was still holding her running top. He thought about the many mornings she'd come back from a run and stood outside the back door with her hand on her chest, counting her heart-rate. He and Maria would watch her from the kitchen window, pop the kettle on, wait for her to come back inside with red cheeks and words split by her breath and statistics on her pulse. For a moment he thought he could feel the echo of it in the cloth, but then he realised it was his own heart, racing, breaking. Where Ruth had been, there was silence.

Chris left the shop, stunned.

He walked a few steps then crouched down on the cobbles, head in his hands. Nausea surged. Tears came. He could do nothing to stop either of them. Passers-by chattered, buses rattled along the bridges, bagpipe music blared from the tourist shops, tour guides dressed as grave-diggers led groups through the closes, men smoked outside pubs, a street performer egged on a boring crowd.

He should call Farida, but what would he say? She'd ask for facts, and all he had was a limp green dress and the hunch of a kind charity shop worker.

He needed more. He needed to find that man.

Chris stayed where he was on the pavement, barely noticed when the sky rumbled and the morning's misty rain suddenly became a heavy downpour. He was already soaked when somebody touched his arm and when he looked up Tina was beside him, jacket pulled up over her head instead of an umbrella. 'Maureen just told me something,' she said. She was out of breath, but pointed further down the street. 'I asked her about the man who handed in the bags and she remembered him too, says he's said hello to her a few times when she went for lunch. She says she's always seen him sitting on his own, smoking, on a bench outside that coffee shop over there.'

'Has she seen him today?'

Tina shook her head. 'Not for a few days, she says.'

Chris thanked her, then stood up and strode towards the coffee shop, heart thundering so hard his whole body pulsed. The time for answers was here.

CHAPTER 38

The coffee shop owner was called Alberto and had a face made for radio and a lisp so strong it sounded fake. Chris struggled to understand half of what he said but one word came through loud and clear. No, no, and no.

Chris had zoomed in on the group photo from Man With A Heart's blog, pointed at the blur of pixels he and Sandy suspected was the face of Javi Fernandez. 'I know this man's been here before,' said Chris. 'My friend says he sits outside, on the bench. Smoking. Every day. You must have seen him.'

No, no, no.

Alberto explained he owned three coffee shops across Edinburgh and this was the one he worked in least of all. Why? It was so popular that business took care of itself. His baristas served almost a thousand customers every day and would be equally unlikely to recognise suspicious characters lingering outside by the smokers' bench. But of course, Chris was welcome to come in later in the day, see if the baristas on the afternoon shift could help him. He smiled after he said that, then eyed the oversized wall clock with the subtlety of a slap.

Rage burned in Chris, fuelled by grief.

He headed outside to the wooden bench in front of the coffee shop's bay window. He'd wait, watch, grab Javi Fernandez if and when he arrived. He pulled out his phone, but couldn't face making any calls. He didn't want to say out loud what he'd found at the charity shop. Bits of his daughter, left behind.

He'd hoped Alberto would say yes, of course he recognised the man in his photo and yes, of course he knew his name. Javi Fernandez. And yes, he was definitely here with a woman in orange trainers on Sunday morning. He'd hoped Javi Fernandez would be in there, relaxing with Ruth, drinking coffee.

But, no.

Chris sat down on the bench and flipped through the few notes he'd cobbled together during the last few hours. They were about espresso in length.

He sighed and leaned back against the coffee shop window. He took out his cigarettes, was looking for his lighter when he caught the scent of exotic spices and deep-fat fryers. Across the road a chubby man with chef's overalls and a pleated grey beard was lifting the metal shutters of his restaurant. Moments later a younger man wearing a football top appeared with a ragged towel which he used to wipe dry the sodden window frame. Chris watched him while he smoked, was halfway down his cigarette when the younger man stretched up and very carefully dried something above the main door.

Chris stood up, narrowed his eyes, stepped closer.

The man was drying two tiny security cameras.

One was slowly turning in the direction of the Royal Mile. The other was aimed at the far end of the street, then moved until it was pointing to the place where Chris was standing. Right in front of that coffee shop.

Again, hope flickered.

He wasn't the only one watching this street.

And so I lived two lives at once.

In one life was Anna and the lies I'd told to keep her close. In the other was Ruth and the lies I'd told her family to keep them as far away as possible. The problem with lies is that they breed and grow and get into a tangle that trips you when you least expect it. Lies maintained for months unravel in days.

The start of the end was last Friday evening when Ruth's mother turned up at her flat without a key or an invitation or any concept of the fact that she'd lost her daughter. I stared at her through the spyhole, pitied both of us.

Before she left she bent down and stuffed a note under the door. It hit my shoe and I wondered if that was the closest we'd ever come to touching. The note explained that an intercom engineer needed access to the flat. It also asked whoever was living there to get in touch if they'd seen or heard from Ruth, said it was Very Important. She'd underlined that part, and the word Please.

And so it was that I realised my freedom was finite.

Ruth had long since rotted but, just like that, her life was dragged back into mine.

CHAPTER 39

Jamal's mouth fell naturally into a smile and his hands were vaguely sticky and he was very happy to help, especially after Chris explained his situation – and promised he'd write a five-star restaurant review in the weekend supplement of the paper.

He took Chris through the back, past sacks of rice and sealed plastic tubs and crates of imported beer and a stainless-steel kitchen that smelled of freshly cut ginger. The tiny airless room Jamal called his office was about the size of a walk-in fridge and, given the temperature, might as well have been one.

Jamal offered the only seat to Chris – and minutes later put a steaming bowl of lentil curry in front of him. On the house, he said. Chris thanked him and quickly spooned it down while his host attached cables to the two laptops on his desk. Jamal explained that the restaurant windows had been smashed three times in the past year so he'd invested in two digital cameras which recorded all day, every day then automatically sent a file to his laptop at midnight, marked with the correct date.

So finding the right day and time was easy. The laborious part was looking at constellations of shuddering, grainy black and white pixels and trying to work out exactly who was on the screen or what was happening.

The two cameras moved automatically, but never lost sight of his restaurant or the coffee shop across the street. Why? The police had concluded that bricks thrown in the last attack had been launched from there. Now anyone who came anywhere near the restaurant or coffee shop was caught on camera.

So if Maria had been there on Sunday, she'd have been recorded.

Jamal opened the right file then left Chris to it, said he'd be in the kitchen if he needed anything. The smell of the little room had switched from oil to onions to garlic to spices that were stinging Chris's eyes by the time he saw her.

Chris recognised Maria the moment she appeared on screen, a life locked inside that running jacket, edging towards the enormous bay window of the coffee shop. He paused the video, noted the time. It was only 8.45 a.m., more than an hour before her accident. He took a deep breath, let the video play.

Maria paused a short distance from the coffee shop then stepped back and looked up as if she was reading the sign. Chris watched her, but kept an eye on the people going in and out. There was a girl who pulled up on a motorbike, tucked her helmet under her arm before she went in;

a boy carrying a guitar case on his back; a couple wearing sunglasses who held open the door for an old man with a pram. Then came a man with his hood up, shoulders hunched, eyes to the ground. He glanced over his shoulder before he went in.

Chris paused it again and leaned towards the screen. Was this Javi Fernandez? His neighbour Jim had talked about a hooded figure at their house, and Wee Mary had given a similar description for the man who'd collected Ruth's lost phone. Tina at the charity shop had said the man was wearing a hooded top too. Was this him?

Chris pulled out his phone and opened the Man With A Heart blog, scrolling down to the group photo Sandy had shown him earlier. They'd guessed Javi was the one on the left of the shot, wearing a wide hat for shade. Chris looked from his phone to the CCTV screen and back but it was impossible to tell if it was the same person. The image quality was too poor on both the blog and the CCTV. They should have asked Man With A Heart to send a better photo.

He sighed and pressed play again, waited for Maria to make her next move. After a few seconds she stepped closer to the window, right in front of the bench where Chris had just been sitting. She stopped there and gazed inside.

It was precisely 8.47 a.m.

Chris kept watching and waiting, but all Maria did was stand and stare intently at someone or something on the other side of the glass. He paused the video again, studied a world on hold. There was nothing extraordinary in this scene. Buses, cars, bikes, doors, windows, pigeons, seagulls, Maria.

Everything stilled, everything silent.

When he pressed play again Maria did something he hadn't expected.

She slumped onto the bench outside the coffee shop window, then dropped her into head to her hands. Chris kept watching, but Maria didn't move.

It was as if she'd remained on pause while everyone and everything around her sprang back into life. Let the doors swing open and a customer drop his change in the street and a smoker light a fag and a student vomit on the pavement, but let Maria stay right there, still as death on that bench.

People and cars and delivery vans and pigeons and cyclists and tour groups passed Maria and paid her no attention at all. Chris pressed fast-forward, watched the minutes fly past. Fifteen minutes, half an hour, forty-five minutes – and still Maria didn't move. If she'd wanted to compete in the race she'd need to have left town by 9.45 a.m. at the very latest.

But still, she sat.

What had happened?

Chris tried to keep his mind from speculating but his brain threw out all sorts of ideas. Had she started feeling unwell? Had she had some kind of turn and become confused? Or she had seen something or someone through the window of that coffee shop that had shocked or frightened her enough to shut down her system? He stared at the screen, each passing second a torture.

The clock had just struck ten a.m. when Maria got up, slowly. Then she turned around to face the coffee shop and once again, stared in the window.

She stood there for more than two minutes, looking through the glass at something or someone Chris couldn't see, no matter how many times he replayed it. The quality of the film was far too poor to see through the window but every time he let it run he squinted at the screen anyway, desperate to see what she saw. He watched Maria too, trying to read her body language. He wondered if it was fear that had frozen her to the spot. What else could it be?

He cursed when a white van appeared from the right of the screen and pulled up directly in front of the coffee shop. A bald man with a clipboard got out of the passenger side, opened the doors at the back of the van and, just like that, obscured Chris's view of the window and the door and his wife. All he could see of Maria was the heels of her orange running shoes.

Chris kept the recording running. Ten seconds passed, then twenty, then thirty. The van did not shift and neither did Maria's feet. When the clock reached one minute Chris reached for the mouse, moved the cursor to the fast-forward icon. He was about to press click when the man with the clipboard reappeared from the left of the screen. He walked the length of the van then pushed shut the back doors. The van reversed slightly before it pulled away and for a moment Maria disappeared completely from the screen. Chris locked his eyes on the back of the van, hoping Maria would still be there when it drove off. She was, for a second.

And then? This was the hardest part for Chris to watch. Then Maria ran.

CHAPTER 40

The head barista shook his head and stuck to his story. He'd seen nothing and knew nothing and could not help. And yes, he was totally sure.

Chris persisted. He'd used his phone to record the footage from Jamal's CCTV so he could email a copy to Sandy and Farida. But right now he hoped images from the film would trigger a memory. He paused the video and zoomed in on the hooded figure. 'This is him,' he said. 'Javi Fernandez. As I said before, I need to track him down, and I've been told his girlfriend works here.'

Alberto sighed loudly. 'And as *I* said before – I wasn't here on Sunday. You'll need to speak to the girls who were working the weekend. Their names are Anna and Alyson, okay? Tell them I said it was fine to speak to you and I'm sure they'll be happy to help.' His eyes flitted over Chris's shoulder. 'In fact, here comes Anna right now. Anna? Glad to see you're on time today. Early, in fact. But have a word with this gentleman before you start your shift, will you?'

Chris turned and got a smile from a girl with a studded leather jacket and a motorbike helmet held in her tattooed hand. 'Give me a minute to dump this,' she said, then disappeared into a room behind the counter.

When she came back a minute or so later, Chris showed her the film.

'This man, here, with the hood. Have you seen him before?'

'Never.'

Chris sensed a lie. She'd answered far too quickly. 'Will you look again?'

Same answer.

Chris let the recording play and when it finished he switched to his photo album, opened an image of the family. The girl flinched, as though she'd been pricked by a pin. She leaned closer to his screen. 'Can you make it bigger?'

Chris zoomed in on Maria's face, watching the girl's eyes. 'You recognise her, don't you?'

Anna shook her head. 'Thought I did, but no. Sorry.'

'She had an accident, Anna.' He stared at her until she looked back. 'And I know she was here just before it happened, looking in that big window.'

Anna looked again at the image on the phone, then back to Chris. For a moment he thought she was going to speak but then a customer bashed her and she turned when they apologised and when she looked at Chris again the moment was lost. 'I should get to work,' she said. 'Sorry I can't help.'

She tried to leave but Chris grabbed her arm, forced her to turn.

'My wife is in a coma, Anna. And my daughter, Ruth, is . . . missing. You understand that? And this man . . .'

Chris gritted his teeth. 'This Javi Fernandez is responsible for all of it. So, please, if you know anything, tell me.'

'Get *off* me!' Anna protested, pulling her arm from his grip and rubbing it.

'You. Out. Now.' Alberto leapt from behind the counter, forced Chris out of the door and on to the street. 'Come back and I'll call the police. Get it?'

Chris flushed, heart thundering. 'I didn't mean to hurt her.'

'They all say that,' said Alberto, then stormed back inside.

Chris felt dazed. He knelt down, tried to calm his breathing, willed all of this to pass. When he eventually got to his feet he realised he was standing in the same spot Maria had stood. For a moment he stared in the same window, wondered again what or who had kept her there; and what had made her run.

And when he turned he walked away in the same direction she'd fled.

He clicked his pen on and off in his pocket as he walked the route Maria had run, trying to calm himself and trigger logical thought.

He knew for sure now that Maria had registered for the 10km on Sunday morning but that she'd been staring in the coffee shop window when she should have been lining up for the race. But he didn't know who or what she'd been looking at. He knew she'd left there running and ended up in Fleshmarket Close, but didn't know what she'd been running to, or from. He knew Javi Fernandez had emailed her to say sorry shortly after the accident and that the email was titled *Me and Ruth*. But he didn't know what he was sorry for and whether or not there had been any contact between them previous to that.

He knew he loved Maria but that, at some point, she'd lied.

He kept walking when he reached the crossroads connecting the bridges and the Royal Mile, head too full to notice he was going the wrong way. He squeezed past jostling queues at bus stops, stepped over squashed chips and the damp cardboard sign of a homeless girl. Traffic edged along the bridges towards Princes Street, tail lights turning puddles red. On one side the early winter sunset sucked all colour from the lumpy summit of Arthur's Seat and, on the other, floodlights illuminated the castle and the rock that held it. Christmas decorations strung across the street started flashing green and red, but Chris barely noticed. He was lost in thought, only realised he'd missed his turning when a stranger asked him for directions to the university. He looked around then cursed himself and turned, back towards the place Maria was found.

He was almost back at Fleshmarket Close when he got a whiff of bacon rolls from a greasy spoon he'd gone into earlier. The waitress, Janine, had been working on Sunday morning but, like most people, hadn't seen or heard a thing until the ambulance arrived. He'd left his phone number with her anyway, asked to her call if she heard anything at all. She was clearing tables now but she glanced up when Chris passed the door, eyes wide. She waved him inside.

'I was hoping you'd pop in again,' she said. 'I tried to phone you earlier but it wouldn't connect – I must have taken down the wrong number.'

'Did you remember something?'

'No, but James did, the owner. He phoned me not long after you'd left and I mentioned a news reporter had just been in, said you were looking for information on that poor woman they found in the close. I told him what you'd told me – the time she'd have been here, what she looked like, and the fact she'd been wearing orange trainers. That was when James said it must be the woman he'd spoken to before opening time on Sunday. We don't open until ten but James had the metal shutter up early, said a woman in orange trainers had popped her head in the door around eight forty-five, said she was looking for a lassie called Anna and asked if *this* was the coffee shop where she worked. James said no, told her it was just me and him working here.

'According to James she looked a bit confused, then pulled out a note a friend had given to her. She'd been told to look for Anna in a wee café near the crossroads with South Bridge, she said. Something to do with a flat in Portobello? Anyway, James told her the only other coffee shop nearby was that hipster one opposite the curry house. Told her she was in luck because it opened early on a Sunday. Then he pointed her in the right direction and off she went.'

'Is James here?'

'Not today, I'm afraid. His wee boy was up all night spewing, apparently, so he's taken him to the doctor. Can't come in until he's better.'

'Could I get his number?'

'I sure he wouldn't mind. He's usually got his phone on silent, mind you.'

'Thanks for the warning.'

Chris got a phone number for James and gave his own to Janine. Then he thanked her and left.

And so it was confirmed.

Maria had been looking for Anna, the girl he'd spoken to in the coffee shop opposite Jamal's restaurant. The note Maria had must have been from Madeline, the Portobello neighbour who'd taken the same bus as Ruth's tenant and his girlfriend. That meant Anna's boyfriend was renting Ruth's flat.

But was her boyfriend the same person who'd dumped Ruth's clothes at the charity shop? The same person who often sat and smoked on the bench outside the coffee shop? Was Anna's boyfriend Javi Fernandez?

Chris thought of Ruth's money in his bank account, and the email he'd sent to Maria moments after her accident. Its title, *Me and Ruth,* then an apology. Was Javi sorry because he'd been cheating on Ruth with Anna? But why tell Maria? And why would nobody have told him anything about it?

Even if he had the answers to those questions, it didn't explain why Maria had fled the coffee shop instead of going inside to tell Anna about the intercom problem at Ruth's flat. Somebody needed to speak to her, force out the truth.

Farida McPherson was the right woman for that job.

He pulled out his phone to call her but it started ringing before he dialled. *Rachel.* He answered quickly, hoping for news on Mikey. Instead he got five words, squeezed out between sobs. There was no room for questions, just assurance that he'd do what was asked of him.

You need to come, now.

When Ruth's mum left I opened a bottle of wine and rolled some tobacco and filled my body with both in a vain attempt to smother one simple, solid fact.

It was not yet over but it was ending.

Ruth's mum had found me and soon enough she'd be back. She'd knock longer and louder and if I still didn't answer then she'd find keys or someone strong enough to break the lock or maybe the police would come with dogs and a metal ram that would splinter the wood, and any peace left in her.

She'd see what lay behind the door, in a flat that still stank of Ruth.

But if there were police there would be reporters writing stories I'd hate to read and printing photos that would make Ruth look much happier than she ever really was, and when they finally tracked me down there would be endless quotes from people claiming they knew me when I was little. They'd sneer and brand me a freak, say they always knew I'd end up doing Something Like This.

I would not allow it.

I went to the bedroom and opened Ruth's old wardrobe, tried not to breathe in the scent of her. Once I'd got rid of her I'd got rid of her clothes and shoes and jewellery too, but I'd stashed other pieces of her life in the bottom drawer – photos, letters, keys, her old mobile phone. It hadn't been

switched on for weeks. I plugged it in, lit a fag, was half-
way down my second by the time the phone lit up and
started beeping. There were a few old messages but noth-
ing that merited my time or attention. I stuffed her phone
in my pocket and left the flat without a plan or any idea of
how the day would end.

But I knew one thing for sure.

The time had come to tell my side of the story.

CHAPTER 41

Chris could smell the sea the second he opened the car door.

He sucked it in; filled his nose and lungs with the scent of salt and the sharpness of a bitter east-coast breeze. He looked towards the golden-grey beach that hugged the village where Rachel and Mikey had set up their home, watched waves roll into the harbour wall then swirl and remake themselves.

Rachel was waiting for him in the street outside the house. The door was closed, her lips pursed. She gently shook her head as he approached and Chris wondered if it was a rehearsal for what came next: a silent apology in advance.

'Cold this afternoon,' she said.

'Forget the small talk, Rachel. Is Mikey here? I've not heard a thing from him since yesterday and he won't answer my calls or texts. If you know where he is, you need to tell me. I really don't need the extra stress right now.'

She looked away from him, chewed her lip. 'I've no idea where he is,' she said. 'But he's done this before – thinks it's fine to bugger off and not tell anyone, so long as he feels better. He's so selfish, Chris. And I'm sick of it.'

'Rachel – why did you ask me to come here?'

She glanced over her shoulder, towards the path that led down the side of their house. Chris followed her eyes. Was there movement there? It was probably just leaves, was too dark to be sure.

'What's going on, Rachel?'

'I wish I knew,' she said. 'First of all – Carmen called; she told me you'd been in to see her. So I know you know about Mikey's business going bust. He's penniless. And I'll tell you something else. Money – or the lack of it – is one of the reasons me and Mikey have been fighting so much. But that's not the only reason.' She sighed, and when she spoke again her voice was trembling. 'I've been convinced he's having an affair. Mikey denies it, of course, tells me I'm paranoid. But your voicemail message about Max McAndrew confirmed my suspicions.'

'How?'

'You told me Max saw Mikey *with me* at the casino, the night before Ruth was due to leave for Spain. The night he left her at the Alba with Max.'

'Aye, and I was just about to ask you about that,' said Chris. 'Why didn't you tell me you were there too?'

'Because I wasn't,' said Rachel.

Chris stared at her, hesitant.

Everyone else in the family was lying – so why not Rachel? But he was a man of instinct, and something in his gut told him she was telling the truth.

'So where were you?'

'I was at home the whole night. Right here, in bed, waiting for Mikey to come back. He must have been with some other woman when Max saw him at the casino. Max McAndrew doesn't know me, Chris – and he certainly couldn't identify me in the street after a big night on the beer. I'm not the only blonde woman in Edinburgh, you know. That's why I was so upset when I got your voicemail. First, it confirmed Mikey's been seeing some other woman and lying to me about it. And secondly, you trusted Max McAndrews's word over mine.'

'Are you saying Max can't be trusted?'

'I've no idea,' said Rachel. 'Max and I have never actually spoken – but he was well known at school because he was such a geek. He was in Ruth's year and they used to be friends but then for some reason he started giving her loads of shit all the time. He was the boy she punched that time. Remember?'

'Hang on – Max McAndrew was the person Ruth bullied?'

'I'd say it was more the other way round. But she gave as good as she got in the end. I'm assuming by your reaction that he didn't mention that to you?'

'No, he didn't.'

'Then I think you've got your answer about whether or not he can be trusted,' said Rachel. 'I'd have thought a journalist like you would have checked the facts before you started throwing accusations at family members.'

'I didn't accuse you of anything, Rachel.'

'Not directly. But it's obvious you think I'm keeping stuff from you and Farida. Do you think I'm that stupid? It's not me who's done something wrong, Chris. You need to look closer to home if that's what you're looking for.'

'Meaning?'

'Meaning it's Mikey who's been lying. And not just to me.'

'Lying about what?'

'About what happened the night Ruth went missing. What Mikey has failed to mention is that he went missing for most of that night as well.'

'Rachel. Please. I'm really not in the mood for riddles. Just tell me what happened. Take your time, but for Christ's sake tell it straight. Plain English, from the start.'

Rachel sighed, making her fringe flutter on her forehead. 'Ruth arrived here early evening, in one of her moods. They had a few beers here then Mikey suggested they go to the Alba for a couple of pints. Ruth said she couldn't stay out late because of her early flight but off they went, already steaming drunk. I went to bed as soon as they left, but I couldn't sleep. I was too furious.'

'Furious at who?'

'Mikey.'

'Why?'

'Because he was so drunk, because he always gets drunk when Ruth's here. Because he always chooses her over me if he gets the chance.'

'I get the picture,' said Chris. 'So you went to bed angry. Then what?'

'I was awake almost all night. Every time my watch beeped to say another hour had passed I got more and more furious, and when it got really late I started getting worried. I tried calling Mikey at three a.m. but it rang out. Same happened when I tried Ruth's phone. Even if they'd gone into town, the clubs would have closed by then. He should have been home. They both should.'

'Did you call the police?'

'I thought about it, but every time I went to phone I convinced myself I was being melodramatic. He'd often be out all night when we were students. I convinced myself he was just having a crazy night, a final farewell to Ruth. In the end I must have drifted off and the next thing I know it's seven a.m. and I hear the front door being opened. I waited in bed, silently raging, assuming he'd come upstairs and apologise – or at least explain where he'd been.'

'But he didn't?'

'I heard him go into the kitchen, put the kettle on, make some toast. All the usual morning noises.' Rachel took a deep breath. 'But then I heard the washing machine.'

'And that's not usual?'

'Not at that time. And not after Mikey's been out on a mad bender. So I got up, went downstairs, asked him what was going on. God, he looked like shit. He was hungover to hell, said he'd talk to me in the morning. I said it already was morning and he just rolled his eyes at me then went upstairs and conked out. I went to work after that, didn't see him again until evening. He'd made a special dinner, bought me flowers – all the same clichés I always fall for. He apologised, I accepted.' She shrugged. 'And I thought that was that.'

'Did he tell you where he'd been?'

'Gambling. He went on and on about this new casino in town, open twenty-four hours. No windows, no mobile reception and all the booze you want so long as you've got money on a table. He said he left the pub before Ruth and claims he went off to the casino with some other pals. Said he had a bit of a winning streak and totally lost track of time. If Max is telling the truth then we know Mikey didn't get past the door – but at the time it seemed credible enough.

'I asked why he'd put on a wash when he got home and he looked a bit sheepish, told me he'd got wasted on all the free booze at the casino, ended up spewing all over himself. It's hardly standard Mikey behaviour but I had no reason not to believe him. He often goes wild on nights out with Ruth.'

'Is that one of the reasons you don't like her?'

Rachel blinked a few times, surprised. 'Is it that obvious?'

'Aye,' said Chris, 'it is.'

'I'm sorry. I just . . . I think she's a bad influence on Mikey.'

'You're entitled to your opinion.'

She looked down at her hands. 'Should I go on?'

Chris nodded.

'I thought Mikey seemed a bit distant, but he blamed it on the hangover, said he'd be back to normal in no time. But he wasn't – and you know what? He hasn't been himself since. I could tell right away that he was keeping something from me but I kept giving him the benefit of the doubt, convincing myself it was nothing to worry about. Then a few days later we had high winds and all the bins blew over during the night. The noise woke me up so I went outside in my pyjamas to clear up. And that's when I found it.'

'Found what, Rachel?'

'Follow me.'

Chris followed her down the side of the house, helped her open the side gate. It always jammed in wet weather, had done for years. They left it open behind them, then headed down the gravel path that led to the outhouse.

It was an unremarkable building from the outside, whitewashed bricks and black downpipes and a slanting roof with dozens of squint and missing slates. A thin covering of brown moss grew on those that remained.

White paint flaked off the frames of the little square windows and the rotting wooden shutters that closed with rusting hooks. The door was new: Mikey had replaced it himself last summer, using more enthusiasm than skill. It looked good – glossy red paint and shiny brass fittings – but didn't sit flush to the wall and floor. It shuddered then stopped when Rachel tried to open it and she had to push it hard with her shoulder.

She leaned in and turned on the light. It flickered a few times then stayed on, illuminating dust caught in the air, but doing little to brighten the gloomy interior. Rachel stepped back and motioned for Chris to go in before her.

The first thing he saw was wetsuits, black and limp, strung up like headless shadows along the back wall. Plastic crates loaded with snorkels and flippers had been pushed in underneath. The rest of the place was chaotic, a place to put all the things they didn't want or need but couldn't bear to throw away. The old family sledges were there, and the swing-ball set – thrown out by Maria, scooped up by

Mikey. Chris was surprised to see two plastic boxes packed with old newspaper cuttings. He'd kept all of his front pages throughout his news career, boxes filled with memories of stricken lives he'd briefly been a part of. When he'd been shunted to the features department he'd loaded those boxes into the boot of Maria's car, told her they were hers for the dumping.

But here they were, kept.

'So what is it, Rachel? What did you find in the bin?'

She knelt down next to a set of wooden shelves loaded with transparent plastic boxes containing DIY tools. She opened one of the boxes, pulled out a grey hooded top.

'This,' she said, handing it to Chris. 'I bought this for Mikey's birthday. I was upset he'd chucked it without telling me. But I soon realised why. I don't know why I kept it, but I did. And I don't know why I never told anyone, but I couldn't. I mean, it's Mikey. My Mikey. I suppose I kept hoping I'd find an explanation for it. But I never did, and now . . .'

Chris pulled out his phone, switched on the torch and stared at the hooded top in his hands. He looked at Rachel but she was staring at the floor, offering no comfort simply because she had none left to give. She was still and silent and Chris the same. He stared and stared at the hooded top but he didn't notice the brand or the colour of the little bird motif on the chest and sleeves.

He only saw the blood.

CHAPTER 42

Chris sat in his car for a long time after Rachel went back inside. He'd wanted to call Farida McPherson right away but she'd convinced him to wait, to try to speak with Mikey themselves before they got the police involved. They'd both keep calling Mikey's mobile and she'd phone around his friends too, ask if they'd seen him. Rachel wasn't sure where Mikey had been sleeping since the break-up, so she would check their joint bank account online too, see if there were any payments to hotels. If they'd heard nothing by the next morning they'd contact the police then, tell them to come to the house.

Chris gripped the steering wheel, wishing he'd washed his hands after touching that top. That blood.

But whose blood was it?

He felt sick to his core, thinking of all the lies Mikey had told, now exposed. What kind of secret merited so much deceit? Anger raged in him, but underneath there was something else, something softer: that familiar ache of loss, of grief not diminished by time. He thought about suffering and how well he'd always hidden it – and the damage that had caused. Like father, like son.

Another wave crashed against the harbour wall and with it came the thought of that body in the water, smashed against cliffs. He thought of both his children and of the agonising possibility that one might have hurt the other.

Chris got out of the car and went to the harbour, stood as if he felt strong – feet planted wide and firm on the sea wall, eyes fixed on the dark horizon. The sea raged and the wind whipped his cheeks and the tears would not stop and his heart stung like a bloody wound plunged into salt water.

He *had* to call Farida.

Yes, he'd made a promise to Rachel, but it was the right thing to do. He knew that, he knew that, he knew that. But he held back. One question still tormented him. He knew Javi Fernandez had connections to Ruth and to Maria. But was there a connection between Mikey and Javi Fernandez as well?

He filled his lungs with sea air then headed for his car, had almost reached it when he noticed his mobile phone on the dashboard, screen lit up.

Christ. Had somebody called?

He broke into a run, grabbed his phone just as a text message came in, telling him he had a new voicemail. He slumped down into his seat and listened, was both relieved and disappointed when he heard Sandy's voice.

'Hey, Chris – we need to talk about that CCTV footage you sent me from the Indian restaurant. I assume you sent it to Farida too? If not, do it. I'll get his image on the front page if Farida thinks it'll help. That van fairly spoils the view but at least now we know Maria was the chaser, not the chased. And in my book that's progress. Take care, Chris. Bye.'

Chris stared at the screen long after Sandy ended the message, his mind slowly processing the words like an old mobile phone running low on memory.

Maria was the chaser, Sandy had said, *not the chased*.

Clearly he'd seen something Chris had not.

Chris flipped to videos and pressed play, then watched Maria come to life on his screen. There she was, staring into the window of that coffee shop. The world seemed to shudder when a big wave smashed into the harbour wall. His heart did the same when he reached the part where the van pulled up beside her. Its back doors were pulled open, blocking his view of Maria, except the heels of her orange trainers. Just like before, he kept his eyes on that tiny part of Maria and, when she ran off screen, nobody followed. He pictured the route she'd taken and the place she'd ended up. He'd been there, seen it for himself.

But then he rewound, saw the part he'd missed.

When he'd watched the film before, he'd kept his eyes on Maria after the van pulled up; watched her run off then waited to see if anybody else ran after her, in pursuit. Nobody had. But now he kept his eye on the coffee shop instead. He watched the white van pull up, block Maria from view. But then, instead of looking at the back of the van, Chris kept his eyes on the front – and realised that the door of the coffee shop was partly visible above the curve of the bonnet. A couple left the café, then a boy on a skateboard arrived – just as a man on the inside pulled open the door. The van bonnet hid most of his body but his face was in view. Chris watched him look right, look left, then run – just before the van pulled away. Maria ran in the same direction a few seconds later.

Chris rewound the footage, paused when the man was standing in the doorway. The image quality was poor and the man's hood obscured the details of his face – but there was something in the way he held himself that made Chris's chest tighten. He zoomed in closer but the image blurred. Chris cursed himself for leaving his laptop at the hospital. He needed to go back there, now. He had to see this on a bigger screen.

He started the engine and called Sandy on his hands-free as he drove.

'Chris? I can hardly hear you. It's a terrible line. I'm driving – on my way to Lesmahagow of all bloody places, and you know what the signal's like up that way. Absolutely dreadful. Worth writing a story about – but not today. We've got a murder. Body in a wheelie bin, believe it or not. I'm sorry I couldn't stay with Maria any longer, but I told the nurses not to let anyone in – unless they're family. Still no word from Mikey?'

Chris swallowed hard. 'No.'

'And no updates on the body at Brewster Bay?'

'No,' said Chris. It was the only word he could manage.

'And have you called Farida?'

'No.'

'Worth chasing her up, I'd say. I'd best go, Chris. Take care.'

When Sandy hung up Chris called the hospital, reinforced the warning not to let anybody anywhere near Maria. Only me or Sandy, he said. They didn't ask questions and he couldn't have answered them if they had. His voice was lost in the sobs that choked him and shook his whole body all the way back to hospital.

He parked the car and took two deep drags of a cigarette before he went inside and headed for intensive care. He heard the shouts as soon as he opened the double doors leading to Maria's room and he could see someone grappling with security guards at the far end: a man, with a beard, shouting in Spanish.

I pretended I was asleep in the taxi so I didn't have to answer the driver's questions, got him to drop me at the end of the street that led to their house. Hood up, head down, I headed for the railway embankment behind their back garden, a place where Ruth used to be with me in secret, smoking joints after school. I sat for hours on leaves and moss, my back against that silver-trunked tree she could never remember the name of. This was the place Ruth came when the bullying was at its worst; a place she knew she would be not be seen by anyone but me.

I kept daring myself to climb the wooden fence the next time a boiled kettle steamed up the kitchen window at the back, pictured Ruth's mum leaning forward to wipe the glass with a soft cloth. She'd look up when the security light flickered on, illuminating the lawn. She'd see me there, standing alone in her garden, and she'd know right that second that she'd lost another daughter.

I tried to picture her face in that moment of realisation. She'd think back to That Day, and suddenly it would all make sense. She'd realise it was me who'd convinced Ruth to split herself open. And, finally, she'd understand why.

CHAPTER 43

The security guard noticed Chris before the man did, rolled his eyes at him as if they were in on a secret. 'Calm yourself, pal, and let this gentleman past.'

The man turned, mouth jammed open but empty of words when he saw Chris coming towards him. His body loosened and for a moment the air around them held only the sound of his breath. It held the reek of alcohol too, the unmistakable scent of that man. Mateo.

'Something happened to Maria,' Mateo said urgently, shaking off the security guard and stepping towards Chris. 'Just as I got here. One of the machines started flashing. An alarm sounded. And then she tensed up, started making groaning noises. Best she could manage with that ventilator.'

Chris felt sick, imagined the terror of waking up and realising your throat had a tube rammed down it. And worse, realising that your life depended on it.

'Had Sandy noticed any change?'

'Sandy?'

Chris stared at him. 'Sandy Hamilton. Tall guy, white hair, tweed suit.'

Mateo bunched up his lips, shrugged in a way that seemed deliberately exaggerated. 'He didn't mention it, but he seemed in a rush to leave.'

'And there wasn't anybody else here, in Maria's room?'

'Not that I noticed.'

'You're sure?'

'I'm not blind, am I? If you choose to leave your dying wife on her own, that's your decision. But please, don't pass your guilt on to me. Where have you been, anyway? You can't just abandon my sister when she's in this state. She was on her own the last time I came to visit, too, you know. I strolled right in, no questions asked. Lucky I was here to bring a card. Sunflowers. Her favourite. And the only card she has, may I add. I'm a good brother, Chris. You should be thanking me. If it weren't for me, the doctors would not have been alerted to the change in Maria's condition.'

'So what's all this about, then?' Chris motioned to the guard. 'If you're such a good citizen, why was security called? It's not for nothing.'

'I wanted to stay with her after the alarms sounded.'

'And?'

'And they wouldn't allow it.' Mateo shifted his eyes towards Maria's door. 'It seems that in Scotland a man can't even hold the hand of his dying sister without breaking some absurd rule. I do not want Maria to die alone, Chris. I protested, told them it was my right to be with my own flesh and blood. But they won't let me in – and they won't let you in, either, so don't even try.'

Chris looked towards Maria's room. 'But did they tell you what happened? Did they say . . . this was it?'

'No,' said Mateo. 'But they didn't say it wasn't.'

Just then a doctor with long ginger hair left the glass-walled staff area and headed quickly towards Maria's room. Not running, but not walking. A security guard wearing a suit two sizes too big was blocking the doorway, a standing stone with a shaved head. He nodded to the doctor then opened the door.

Chris ran towards them. 'My wife,' he said. 'Can I see her?'

The guard quickly shut the door then stood in front of it. 'Off limits, pal.'

'You know what's happened?'

'Ask that numpty.' The guard nodded towards Mateo. 'Unless he gets lifted first. A night in the cells would sort him out. Dry him out as well.'

Chris stared at Maria's door for a moment, trying to decipher the muffled sounds from inside. If there was panic he could not sense it, and if there was loss he could not yet feel it. He started knocking on the door, said Maria's name over and over, until the security guard asked him to stop.

'You and your Spanish pal really need to keep the racket down. I know this is a nightmare, I do. But you're not the only ones in here with a sad story.'

Chris went and stood with Mateo, leaning against opposite walls. If they'd both stretched out their arms their fingers would have touched, but they did not.

Chris stared at the floor, trying to ignore Mateo's attempts at small talk. He talked about the shit weather in Glasgow and the excessive cost of his rehab clinic and his determination to give up the drink once and for all.

'Och, come on, Mateo. Your breath alone could pickle a liver.'

'My sister's *dying*.'

'I'm well aware of that.'

'You've got no idea of my struggles, Chris. And if it's the money you're bothered about, I fully intended to refund Maria once I'm better. I always do.'

'What money?'

'For the clinic.'

'Christ. How much money are we talking about?'

'A few thousand.'

'And when did she give it to you?'

'It was transferred into my account on Sunday,' he said. 'But I'd asked her for a loan the last time we spoke. I've spent thousands on that clinic already but I need a few more months. I want to get better this time, Chris. Anyway, Maria told me she couldn't touch her savings and would speak to you about using cash from your joint account. She's not been in touch since then so I assumed she'd decided against it. But suddenly, the money arrived at the weekend.'

Chris thought of his bank card, the failed transactions, and Victoria's voice telling him their money had been sent to M. Hidalgo. He'd assumed it was Mikey, since the bank always used both his surnames. Michael Morrison Hidalgo. But here he was, the other M. Hidalgo. Mateo.

Christ. So Mikey was relieved of one crime.

But what about the others? He thought again of that bloodstained hoody and then it came: the memory of the helicopter, the lost life it lifted to the sky. He checked his phone, then tried yet again to call Mikey. It had just switched to voicemail when Maria's door was finally opened.

Chris turned with the hinge, trying to read the eyes of the red-haired doctor when she walked towards him with a clipboard in her hand.

'Mr Morrison? If you'll come this way, please.'

She touched his arm, guiding him towards the visitors' room with the gentle precision of a novice driver. Chris followed her, but glanced into Maria's room just before the security guard closed the door again. Was she dead? He couldn't tell. But from here she looked as if she was carved out of marble. Chris smiled and for a moment let love drown out his fear of death.

Maria was beautiful, even when she was cold.

CHAPTER 44

Chris shifted the itchy hospital blanket away from his face and sat up. Sunrise was at least two or three hours away – but his head was far too busy for sleep.

He reached over to Maria's bed, found her pulse and felt hope.

After four full days in a coma, she'd woken up.

She'd opened her eyes shortly after Mateo had arrived and made a brief attempt to communicate with him and the nurse he'd quickly grabbed from the corridor. She'd moved her left arm towards her leg then closed her eyes again and returned to her previous state of total stillness. The doctor had told him they'd be running several tests to monitor significant changes in her condition.

But I'm confident she's improving, the doctor had said.

Chris had cried and she'd squeezed his arm, suggested he got some rest.

And here he was, trying, failing.

He checked his phone but it was far too early on a Friday morning for anyone to be awake except dedicated runners and parents of newborns. Carmen had texted the night before to say she'd still not managed to get hold of her sister to check the dates of her mum's visits to the clinic where she'd seen Ruth. She promised to be in touch as soon as she knew more. He'd also got a text from Rachel, pleading again with Chris not to tell the police about the blood on Mikey's hooded top. *Not yet.*

But from Ruth and Mikey there was silence, nothing more.

He got up, opened the wardrobe and pulled out the laptop. This was what he'd meant to do last night. He'd take yet another look at Jamal's CCTV footage, but this time on the big screen.

And there she was. Maria, staring in the coffee shop window. Maria, blocked by the van. Maria, running. He rewound a few seconds, then paused the film when he saw the face of the man who started running moments before Maria did. He then brought up the photo of Javi Fernandez from the Man With A Heart blog – and compared the two faces on the big screen of the laptop instead of the tiny screen of his phone. There were definitely similarities.

He'd forwarded the video to Farida at the same time as he'd sent it to Sandy, but so far he'd heard nothing back. It was too early to call her so he did yet another round of checks. First, he scoured his and Maria's email. There was nothing from Ruth and nothing from Javi. After that he checked Ruth's social media to see if she'd posted anything new. *You never know*, Sandy had said. And so for a moment he allowed himself to imagine logging on and seeing a selfie of Ruth with a silly hashtag and smile and a pulse and without the slightest idea of the drama the rest of them were suffering.

Not today, pal.

From there he did a search for Javi Fernandez, opened the Instagram account Sandy had told him about. The last post was that photo showing two pairs of feet, pointing skywards. It was dated a few days before Maria's accident and there had been no activity on the account since then.

Chris started scrolling through other images on the account – but they were all just as meaningless as Ruth's posts. Landscapes, beaches, meals, buildings – nothing that gave an opinion or showed any trace of personality whatsoever. But as for *where* they were taken – in Spain, in Scotland, or elsewhere, most were too abstract to place. Why bother posting them at all if they said nothing? His heart squirmed in his chest when his brain produced a reason. They'd all been deceived by the photos on Ruth's pages – and maybe they were falling for the same trick with Javi.

He'd find out soon enough.

He grabbed a coffee from the machine and started working through Javi's images one by one. He checked for copyright icons, compared Javi's photos to images from internet searches, repeated all the work he'd done with Ruth's account. After an hour he'd checked hundreds of photos but his notepad was still empty. So far all images appeared to be his own, a representation of this man's life in small squares. And so far one thing was clear – there was not a trace of Ruth in it.

He sipped his coffee, kept on scrolling through photos until he reached March 18th, the last day they'd seen Ruth. No photo had been posted that day, but Javi Fernandez had posted a photo the next morning – the image of the sky at sunrise, a square of red and orange streaked with wispy clouds.

The title was *New Day, 0319.*

Chris clicked on the photo to enlarge it. There was a bird in flight near the top corner. Above it was a black triangle which Chris guessed was the overhang of a roof. He realised then that the photo had been taken through a window.

He turned the screen away from Maria's bedside lamp so he could see the image in better detail. Suddenly he noticed spots of light and faint straight lines that did not belong in the sky; that did not come from outside.

They were reflections on the glass.

He could make out the shape of lamps and furniture and picture frames on the wall behind the camera – and the ghostly outline of the person holding it.

Then he spotted a different smudge on the sunrise sky.

Neatly sandwiched between one cloud and the next was a trail of old glue tracing the outline of a sticker that had been stuck there for years.

And just like that, Chris knew exactly where that window was. It was the kitchen window of their old flat in Portobello, the one Ruth now owned.

Ruth had pulled the sticker out of a cereal box one morning before primary school. Chris had lifted her onto the draining board and she'd stuck it on to the window, as high as she could reach. He remembered the way she'd carefully smoothed down the edges with her little fingers, and how she'd loved looking up at it from the street.

When they'd bought the house and moved out of the flat Maria had carefully peeled off the sticker, then tried and failed to remove the sticky residue it left behind. But there it was, unchanged, more than twenty years later.

Finally, proof.

Javi Fernandez had been at Ruth's flat the day she disappeared.

And if he was there then, maybe he was there now.

Chris packed up the laptop and went to the visitors' room. Security had agreed to let Mateo sleep there on the condition he calmed down and sobered up. Chris shook him until he woke up. 'Look after Maria,' he said, then headed to the car. He knew where he was going, but did not know what he'd find.

I fled Ruth's parents' house instead of confessing, and two days later I fled again when her mother tracked me down in the coffee shop where Anna worked. I fled technology too, disconnected myself from mobiles and landlines and internet. I fled doors that were knocked on and handwritten notes pushed underneath. And what was I fleeing? The part that came next.

I'd have fled from Anna too, but when she turned up at my flat four days later she pushed open my letterbox then said out loud a name she should not know.

'Who's Ruth?' she said.

When I went to the door I saw that another note had been pushed under – but it was caught under the doormat in the hall and had been hidden from me until now. When I pulled it out I saw Ruth's name, and her dad's.

So he'd been here too – and the note said he'd be back.

Anna talked to me through the letterbox, told me a man called Chris had come to her coffee shop, looking for me – and for his daughter.

When I opened the door Anna handed me a newspaper.

MISSING, the headline said, above the photo of Ruth's face.

They'd edited the image, chopped out the context. It was one of Ruth's favourites, taken during a family hiking holiday on the Isle of Harris when they'd followed an ancient route called the Coffin Road. In the old days the islanders *would carry their dead across the island for burial, put death in a box and walk from the rocky east coast to the wide sandy beaches of the west.*

I wondered if they'd thought about that when they handed that photo to the police: the weight of Ruth's body carried on the shoulders of grieving relatives, the shifting walls of a sandy grave, the cries of the gulls drowning out their own, the endless tides that would sweep in and suck old bones out to sea.

I looked at Ruth's face in the newspaper and imagined the line drawn around her by the editor, separating her from the place she should be. Ruth, cut and pasted. The rest of her world blanked out, regarded as irrelevant. Left on the screen but off the page would be the image of a smiling mum and dad, arms curved around an empty space that matched the shape of their daughter.

I read on, and only then did I find out about the accident on Fleshmarket Close: that she'd chased me, fast, then fallen; that a coma now held her still.

I felt sick and entirely responsible and wondered if she was already dead.

I imagined Ruth's dad in hospital, clutching the limp hand of his wife in one hand and his mobile in the other. He'd jump to his feet if I called from Ruth's phone, walk away from the bed as if he didn't want to announce her mum's death in front of the body. He'd already have pictured Ruth beside him at the funeral; would see the face of his dead wife in hers. Then I'd speak and he'd wonder why it wasn't his daughter's voice he was hearing.

And he'd realise he'd lost two worlds at once.

Anna touched my arm, pulled me out of my thoughts and back into that room. You look like you've seen a ghost, *she said. I took her hand, and, for the first time in all the months since we'd met, I led her into the bedroom.*

She was about to see one for herself.

CHAPTER 45

Chris's knees cracked when he bent down to the level of the letterbox then pushed it open and peered inside. All the lights were switched off but the sunrise was slowly diluting the darkness. The walls were the same pale green they'd always been. He and Maria had helped Ruth to paint them when she'd moved in and tried to make their old family home her own.

The lampshades in the hall were the retro ones Ruth had bought from one of the charity shops on Portobello high street – and he guessed the framed photo on the side wall would be that picture of her and Maria during their cycling holiday in the Highlands. The door that led to the sitting room was half-open but he couldn't make out any details from that distance. He could make out the bad smell, though, a reek that reminded him of old folks' homes, places air never reached. Crouching down in front of the door, Chris peered again through the letterbox into the hall he'd walked through so many times.

'Hello?' he said. 'Anyone in there?'

His voice was soft at first, but it hardened and the volume was upped a notch every time he said it. He knew neighbours would hear and make up their own version of events. Chris didn't care, had no idea how many times he'd said it when he heard footsteps behind him; and he had no idea who he'd see when his eyes adjusted to the glare of the strip-light that suddenly switched on above him. It came on whenever somebody climbed the stairs, triggered by a sensor. Chris stood up, turned at exactly the same time as a young woman in running gear reached that top step, her tattooed hand gripping the banister.

For a moment they both froze.

Chris saw recognition in her face, the same way he'd sensed it in the coffee shop when he'd shown her the photos of Javi and Maria on his phone.

'Anna, isn't it?'

She turned and ran.

Chris followed, taking two steps at a time, left hand gripping the metal banister to keep his balance. But Anna was more than thirty years younger and wearing trainers and clearly harbouring a secret she did not want to share. She was already in the entrance hall when Chris was slowed by a boxer dog bounding out of a flat on floor three. He leapt to one side to avoid it, banged into the banister – then looked over just as Anna was opening the front door.

He was never going to catch her.

She was nowhere to be seen by the time he made it out on the street. He walked out on to the road, looked downhill towards the beach, and up towards town. Nothing, nobody. For a moment he just stood, willing his heartbeat to return to a normal pace and hoping she'd creep out from behind a parked car or the recycling bins a few doors down.

But nobody came.

He went back inside, was about to climb the stairs when he noticed Ruth's mail box was even more tightly packed with junk mail than it had been the other day. He pulled out the whole pile, then sat on the stairs and flicked through the envelopes while he got his breath back. Most of the names meant nothing to him and weren't even meant for Ruth's flat. But then he saw that name.

Javi Fernandez, at his daughter's address.

The envelope had *Confidential* printed along the top and beneath that word was the name of the Glasgow-based firm who'd sent it. Chris hesitated then stuffed the letter into his pocket. He'd keep hold of it, read it later.

As far as Chris could tell most of the remaining letters were intended for former owners and tenants of other flats, junk mail pulled out of one mail box and stuffed into another. If Maria still lived there she'd have carefully sorted through them, written *Return to Sender* on the envelope and left them on the table by the back door where the enormous free phone book used to be kept.

He stood up, turned around – and there it was.

That old table, and a pile of envelopes on top of it.

He approached it slowly, with caution, anxiety clawing at his chest. His fingers trembled when he picked up the letters, flicked from one to the next. They were all junk mail – and they were all addressed to either Ruth Morrison or Javi Fernandez. But that wasn't the only thing they had in common.

The same message had been written on the front of every envelope, all in the same hand-writing. *Return to Sender*.

Chris's hands trembled as he opened the envelope at the top of the pile and pulled out the letter. He didn't read beyond the top line. All he needed to check was the date in the top right-hand corner, and just like that, he knew.

CHAPTER 46

Chris heard the beep of alarm clocks and snippets from morning radio shows and babies crying as he climbed back up the stairs to Ruth's flat, but when he got there he didn't ring the bell or knock. Instead he crouched down in front of her door once again and pushed a plant pot to one side.

He reached for Maria's purse, took out the scrap of paper he'd found in it the previous morning. He'd assumed the four-digit code was a PIN number but now he had a different idea. It could be the code for the key safe.

It was Billy Mason who'd reminded him about the safe, said Maria had refused to open it and take out the spare keys because *by law* landlords needed permission from tenants before entering a flat – and permission was exactly what Maria had been trying to get when she'd gone to that coffee shop.

It should have been easy.

Find tenant, fix intercom. Problem solved, everyone happy.

But Chris had watched Jamal's CCTV footage enough times to know that while Maria had made it to the coffee shop, she definitely hadn't gone inside.

Why?

Maybe he'd find the answer here, now, behind the door.

His hands shook as he turned the dials on the security box then pushed the little red button that released the lock. Nothing happened. He hunched lower, moved closer, checking if one of the numbers was out of place. They were all where they should be. He spun the dials again anyway, repeated the process – but got the same result.

The code had been changed.

He stood up, stepped back, leaned against the banister and stared at the door as he mulled over his options. He could try to crack the code for the key safe, or break it open or wait until the person inside needed to leave. He could go home and find a spare set of keys or he could call Farida McPherson and ask if the police would help him gain entry. Or he could kick down the door.

He was still debating it when his phone rang. He stared at the screen for a few seconds before he picked up, heart thundering. He didn't believe the name on the screen until he answered and heard the voice in his ear.

'Dad? It's me.'

Mikey, alive.

But still a liar.

He barely let Chris speak, filled the space between them with apologies and invented excuses about business meetings and feeling unwell and crashing out for hours and Rachel failing to wake him and phones being perpetually on silent. He'd just woken up to find dozens of missed calls from Chris and Farida.

'I'm so sorry, Dad. Any change?'

Chris almost laughed, felt the bitterness of it all sting his tongue. *Any change? My daughter has disappeared and my wife is dying and you, son, are a bloody liar.* 'I'll tell you when you I see you,' said Chris, and ended the call.

He stared at his phone for a few seconds, brain whirring, then dialled a number he knew off by heart. Then he held his ear to the door and waited, waited, waited. Inside, a phone started to ring. Chris felt his legs give way, steadied himself on the doorframe. But he kept his ear in place, desperate to hear what happened next. One ring, two rings, then someone silenced the phone. Now there was no doubt. There was someone inside. But who?

Chris wouldn't believe it until he saw it.

He hunched down and started spinning the little metal dials on the key box. He entered all the passwords they'd ever used on the burglar alarm at the house. Nothing. He entered all significant dates he could think of – births and deaths and graduations and weddings. Nothing. He entered their ages in different combinations. Nothing. When his back started hurting he sat down, leaned against the banister with his feet pointing towards the door and tried to think logically. The sunrise made the skylights above him glow red, then orange, then for a few minutes he was illuminated in pale golden light. Chris screwed up his eyes, thought again of that photo posted by Javi Fernandez the day after Ruth went missing – an image of the sunrise taken from her kitchen window.

And just like that, he remembered something else.

He pulled out his phone, pulse racing as he searched for the right page then scrolled down to the picture he held in his mind. And there it was.

The title. *New Day, 0319.*

He turned the dial to 0319, heard a click, opened the key safe, got the keys, turned the lock – then stepped into the still, silent gloom of that windowless hall.

Ruth's body was barely recognisable when Anna finally saw it, wrapped in sheets that smelled of me. Her breath quickened and she held a hand over her mouth as if to stop the wrong words slipping out. For a long time she just stood, looking then looking away, over and over and over. Then she slumped to the floor and sat cross-legged at the end of the bed. I did the same, head down, arms wrapped round my knees. She flinched when my legs touched hers.

Then she said, Can you tell me about her?

I got my suitcase from the top of the wardrobe, took out that old photo of Ruth and her mum that used to hang on the wall of the flat. It was exactly the kind of photo that the papers would be happy to get hold of and probably would, eventually: an attractive mother and daughter on bikes, looking strong and adventurous. Two women, together, united by blood and by love.

But if you could slip under the glass of the frame and the gloss of the photo then climb inside Ruth's head and have a look around you'd find a much bleaker scene, and me in the middle of it. Even then, Ruth loved me but did not want to. Every thought of me was coated in guilt, thick and black and toxic as tar. It was enough to drive anyone mad and, to be fair, it almost did.

I handed the picture to Anna, watched her eyes as she studied the pieces of a life long since lost and realised she knew nothing about me. She loved me last week and last night and this morning but I was sure she didn't love me now.

She pressed a finger on to the dusty glass, pointing to Ruth's mum.

So she doesn't know?

I shook my head, closed my eyes. I did not want to read hers because I knew what they would say. They'd say, You let me down. *They'd say,* You lied. *They'd say the thing that scared me most:* You need to finish what you started.

I cried once Anna had left.

It was comforting to think my tears were for Ruth, and for her family; that it was their pain that moved me; that I was strong enough and noble enough to put their suffering before my own. It made me feel like a slightly better person.

Still, the very fact that I stayed there, locked up in Ruth's flat, proved beyond doubt that I was not. The people who loved Ruth were searching for something I'd already destroyed; looking for answers only I could give them. I was the only one who could stop it but still, I chose not to.

My tears were for me and me alone.

I was crying simply because the hardest part was still to come.

CHAPTER 47

The sitting room light blinked a few times then came on, too bright. There used to be shades, but whoever was here now had left the bulbs exposed. The thick curtains were closed. Chris looked at his reflection in the heavy mirror above the fireplace, wondering how many faces it had held on that wall, and whose was there before his.

He couldn't bear it, moved to the kitchen.

A single mug sat on the draining board. Black coffee, half-drunk. The window behind it reflected the room, the same way it did in the photo on Instagram. Chris noticed the trace of that old sticker in the corner – but that wasn't all. A shrinking circle of steam clouded the glass on the inside, inches from the spout of an electric kettle plugged into the wall.

Chris touched it, felt warmth.

Fear surged into every part of him, then sucked away his strength like a rip tide. He swayed a little, steadied himself against the wall. Then, hesitantly, he headed for the hall. There were four doors, all of them open except the one at the end. Ruth's old bedroom. A phone charger was plugged into the wall, and the cord had been pulled under her door.

Was it charging the mobile he'd phoned from outside? Probably – and that meant the person who'd silenced his call was in that room. Now, he'd find out if they'd silenced Ruth as well.

Chris gritted his teeth and forced himself to walk towards the closed door.

The handle rattled when he turned it and stepped into the room, eyes narrowed. Even in the dark he could sense there was someone there. He searched for the light switch with his fingers and flipped it. His insides erupted. He recognised the face of the man on Ruth's bed. So this was Javi Fernandez, right here in front of him.

And, with him, the parts of Ruth that remained.

CHAPTER 48

The first word between them was her name, said softly.
'Ruth?'

The answer was a shake of the head, but no apology.

'I won't answer to that name now,' he said. 'Call me Javi.'

Chris flinched when Javi spoke. His words were wrapped in a lilt Chris knew was of his own teaching, but the voice was deep, had broken and become someone else's since the last time they'd spoken, nine months earlier.

'I thought you were dead. I never for a second thought . . .' He swallowed hard, tears stinging like acid as every lie untangled itself. Ruth's flat, Ruth's room, Ruth's bed, Ruth's body and bones and blood. But now, she was Javi.

Disbelief turned to elation, anger to guilt. Chris felt dizzy, noticed the ache of grief too, though he wasn't yet sure what he'd lost. He closed his eyes, tried to find a place in his head that was still, that could make sense of what he was seeing. He'd pictured a daughter, dead, flies sucking on the scraps of her. He'd pictured a stranger with a grudge and no remorse and blood on his hands. He'd pictured police and his name in the paper for the wrong reasons. For a moment he'd stopped willing Maria to wake up, because the world she'd left behind had betrayed her, left a gaping hole far bigger than he'd ever have been able to fill.

'*Christ.*' He had no other words.

Javi looked away and hugged his knees to his chest, same way Ruth would do when she was little and they'd given her a row for breaking rules.

'I saw the paper.'

'About your mum?'

He nodded. 'It was me she was chasing.'

'I know.'

'I didn't know she'd fallen, Dad.' Despite the scrappy beard, Chris saw the sudden flush of red on Javi's cheeks. The same thing happened to Maria when she was upset but trying to be strong. 'I'd have helped her. You know that.'

'Aye.'

'How did you find me?'

Chris held up the glossy envelopes in his hand, junk mail with *Return to Sender* written by hand on the front. The letters were dated last week and the writing was Ruth's. He'd seen that same writing in school homework jotters and in the letters sent home from university and on the family calendar hanging in their kitchen. Those curves and lines belonged to Ruth and Ruth alone.

'I saw the letters downstairs, recognised your writing,' said Chris.

'Some things don't change,' said Javi, then he rolled up his sleeves, exposed the faded tracks carved out on the underside of both arms.

These were the scars of That Day.

'So this is why you did it,' said Chris.

Javi nodded then traced a finger along one of the lines, the same route the blade had taken.

His beard was thin but Chris knew it hid another scar; a pale pink line on his neck that he'd pressed on when it was still bleeding.

'I was convinced there was something really wrong with me,' said Javi. 'I had no idea there was any other way out. I had no concept of . . . *this* . . . at all.'

'*This* being . . . *what*, exactly? What's the right word?'

'You can use whatever word you want – or you could just call me Javi.'

'I'll try,' said Chris, eyes tracing the line of the scar beneath Javi's scrappy beard. His neck looked more solid now, and too wide for that butterfly necklace bought by Maria.

Chris pulled it out of his pocket. 'I think you lost this.'

'How—?'

'Long story,' said Chris, handing it over. Javi's face lit up in exactly the same way it always had but it looked broader now, a circle becoming a square.

Javi smiled and tightened his hand around the necklace. Chris noticed thicker wrists, fatter veins, heavier eyebrows. But the eyes were unchanged – the sparkle they took on, from tears held in far too long. He stepped closer to the bed, wished again he could somehow fix that part of his child that hurt.

'Why didn't you tell us?'

'I felt like a freak, Dad. My whole life I knew I was a boy – I just knew – and I thought eventually everyone else would realise it too. And I'm not talking about *feeling* like a boy. I'm talking about *being* a boy. Then I start my period and suddenly the whole world tells me I'm a girl and I need to fit that mould.'

Javi stretched over to the bedside cabinet and pulled a crumpled letter from the drawer. 'Read this,' he said, then handed it over.

There was blood on the envelope: spots of Ruth, half her age.

She had still been gripping the knife when they found her That Day, age thirteen and leaking life on to Uncle Mateo's terrace. She'd pushed down hard enough to split her skin but not hard enough to escape it. When a suicide letter couldn't be found they'd asked Ruth for answers instead. She'd told them about bullies and feeling ugly and always being left out. But she did not tell them *this*. She'd rather have died than live without being the boy born under her skin.

Ruth, gone but not dead.

His daughter, now a son.

There was no way it could be misinterpreted. There were no lines to read between. There was only a before and an after. There was only a then and now. There was the end of the world that Chris knew and the start of a life that was shaped very differently.

There was Ruth, and now – in her place and in her body – there was Javi.

CHAPTER 49

Javi watched his dad read his suicide letter, fifteen years after he should have. He noticed flinches. Chris was like a bird-watcher glancing between a pocket guide and the specimen captured in his sights: comparing features and subtle details, keen to be sure the beast described on the page matched the one he could see.

After a while Chris sat the letter on the bed, apart from the last page. Javi noticed his dad's fingers were touching the two closing words. His signature.

'I used to practise it in secret,' he said. 'I'd sign my name over and over, then I'd tear up the paper into tiny pieces and dump it separate bins on the way to school. I was terrified you'd find them and ask me who Javi Fernandez was.'

'You've known all that time?'

Javi nodded.

'And always . . . that name?'

'*My* name.'

'Why choose a Spanish one?

'It's not a rejection of you, Dad, if that's what you're thinking.' Javi kept his eyes on Chris. 'It's hard to explain but I've just always felt that my Spanish side was more masculine than my Scottish side. The way I speak, the way I hold myself. To be honest it never even occurred to me to choose a Scottish name. I've always looked at myself and seen a Spanish boy looking back at me.'

'Fair enough.' Chris looked away, bit down on his bottom lip.

'I used to do the same thing you've just done, Dad. I couldn't look at me either. Every time I saw myself, I'd turn away. Or I'd try to see Ruth, be her.'

'But you *are* still you, right?'

'I'm not Ruth, if that's what's you're saying.'

'I know but . . . I mean . . . underneath it all . . .'

Javi waited, wordless, while Chris cleared his throat, as though the end of his sentence was still lodged there and he was struggling to shift it. When that didn't work Chris sighed then reached for his hand instead, held it. Javi could feel Chris's racing pulse, doubted his dad had ever touched him so softly before. Touch in their family had always been something practical, a means to an end. Mikey, helping him make the perfect knot in his tie before they went to school. Mum, holding his head still while she fished a lash out of his eye. And Dad, pushing down with all his weight and both hands, doing everything he could to stop life leaking out of his only daughter.

'Do you still think about That Day, Dad?'

Chris nodded. 'Whenever you're not with us.'

'I'm hardly ever here.'

'Then there's your answer.'

Javi pictured the vast sky and the sweet smell of that fig tree and the cheerful song of that blackbird above them and the ants, swarming to the spot.

'It yanks me out of sleep all the time,' said Chris. 'I lie there, eyes wide open, wondering where you are, and if you're sleeping. Sometimes I imagine we're lying awake at exactly the same time, both of us replaying exactly the same scene again and again in beds that are thousands of miles apart.'

'Did you talk about it with anyone afterwards?'

'Just the police.'

'That's not what I meant.'

Javi thought again of his dad's trousers, stained at the knees. His shirt speckled red, as if someone had filled a balloon with his child's blood then popped it in front of him. He thought too of his blood in their bed, the night they brought him home from hospital. They'd let him sleep between them but the sheet all around him had stayed cold. He'd scratched, bled on to their pillowcase.

They'd washed out the stains.

Javi got up and stood with his back to the window and Chris sat on the bed, still holding that letter. Both were reflected on the glass and even though it was freezing outside the room felt stuffy, as though there wasn't enough space for both men, for the questions and the answers they'd held inside for so many years. Chris asked too much, too fast. But finally, he got answers.

Javi talked about meeting Max McAndrew at the Alba the night Ruth disappeared. Max, who looked at Ruth and saw who she really was. Max, who'd always known, and loved her anyway. Max, who'd whispered exactly the same thing to her at school and got a punch in the face instead of a thank you.

Javi talked about leaving the Alba, alone. He talked about walking back to the flat, mind made up, and knowing his body would soon follow. He talked about a decision that was made *not* so he could run away from anything or anyone – but so he could finally acknowledge and embrace a quiet strength and a hidden self that had always been there, gagged but still breathing.

It wasn't like That Day. It wasn't about ending a life. It wasn't about fear, and running from it. It was a slow but confident step in the direction of home.

And so he went to a private clinic in Glasgow instead of the airport, took hormones instead of flights. He talked about the doctors there and the novelty of feeling understood. He talked about injections and mood swings and the luck of having the genes of a swarthy Spaniard. He talked about the panic felt when he went there for one of his psychological assessments and saw Carmen with her mother, waving and calling out a name he'd only just changed. Carmen, who'd once kissed Ruth; who'd sensed she was different and was then pushed away. He talked about a chest now hard to the touch, a round world made flat by cuts and tucks. New scars, not yet healed. He talked about deed polls, the validation he'd felt when he collected his new passport and finally saw a self he recognised. He talked about leading tours in autumn that Ruth should have led; about learning to take her place and why he'd started with strangers. Clients accepted Javi as Javi and had no reason to think he'd ever been anybody else. They simply let him be. And he talked about choice, was asked if he'd had any.

'Do you really believe anyone would choose this, Dad? Do you think I weighed up all my possible futures and decided this was the easiest option?'

'I'm not saying that.'

'Then what are you saying?'

Chris sighed. 'I just wonder if you could've found a place in between.'

'That's where I've been my whole life, Dad.' This time it was Javi who looked away. 'Do you want to know what that feels like? It means never being *anyone* fully. It means never being authentic. It means never being yourself. It means never feeling good enough. It means your mind never being totally still. The *place in between* is exactly the place I tried to escape from That Day. You've no idea how it feels to wake up and start every day wishing you could end a life. I didn't do this for the fun of it. I didn't do it to hurt your feelings or prove a point. I didn't do it with anyone else in mind. Not even you.'

'But why so many lies?'

'I had to lie to give myself space,' said Javi. 'I couldn't just switch from Ruth to Javi overnight and slot neatly into exactly the same world I had before.'

'But when were you going to tell us? Why keep it from us for so long?'

'I kept it from myself for even longer,' said Javi. 'And I *have* tried to tell you, loads of times. I even got as far as phoning the house a few times recently, determined to explain everything, but I could never go through with it.'

'So *you're* our silent caller?'

Javi nodded. 'I changed the settings on my phone, made sure my number was blocked so you couldn't call back.'

'And you never thought those calls might worry me and your mum?'

'I didn't do it on purpose, Dad. But I'd hear your voice and panic. And I was scared to tell you, in case I was wrong; in case it changed, somehow.

'You know, for years I believed that if I just looked hard enough a more acceptable answer would eventually appear. I thought that, if I persevered, something would eventually click in my head and everything would make sense and I'd feel comfortable as Ruth. I blamed myself for not trying hard enough to be happy with my lot.'

'And are you happy now, like this?'

'Happier.' Javi turned away from Chris after he'd said it, came face to face with himself in the window. 'Maybe there are things I'll miss, Dad, but I won't miss the conflict. My whole life has been one big fight against myself.'

'You want to tell me when it started?'

'Twenty-eight years ago, I'd guess. When you and Mum made me.'

'You really believe that?'

'I know it.'

Chris gently touched Javi's shoulder, waited for him to turn around before he spoke. His voice wobbled, hinted at tears held in. 'I remember when you were wee you'd come into the bathroom when I was shaving, slather toothpaste all over your face and plough tracks through the white with your toothbrush. You remember?'

Javi nodded.

'We never tried to make you anything you weren't. We were totally fine with you being a tomboy. I quite liked it, actually. Made me worry less.'

'This is more than that.'

'Och, I know, but . . . *Christ*, you should have said.'

'I couldn't say it out loud,' he said.

'Even to us?'

'Especially to you.'

'But why not?'

Javi sighed, and for a long time he stared at his reflection in the window, chest rising and falling faster than it should.

'Because of Heather.'

Chris screwed up his face. 'What's Heather got to do with it?'

'You'd already lost a daughter.'

'But that wasn't your fault. It wasn't anybody's fault.'

'I know that,' said Javi. 'But I also remember what you said to me, That Day. I remember the weight of you, pushing down. I remember your hands on my neck and my blood on your face and I was so angry, Dad, that you were changing the ending I'd chosen for myself. I could tell that you were speaking but all I could hear was your watch ticking in my ear, every second passing like normal, like nothing special was happening. Then suddenly I heard what you were saying, over and over. *I can't lose another daughter, Ruth.* That's what you said. And that's what made me want to survive it. I promised myself that if I lived I'd hide the letter and force myself to forget all about . . . *this*.'

'And you've carried that pain since then.'

Javi nodded.

'Christ.'

For a long time both men were silent, and both jumped when Chris's mobile phone started to ring. He ended the call, cursed when it rang again. 'It's Sandy,' said Chris.

'Answer it.'

'Chris? Sorry if I've woken you. But I just got to the news room and bumped into Andy, the court reporter. He's given me a tip-off, Chris – and I'm sorry to say it involves your family. Specifically Mikey. You sitting down?'

'Aye.'

'Then keep sitting,' said Sandy. 'I don't know the full details but he's been charged with assault. Got into a fight outside the casino, floored someone. Last March, same night Ruth went missing. It finally came to court yesterday – so that's where he was and why he wasn't answering your calls. Not sure what it means in terms of the investigation, but he's not been telling us the full story.'

'I'll call him.'

'Sorry it had to come from me,' said Sandy.

Chris made excuses to end the call then sat staring at his phone, stunned that life could possibly hold any more surprises.

'Has something happened?'

'I'll tell you later. Come on, we should get to the hospital.'

'You don't mind me coming?'

'I want you there.'

'What about Mum?'

'You'll be the first person she asks for when she wakes up.' Chris stood up, looked at Javi; a man with a patchy beard and, suddenly, his daughter's smile.

He said he'd wait in the car while Javi showered and changed. He was relieved to be on his own for a few minutes, only realised his hands were shaking when he struggled to get his keys into the car door. He closed his eyes, had no idea how to be, what to feel.

Ruth was gone, but here; here, but not.

When Javi appeared on the stairway of the tenement a few minutes later, the intruder light above the front door illuminated, transformed him into a familiar silhouette. Chris tooted the horn, leaned over to the passenger side and pushed open the door. But he was not yet ready to call out that new name.

He'd have to teach himself the name of his own child. How could that be? He wondered if it would ever feel normal to say that name when he saw that face; if eventually he'd forget about his daughter, his Ruth. He had no idea how to grieve a loss like this one. What happened, now, to the life she'd lived?

Even Javi couldn't answer that one.

They spoke about the weather for the rest of the drive, felt the force of it blast their faces when they opened the car door at the hospital. Chris swore then pulled his door shut again. 'You ready?'

Javi stared straight ahead, swallowed hard, then nodded.

They both kept their eyes down and their mouths shut as they pushed through the double doors and walked together down the corridor. When they passed the visitors' room Chris popped his head in and saw Mateo conked out and snoring on one of the chairs with a rolled-up jacket for a pillow. Javi stared at him, said nothing, but Chris knew where his mind would be. The brandy and the knife had belonged to Mateo and the grout on his terrace had been stained by bits of Ruth, seeping into the pores.

'Have you seen him since?' said Chris.

Javi shook his head. 'I've always felt too guilty.'

'You? He's to blame for it.'

'Blame doesn't even come into it, Dad. It was my hand on the knife.' Javi turned and left then Chris followed, showed him the way to his mum's room. He knocked lightly then opened the door, noticed immediately that the room was much quieter. Chris's heart started thundering when he realised why.

'They've removed her ventilator,' he said, unable to contain a smile as he watched Maria's chest rise and fall on its own. 'I'll go and speak to her doctors then wait for Mikey. You should go in. Talk to her.'

Javi stayed where he was. 'Will she hear me?'

'The doctor says she can.'

Javi nodded.

'Say what you need to say,' said Chris, then turned and left.

CHAPTER 50

I know that this will scar you, Mum.

I know my legacy will be a lifetime of uncomfortable moments when old friends write and ask how I'm doing or when strangers ask about your children.

Like mother, like daughter, you always said; and in some ways I think that's all you ever wanted from me – and *for* me. How will you explain it now?

I'm worried you'll be ashamed of me. I'm worried you'll waste inordinate amounts of time wondering why I didn't turn out as you hoped; what you could and should have done differently. You might think you could have protected me from this, but who I am cannot be stored in a jar with a safety cap, then put on a shelf and kept out of reach of your children. Nature does not care about your plans for Ruth's future. Guess what? *I* am Ruth's plan for the future.

Don't ask me what happens to her past.

I picture you trying to pinpoint the precise moment and reason Ruth ceased to exist. Your mind will never be free of questions and underneath it all you will be sad, because you'll miss the me you thought I was. I wish I could say your pain was my main concern but I was more worried about my own, and ending it. This is the only way to make things better.

I got tired of fighting. I got tired of hiding. I got tired of running away because I realised that he will always follow. It didn't matter where I went or who I tried to hide behind. It didn't how many times I changed my address or my hair. Still I could never find a way to cork the love that leaks out of me when I see him looking back at me in the mirror, with that face. My true face.

For me, he is more than beautiful.

I've wanted to tell you this so many times, Mum.

I always used to try after tea when Dad would go through to the sitting room and we would stay in the kitchen with dirty dishes and a hungry dog and you'd nudge me and ask me why I was so quiet and I'd shrug as if I didn't know. I'd stand there with a dish towel in my hand and a tightening knot in my throat, my head a chaos of imagined conversations that never ended well.

This is not how I raised you, you'd say. *It's not who I raised you to be.*

But you do not know me, Mum.

When I was small you packed my lunch and my gym stuff and me off to school, saw nothing of my life until I come back and told you it was fine. You knew only what you were told by me or by Mr Forsyth that day he called you in for a chat. Everyone stared and a few of the bad ones sniggered when I was called out of class but you didn't look at me at all when the headmaster led me into the office, nodded for me to sit in a chair made for children half my size.

I've told your mum what's been happening, he said.

What's Been Happening. Three words to neatly package up my torment. When he called me a bully I stared at the floor, felt gravity push all my tears to the front. You sighed and said *Oh, Ruth*, assured him we'd talk about it.

The next hour was a drum roll.

In the car you switched on the radio and when we got home you made two mugs of sugary tea and gave me a biscuit usually reserved for birthdays. For a while I thought you'd forgotten about our talk but then you put down your mug, put a hand on my shoulder and told me there was Never An Excuse for that kind of behaviour. I tried to tell you what had really happened but you said you didn't want to hear, said I should Learn To Act Like A Proper Young Lady.

When I cried you looked away and when I followed your eyes they were on that photo in the silver frame. Heather, one week old. Heather, as old as she'd ever be. You cried then too and I knew you wished I'd died instead.

I knew right then that what I was should be hidden, and, even when you held me, it hurt. I wanted only to be the daughter you wanted me to be. I wanted you to boast about me in the staff room at work and miss me when I went away for camping weekends with the Girl Guides. I wanted you to smile when we looked through old photo albums and say things like *My little girl – a grown woman!* And even though you'd never say out loud that you loved me I wanted to feel it in the way you looked at me and the things you said about me in the Christmas newsletter to the 284 friends on your list. On my wedding day you'd tell the world you *couldn't have asked for a better daughter* and everyone would know that you meant it and understand why.

And so I built a wall; decided that the love I felt for him would no longer flow freely. I'd force it into a part of myself where I would never go, never look, never acknowledge. I believed that if I left it there for long enough the love would dry up and disappear and that would be the end of it.

Instead, I missed him.

There was no deliberate remembering. It was a barely noticeable sense of loss; the recognition of a sadness that I usually ignored. I'd feel a momentary tug in my chest, the fleeting sensation that something or someone was absent.

But I'd never take a closer look. Instead I'd fill that hole with beer or vodka or hash or bits of boys I knew I'd never love as much as him. When it was over they'd ask if I was okay and I'd look at them and wonder who they thought I was. If they knew I was Javi underneath they'd wish they'd been drunk enough to forget it, or at least use that as an excuse.

They'd wish they'd trusted their instincts.

And so it is with me, Mum.

For years I saw the world through your eyes. If you'd held me upside down and shaken me, all of my beliefs would have fallen out of my ears, each one a yellow Post-it note with words in your handwriting. *This is the right way to cut peppers. Fat people are lazy. Water must not be drunk from a mug. Sex is embarrassing and should not be discussed. Never dry hands on a dish cloth.*

And this one, of course: *I know what's best for my daughter.*

It was years before I held my beliefs up to the light to see what they were really made of. I discovered they had no real substance. They were outdated. And, worst of all, they were not really mine. They'd been handed down through the family like old manuscripts or antiques, held dear, assumed to have value. I'd never contemplated the fact there could be viable alternatives to the rules I lived by. Right, wrong. White, black. True, false. Good, bad. Girl, boy.

My judgements were instant and automatic. My beliefs were actually habits I'd never realised I had permission to break. But Javi broke them for me.

He always came to me when I was drinking, tempted me to hold his reflection for longer than usual on mirrors and windows; to capture him in selfies on my phone. I used to drink to escape him but often the drunker I was, the closer we came to touching.

That's what happened that night at the Alba. I saw Javi reflected in the mirror behind the bar – and I decided that, this time, I wouldn't look away.

I kept on looking, even though I knew exactly where that look could lead me: to the end of everything, or to the start of something else. That night it led to my bedroom, blinds pulled shut. It led to scissors in my hand and hair on the floor and clothes changed. It led me to the face I'd missed. It led to the one place I feel complete and completely at home. Finally, it led me back to him.

And this time, Mum, I've asked him to stay.

CHAPTER 51

Chris waited by the double doors and caught Mikey as soon as he pushed them open. 'I was just heading to the canteen,' he said, and as they sat picking at their breakfast he explained about Ruth and Javi, and about the two of them, together.

Mikey put down his coffee cup and picked it up, then put it down again. 'And it's permanent? I mean, she won't change her mind?'

'It's too late for that.'

'So, Ruth's just . . . gone?'

'I think Ruth would say she's been Javi the whole time.'

Mikey shook his head. Chris placed a hand on his back and wished Maria were there to hold them both. Sometimes that was all it took to make life feel better. But Mikey's body was rock-hard, tendons stretched far too tight.

'Why wouldn't she just tell us, Dad?'

'I suppose we all hide things, don't we?'

'Aye.' Mikey drained his cup and pushed it away. 'You know the stupidest thing? The whole time Mum was pregnant with Ruth, I was desperate for it to be a boy. I knew you and Mum really wanted another daughter, after what happened to Heather . . . but I kept wishing for a wee brother anyway. I knew that if you had a wee girl, she'd be the favourite. Nothing I did made you and Mum feel better. But Ruth did.'

'You honestly think that?'

'It's not about thinking, Dad. I was there. I know what I felt.'

'And what do you feel now?'

Mikey shrugged and went silent.

Chris took a bite of his bacon roll, hoping the pause would help him push out the words he knew he had to say – in spite of the pain he'd knew they'd produce.

'I know, Mikey.'

'Know what?'

'Everything. I know you got into a fight after you left Ruth at the Alba that night, and I know you spent most of yesterday in court. I know you and Rachel have split up. I know your business has gone bust. I know you've been suffering and that you've kept all of it hidden.'

'Me and Ruth have got something in common after all, then.'

Mikey turned away from Chris and stared at the morning sky through the canteen window. White clouds against the grey, not a blue patch in sight. Tears came, silently, creeping down his cheeks and onto his beard. Then came words.

'How did you find out?'

'Contacts.'

'You mean Sandy?'

'The who is irrelevant. But will you *please* talk to me now, Mikey? I want to know where you've been for the past day and a half; why you didn't even bother to send a text. Christ. I've been worried sick. I thought . . .' He sighed, shook his head. 'You can start by telling me why you ended up in court.'

Mikey nodded then tightly closed his eyes.

'First, I'm sorry for disappearing on you, okay? It was out of order. But I was absolutely mortified about ending up in court. I didn't want anyone to know. Especially you. And especially now. And as for why I was there . . .' He sighed. 'I got into a fight, after I left Ruth at the Alba. I went to the casino with some pals, all of us totally wrecked. One of the bouncers refused to let me in and it got out of hand. I threw a punch, burst his nose, knocked him over. Two seconds later the police turned up and I spent most of the night in the cells, sobering up. But they caught me with blood on my hands, literally.'

'And blood on your clothes too, right?'

Mikey stared at him, his face a question.

Chris answered, telling him about Rachel and the blood-stained hooded top, the fear that somehow it was all connected: blood, lies, and a missing sister.

'You thought I'd hurt *Ruth*? Jesus. I can't believe it.'

'And I can't believe you lied to the police,' said Chris, shaking his head.

'I was trying to protect Rachel, and you.'

'Bollocks. You were trying to protect yourself,' said Chris. 'Next question – who was the blonde woman you were seen with at the casino?'

'How do you . . . ?' Mikey sank his head into his hands. 'I've been having an affair, Dad.' He took a few deep breaths and when he spoke again his voice was unsteady. 'That's one of the reasons I left the pub before Ruth, so I could meet her at the casino. I wanted to see her, but I didn't want Ruth to know. And as for Rachel . . . I know she knows, even though I've been too ashamed to admit it.'

'She told me you'd been distant,' said Chris.

'Sounds like she told you a lot of things.'

Stares replaced words and for a few minutes the only sound was the clatter of china and cutlery at the serving station, automatic doors opening and closing.

'You've made a right bloody mess for yourself.' Chris stood up, rested a hand on Mikey's shoulder. 'But I'm on your side. You know that, don't you?'

Mikey nodded but did not look up. He just sat, spinning his wedding ring round and round on his finger. Chris reached for his own, did the same.

'We should go back.'

'Give me a minute, will you?'

'Take your time,' said Chris. 'There's one more person I need to tell.'

He left Mikey in the canteen and went to stand just outside the main entrance. He stared at his phone for a long time before he pressed the call icon, was still debating what to say when Farida answered, her voice barely audible over the hum of blended conversations, a burst of laughter nearby.

'Farida? It's Chris. I've got—'

'I'm not really hearing you. Give me a minute.'

A door opened and closed and when Farida spoke again her voiced echoed, making Chris think she was now in a bathroom. 'Chris? You hear me now? Good. I was actually just about to call you anyway. I got your email and the CCTV picture you sent. And my first question is – how did you do it?'

'Do what?'

'Get that image?'

Chris sensed an accusation, put up his defences. He didn't want to bring Jamal into this. 'Contacts.'

'Mind telling me who?'

'Is something wrong?'

'Quite the opposite. I want to congratulate them. Whoever your contact is managed to get a far better image of the suspect than any of my officers here.'

'*Suspect*?'

'The man who used Ruth's cards. My team just sent me an image caught on CCTV a few hundred metres from that supermarket. It's clearly the same person but yours is supremely better quality. There's no doubt now, Chris. The person who used Ruth's card is the same person in the image you sent me from the coffee shop. The one who ran off just before Maria did. Man with the beard. And it actually looks like Maria was chasing the man, not the other way around. I suggest you speak to Sandy asap. If we get this into the newspaper tomorrow I'm confident we'll track down the suspect fairly quickly and find out why he has Ruth's bank card. It's possible he might lead us right to her.'

'That's just it,' said Chris. 'He already has.'

'I'm sorry?'

Chris walked as he talked, neutralising dozens of lies with a single, solid truth. When he finished explaining he heard another door open and close at the end of the line and he could tell Farida was outside. He heard the sound of a siren, voices from the police station getting quieter as she moved further away.

'Chris, are you telling me your daughter is transgender?'

'Aye.'

'So we have no missing person?'

'No,' said Chris, then realised Ruth would *always* be missing, now. And missed. But was anyone really lost if there were still four seats at their table?

'And your wife discovered this a few minutes before her accident?'

'Aye,' said Chris. 'Maria was called to Ruth's flat last Friday by a neighbour who needed access, to fix the intercom. The tenant wouldn't answer the door and nobody had a phone number so Maria decided to contact the tenant in person – oblivious to the fact the tenant was actually Ruth.'

'But it was Ruth living as Javi?'

'Aye. Anyway, a neighbour told her the tenant's girlfriend worked in a coffee shop in town. That's where Maria went on Sunday morning, thinking she'd be there and back in half an hour, in time to start the race.'

'But we know that didn't happen in reality,' said Farida. 'Instead she got to the coffee shop and came face to face with Ruth, now fully transitioned and presenting as Javi Fernandez?'

'Aye.' Chris could hardly believe the question, never mind his answer.

'Then Javi fled when he realised his mum had seen him? Maria followed, at pace – and fell a few minutes later on the stairs in Fleshmarket Close. Makes sense. It confirms what we originally suspected – and what we've traced on CCTV. Your wife's fall was an accident. No suspicious circumstances.'

'Case closed, then?'

'For me, yes. But how is she?'

'Improving. They've finally taken her off the ventilator.'

'Ah, that's great to hear,' she said, and even down the phone Chris could tell she was smiling. *Christ*. There was a first time for everything. 'And what about Mikey?' said Farida. 'Have you heard from him as well?'

'He's here too. We're all here, at the hospital. The four of us.'

'About time you had some good news. You must be feeling very relieved.'

'That's one word for it,' said Chris, and his mind went again to Brewster Bay, to that body lifted up and carried off. Whoever it was, it was somebody's child; another family's tragedy. But this time around, that loss wasn't his.

CHAPTER 52

Javi held one of Maria's hands in both of his. He searched for her pulse in her fingertips, overwhelmed by grief and by love when he found it. When tears sneaked out he laid his head on her bed, face down. And when Chris and Mikey came in he wished he could stay there, keep his face hidden and, with it, the need for more explanations. He doubted the questions would fully end, ever.

'I always wanted a wee brother, you know.'

Typical bloody Mikey, making a joke to smooth over jagged edges. Javi looked up, tried to ignore Mikey's flinch when their eyes met for the first time.

'You look like shit, Mikey,' he said, matching his brother's tone.

Mikey laughed. 'And you look . . . different.'

'I'll take that as a compliment.'

'Got yourself a girlfriend as well, Dad says. You don't hang about!'

'I've waited long enough, no?' For a moment there was a smile between them. Then Javi looked at the bed. 'You know Mum was chasing me, right?'

'Aye. Dad showed me the video,' said Mikey. 'Now I want to know what happened on your side of the window. Assume it was you she was staring at?'

Javi nodded, turned back to look at his mum. Chris had shown him the CCTV footage when they were at the flat so he knew that when she'd first arrived, his mum had watched him through the window for more than a minute, without him noticing. Then she'd sat on that bench for about an hour – stunned, probably. When she'd stood up again and looked inside he'd been working in the same place as before. And that was when their eyes had met.

'Anna's always run off her feet on a Sunday morning so I went in to give her a hand,' said Javi. 'I was clearing the table by the window, stacking cups and wiping away crumbs, and the whole time Mum was on the outside, looking in. The glass there always steams up on rainy days but she must have recognised me anyway, or she'd have come inside.'

'And how did you notice her?'

'I had the vague feeling I was being watched but I thought it would be a smoker at the bench or some numpty taking a selfie. The usual. Instead I looked up and I saw Mum, looking right back at me. I couldn't believe it.'

'And you're sure she knew it was you?'

'Totally sure. She did that thing with her hands.'

'The prayer thing?'

'Aye.'

Javi remembered the van pulling up behind his mum and a man with a clipboard jumping out of the passenger side.

He shouted abuse at the seagulls that circled and swooped when he opened the back doors to unload stock.

And still, the two of them stood.

He remembered movement behind him; heard the whirr of the grinder and the gurgle of milk being heated; the squeak and puff as someone new sat on the leather sofa. The flick of newspaper pages, the beep of text messages, a tune from his favourite playlist on Anna's phone, connected to the café's speakers.

But most of all he remembered his mum bringing her hands into a prayer position in front of her face. Head bowed, thumbs tucked under her chin, forefingers forced into the corners of her eyes, pinkies pressed tightly together. She did it whenever loss was imminent and accepted as inevitable; like the day they were in hospital visiting Grandpa and the doctor told them about his dementia; like the day they knocked down a deer on the drive home from Skye then watched it die in the undergrowth. And of course, she did it That Day.

'I wiped the window with the sleeve of my shirt then left my hand on the glass. That was when Mum suddenly stepped away from me. It was as if she thought I might reach out and pull her through, drag her into a world she didn't want to be a part of. But I suppose I'd already done that, the moment I turned Ruth's life into mine. I knew it wasn't something Mum could walk away from unchanged. She couldn't shrug it off or hope for the best because in her mind the worst had already happened. Ruth was gone. She'd lost another daughter.'

He'd cried, but couldn't tell if his mum was crying; couldn't move or imagine moving. He'd pictured a statue at church: mother, son, and the gaze between them. Love, captured in stone.

Then his mum had stepped forward again and held her hand against his, on the other side of the glass. He held that same hand now, his palm against hers.

'I'd been dreading that moment for my whole life and suddenly Mum's right there, seeing me exactly as I am,' he said. 'And she smiled, Mikey.'

'But that's when you ran?'

Javi sighed, nodded. 'I know it makes no sense. But I ran because I was ashamed of ever doubting her, of thinking she'd ever offer me anything less.' Javi turned to Maria, focused again on the pulse, the rhythm his own heart had once depended upon. 'I didn't go far. I went to the Royal Mile then nipped down one of the closes and hoped she wouldn't find me. Sounds ridiculous now, saying it out loud. I *knew* I shouldn't have fled so after a wee while I went back to the coffee shop to see if she was still there. But she wasn't, of course. Anna started asking questions so I told her I wasn't feeling well, said I was heading home to the flat. But actually I spent the rest of the morning standing at the crossroads where the bridges meet the Royal Mile, desperately hoping Mum would reappear. I sent her an email too. There was so much I wanted to say – far too much for a text message. But in the end the only thing I said was sorry.

'When there was no reply to the email I phoned the house a couple of times, even left a message. I called her mobile as well, on Monday, but she didn't answer. I was gutted. In my mind mum's silence said everything. After that I switched off Ruth's phone, which is why I missed all Dad's messages.

'I didn't even know about the accident until Anna brought me the newspaper yesterday – and told me Dad had been at the coffee shop, asking questions. I had absolutely no idea about . . . *this*.' Javi stared at his mum, shaking his head. 'And I'm so sorry.'

'It's not your fault.'

'That doesn't mean you don't blame me.' Javi stood up, still holding his mum's hand. He could feel his own heart now too, racing. 'Maybe I should go.'

'You can't,' said Mikey.

'Why?' He looked up at them both. Chris was the one to reply.

'Because you're the one she'll want to see when she wakes up,' he said. 'You always make your mum feel better.'

'I'm not who I was.'

'You're here, Javi. That's enough.'

Chris looked at him, held his gaze, said more with a few seconds of eye contact than he'd ever manage out loud. It was a look that held love and gratitude and the desperate fear of loss. It was a look reserved entirely for his youngest child and it was still intact; still theirs.

The Part That Came Next

The rain started just as they left the harbour.

Maria glanced at the sky, knew it wouldn't last; knew they wouldn't really mind if it did. The boat was heavy with the four of them on board but she steered it forward, loving the sound of waves slapping the sides. Their boat was small but could cope with almost anything; it had carried them safely through waves almost twice its height when required. But there would be none of that today. The water was calm, would be clear under the surface.

None of them spoke on the way to the reef but all of them smiled when Maria cut the engine, tossed the little anchor overboard then tugged the rope to make sure it had caught. This was the first time she'd been out on the water since the accident. Winter had been harsh in every sense, but spring had brought with it her release from hospital and the suggestion that her flesh and bones might just recover, might allow her to inhabit arms and legs and hands that moved at her command. Once again, she'd live in a body she recognised as her own.

The boat tilted to one side when Maria peered over the edge. The water looked green today but it had no single colour, would always change and always be the same. When she glanced skywards she noticed a sliver of blue high above them, and when she looked towards the headland she saw a woman there. It was Anna, waiting. Others would have run, but she had stayed.

Gulls passed overhead, clouds changed position and for a moment the boat was illuminated by rays of yellow so bright and straight they looked solid. When Maria turned towards them, her whole face turned gold.

That was the first time sunshine had touched her scars. They were hard to look at but no longer hurt. And they'd fade, eventually, exposed to the light.

Chris leaned over and kissed her, then got to his feet and pulled up the zip on his wetsuit. Behind him Mikey did the same then shouted, 'Let's go!'

And just like that Chris and Mikey were in the water instead of on it. The two of them, transformed from standing humans into floating ones. The two of them, laughing at the shock of it. Maria knew only too well the painful joy of cold water stinging every part of your body, reminding you it was there even when the weight was gone. She laughed with them and for a moment felt as if the whole world was just sky, sea and the four of them, together in a world without walls.

Ruth had always been the last one into the water.

She'd sit in silence, wait until the rest of them were beyond shouting distance of the boat before she stood up and launched herself into the curl of a wave as it broke. She'd loved being out there on her own, a tiny speck of life in the vast sea. That was what she came for: those brief moments when Nature took over and nobody could stop it, or tried to.

Now, Javi did the same.

The boat wobbled when he stepped on to the bench at the front, arms held out to steady himself. For a few moments he turned his eyes to solid ground, to the place where Anna stood. He smiled when she waved at him then he looked back to the sea, following the swells, waiting for the right moment.

And then it came.

Javi leapt head first into a swell big enough to swallow him whole. A splash and then silence. Maria followed the route of his snorkel tube, moving towards Chris and Mikey. She pictured his lungs, fat with life, and wondered how it felt to look through his eyes. Just under the surface was a world that had always been there, but could not ordinarily be seen. Maria pictured shoals of fish inspecting the sandy floor, bellies flashing silver when they turned and caught the light. Some would swim alone, hunting, hunted. But mostly they would move together, one echoing the movements of the other.

Up ahead, Chris, Mikey and Javi would do the same.

Maria lay down on the bench and stared at the heavens. The clouds were thinner now, a delicate veil hung beneath the bright blue sky. *It's been there all along*, Chris would say, and he was right. She closed her eyes, let herself relax exactly where she was and as she was; focused on the gulp of the waves and the song of seabirds she'd never learned the name of. A breeze came and went, brought with it voices from the shore, lives she'd never be a part of.

She sat up, startled, when Javi pushed out of the water beside the boat, blinking as salt water dripped from his hair to his eyes to his beard and then back into the water. 'You okay, Mum?'

'Better than okay,' said Maria, and meant it. 'You?'

Javi nodded, and when he smiled Maria felt a swell in her chest bigger than anything that moved them in the water. She smiled back, meant that too.

He stilled the little metal steps as Maria eased herself into the sea, held her hand under the water when a wave lifted them up and away from the boat. It brought them down beside Chris and Mikey and for a moment they all just looked at each other, four smiles floating on the water. Maria couldn't imagine a world without the sea, and them in it. When the next swell came they flipped on to their backs and surrendered themselves to the endless movement of the waves, let Nature take them anywhere it wanted.

But that day, in that moment, it held them together.

Acknowledgements

Absolutely massive thanks to my brilliant agent, Caroline Hardman. Your guidance has made me a much better writer and your faith has kept me going. To Joanna Swainson, thanks for reading a very early version of this story and getting it on to Caroline's desk! I'll never forget your words of encouragement. Thanks to everyone else at Hardman & Swainson for all that you do.

Huge thank you to Jon Elek, Rosa Schierenberg, Rob Cox and the rest of the team at Welbeck Publishing. Thanks for believing in *The Silent Daughter* and helping me bring this story to life. To my endlessly calm editor, Sophie Wilson – I'm still amazed by your insights. Thank you for helping me transform this book in ways I'd never imagined. To Linda McQueen, your eye for detail is exceptional. Thank you also for feeding my characters after five foodless days.

Thanks to everyone who took the time to read early versions of this book, especially Andrew Hamilton and Ruth Forsyth. I truly appreciate your honesty and definitely owe you a pint. Thanks also to Jenny Clarke for reading the very first draft and convincing me to kill off the pilot.

Thanks to Andrew Kellock for being so nice when Dora phoned to quit her job at the paper. That moment was my first step to here. Thanks to Ashleigh Barbour for answering my long list of questions about the police and to Diane Tunks for all our charity shop chats. You made it the best job ever. Big thanks to Dr Tash Pirie-Burley for teaching me about helicopters and to Dr Julie Peat for answering my baby questions. Any inaccuracies are my own.

I'd also like to thank Chris Montgomery at Worldstrides and Michelle Capocchi at Road Scholar for understanding why I needed so much time off – and for giving me work when the book was written and I was ready to get back on the road.

Kate Stewart and Deborah DeWolfe, thanks for your boundless enthusiasm and interest. You're an inspiration. Safari, thanks for always believing I'd get there. Thanks also to the Cumnock girls for the many online laughs while I worked on final edits during lockdown. For *Club CMV*, *las sillas amarillas* and everyone else at MOB in Barcelona, thank you for making me feel so completely at home in this spectacular city. The next vermouth is on me. Sincere thanks to AJ for introducing me to Juanito. You're both amazing teachers. Thanks Mary Rodgers and Claire Moore for good times and being the first people to pre-order the book!

To Mum and Dad, thank you for raising me to believe in myself. And to the whole family – thanks for all the dinners, beds, breakfasts and encouragement you've offered me over the years. I live far away but the distance means nothing.

And finally, thanks to Mari: for *despertando* so much love in me and bringing so much beauty to my life every single day. Your belief has never wavered, even when mine has. Thank you also for taking the photograph that inspired so many chapters of this book. You're pretty much amazing, and I love you.

Author photograph © María Jose Fernandez Hidalgo

Emma Christie grew up in a book-filled house in Cumnock, an Ayrshire coal-mining town.

After quitting her law degree to study English literature and medieval history at Aberdeen University, she spent five years working as a news reporter with one of the UK's top-selling regional daily newspapers, the *Press and Journal*. Throughout her journalism career, she secretly wanted to *be* every author she ever interviewed.

When she's not writing, Emma works for a US travel company, leading educational journeys across Europe.

Emma can often be found in Portobello, Edinburgh's captivating seaside community. But most of the time she lives in Barcelona with her girlfriend, María Jose, and far too many plants.

The Silent Daughter is her first novel.

www.emmachristiewriter.com

WELBECK

Love books? Join the club.

Sign-up and choose your preferred genres to receive
tailored news, deals, extracts, author interviews and
more about your next favourite read.

From heart-racing thrillers to award-winning historical
fiction, through to must-read music tomes, beautiful
picture books and delightful gift ideas, Welbeck is
proud to publish titles that suit every taste.

bit.ly/welbeckpublishing